Other Books by Harriet Steel

Becoming Lola
Salvation
City of Dreams
Following the Dream

The Inspector de Silva Mysteries

Trouble in Nuala
Dark Clouds over Nuala
Offstage in Nuala
Fatal Finds in Nuala
Christmas in Nuala
Passage from Nuala
Rough Time in Nuala
Taken in Nuala
High Wire in Nuala
Cold Case in Nuala

Short Stories

Dancing and other Stories

AN INSPECTOR DE SILVA MYSTERY

BREAK FROM NUALA

HARRIET STEEL

Author's Note and Acknowledgments

Welcome to the eleventh book in the Inspector de Silva mystery series. Like the earlier ones, this is a self-contained story but wearing my reader's hat, I usually find that my enjoyment of a series is deepened by reading the books in order and getting to know major characters well. With that in mind, I have included thumbnail sketches of those taking part in this story who feature regularly in the series. In response to requests by readers who prefer not to read on Kindle, there's also a copy of *Christmas in Nuala*, previously only published as a Kindle Short Read, at the end of the book.

Several years ago, I had the great good fortune to visit the island of Sri Lanka, the former Ceylon. I fell in love with the country straight away, awed by its tremendous natural beauty and the charm and friendliness of its people. I had been planning to write a detective series for some time and when I came home, I decided to set it in Ceylon in the 1930s, a time when British Colonial rule created interesting contrasts, and sometimes conflicts, with traditional culture. Thus Inspector Shanti de Silva and his friends were born.

I owe many thanks to everyone who helped with this book. John Hudspith was as usual an invaluable editor. Julia Gibbs did a marvellous job of proofreading the manuscript, and Jane Dixon Smith designed another excellent cover and layout for me. My thanks also go to all those readers who told me they enjoyed the previous books in the series and would like to know what Inspector de Silva and his friends did next. Their kindness has encouraged me to keep writing. Above all, my heartfelt gratitude goes to my husband Roger for his unfailing encouragement and support, to say nothing of his patience when Inspector de Silva's world distracts me from this one.

Apart from well-known historical figures, all characters in the book are fictitious. Nuala is also fictitious although loosely based on the hill town of Nuwara Eliya. Any mistakes are my own.

Characters who appear regularly in the Inspector de Silva Mysteries

Inspector Shanti de Silva. He began his police career in Ceylon's capital city, Colombo, but in middle age he married and accepted a promotion to inspector in charge of the small force in the hill town of Nuala. Likes: a quiet life with his beloved wife, his car, good food, his garden. Dislikes: interference in his work by his British masters, formal occasions.

Sergeant Prasanna. Nearly thirty and married with a daughter. He's doing well in his job and starting to take more responsibility. Likes: cricket and is exceptionally good at it.

Constable Nadar. A few years younger than Prasanna. Diffident at first, he's gaining in confidence. Married with two boys. Likes: his food, making toys for his sons. Dislikes: sleepless nights.

Jane de Silva. She came to Ceylon as a governess to a wealthy colonial family and met and married de Silva a few years later. A no-nonsense lady with a dry sense of humour. Likes: detective novels, cinema, and dancing. Dislikes: snobbishness.

Archie Clutterbuck. Assistant government agent in Nuala and as such responsible for administration and keeping law and order in the area. Likes: his Labrador, Darcy; fishing, hunting big game. Dislikes: being argued with, the heat.

Florence Clutterbuck. Archie's wife, a stout, forthright lady. Likes: being queen bee, organising other people. Dislikes: people who don't defer to her at all times.

Doctor David Hebden. Doctor for the Nuala area. Under his professional shell, he's rather shy. Likes: cricket. Dislikes: formality.

Emerald Hebden (née Watson). She arrived in Nuala with a touring British theatre company, decided to stay and subsequently married David Hebden. She's a popular addition to local society and a good friend to Jane. Her full story is told in *Offstage in Nuala*.

Charlie Frobisher. A junior member of staff in the Colonial Service. A personable young man who is tipped to do well. Likes: sport and climbing mountains.

CHAPTER 1

Galle, Ceylon, autumn 1940

Dusk was gathering by the time de Silva and Jane reached their hotel. As they drew up at the entrance porch, two uniformed doormen hurried down the steps to greet them and take their luggage. Another man in a chauffeur's uniform came forward, offering to park the Morris. With a momentary twinge of concern at the prospect of letting anyone else drive his beloved car, de Silva handed him the keys.

A spacious and elegant lobby with white-painted walls, a teak-lined ceiling, and a black and white tiled floor awaited them. On either side, columns supported a gallery that was also made of teak. It ran around three sides of the hall and was reached by an impressive double staircase. De Silva glimpsed doors that he presumed led to the guest bedrooms.

A man in a smart dark suit, hurried to greet them. 'Welcome to Cinnamon Lodge! I'm the manager. If you would be so good as to sign the register, I'll have your luggage taken to your room in the meantime.'

Two porters bore their luggage away and de Silva and Jane followed the manager to the reception desk. Brief formalities completed, he called over a third porter and handed him a key. 'Show our guests to their room.'

'Yes, sir.'

Like the lobby, the room de Silva and Jane found themselves in had white walls and a teak ceiling but in this case, it was mirrored by a gleaming wooden floor. The furniture, which included a four-poster bed and a large, heavily carved armoire, was of a darker wood. Ivory muslin curtains hung at the windows.

Jane let out a little exclamation of pleasure. 'Oh, it's charming.'

The porter bowed. 'I'm glad you are happy, memsahib.' He went over to a door. 'The bathroom is here. We hope that everything you need is provided.' He gestured to the telephone on the nearest bedside table. 'But if you wish for anything else, please call reception and it will be brought to you straight away. Is there something I can fetch for you now?'

De Silva glanced at Jane, who shook her head. 'No, thank you.'

'Then I will leave you in peace to unpack. Dinner is at eight and drinks are served in the bar from half past six.'

De Silva slipped a few coins into the porter's hand and the man smiled. 'Thank you, sahib.'

Jane went to the window and pushed it open wide. 'What a wonderful view!'

De Silva joined her, and together they looked out over the gardens towards the sea.

'I'm glad you approve,' he said. 'We so rarely take a holiday. I thought we should do it in style.'

'We're certainly doing that. I feel very spoilt.'

'Apparently, the hotel was originally built in the early eighteenth century as the private house of a wealthy Dutch merchant who preferred to live outside the city walls.'

'I imagine the city was rather a smelly place in those days.'

'I'm sure it was. When the Dutch left, and before it became a hotel, several Britishers made their homes here.

There are only ten bedrooms in the main building but also two cottages in the grounds for guests who want more privacy.'

Jane turned away from the window. 'I suppose we should unpack and then get ready for dinner, or we won't have time for a drink in the bar.' She frowned. 'I do hope the clothes I've brought will be smart enough.'

He kissed her cheek. 'I'm sure you'll be the most elegant lady there.'

She laughed. 'Somehow, I doubt it, but I'll be satisfied if I can pass in the crowd.'

An hour later, with Jane in a midnight-blue dress that flattered her slim figure, they set off. De Silva wore the dinner suit that usually only came out when they were invited to one of the evening parties that his boss, Archie Clutterbuck, and his wife Florence threw at their official residence in Nuala, but he had known when he booked the hotel that formal dress would be required in the evenings. All the same, he was looking forward to spending his days in more relaxed attire.

He glanced down at the front of his dress shirt. Some of the buttons were straining a little; it was a while since he'd needed to wear it. When they got back to Nuala, it might be wise to ration his consumption of his favourite pea and cashew curry and cook's excellent butter cake for a few weeks. Still, they were on holiday now. He gave his bow tie a tweak to make sure it was straight and offered Jane his arm.

As they descended the stairs, however, the doubts that often crept up on him when he and Jane ventured into unfamiliar territory refused to be banished from his mind. In Nuala, people who knew them had long ago accepted that they were man and wife, or if they disapproved, they were too polite to show it. All the same, there was no deny-ing that a marriage between a local man and a British lady was unusual and might give rise to unwelcome comments in new surroundings.

He pulled himself together. Jane was far too matter-of-fact to be troubled by the prejudices of strangers who they would probably never encounter again after their holiday came to an end. He must try to take a leaf out of her book. Still, he had to admit that he would be glad if they managed to make a quiet entrance to the bar and avoid too many eyes turning to look at them.

A commotion over by the main entrance to the hotel distracted him from his thoughts. In common with everyone else in the lobby, he and Jane stopped to watch the arrival of a tall, slender lady dressed in a black satin gown. White ostrich feathers trimmed its low neckline and the lady's stylish appearance was enhanced by the ropes of pearls and the magnificent diamond bracelet that she wore. Her face was fashionably pale with artfully plucked eyebrows and lips accentuated by scarlet lipstick. One of the three dinner-jacketed men who escorted her carried her ermine stole.

The manager rushed forward to greet the party and ushered them into the bar. De Silva and Jane followed. By the time they crossed the threshold, not only the manager but several waiters too were hovering around the table where the lady and her companions were taking their seats. Their table was in one of the large bay windows overlooking the garden. De Silva was amused to observe that although most of the other occupants of the bar were watching discreetly, a stout lady in a puce dress, who reminded him of Florence Clutterbuck, was doing no such thing and was studying the foursome with blatant curiosity.

The party's orders for drinks taken, the waiters scurried off to fetch them, but the manager stayed a few moments longer before coming back in the direction of the lobby. When he passed the table where the de Silvas sat, he stopped and bowed. 'I hope everything is to your satisfaction in your room.'

Jane smiled. 'Perfect, thank you.'

'Would you like a few moments before I send a waiter to take your drinks order?'

'Yes, please.' Jane lowered her voice. 'Who is the lady at the table in the window? I'm sure I recognise her.'

'That is Madame Elodie Renaud, ma'am. She and her party are with us for a few days. They're staying at one of the two guest bungalows we have in our grounds.'

'Ah, of course. Thank you.'

The manager departed and de Silva reached for the cocktail menu and handed it to Jane. 'The name obviously means something to you,' he remarked, 'but I can't say it does to me.'

'Don't you remember? There was an article about her in the papers a while ago.'

'I'm afraid I don't.'

'She's the widow of Pierre Renaud, the French adventurer. He was killed in a skiing accident a couple of years ago. Skiing was only one of the adventurous activities he liked to take part in. Another was deep-sea diving. He became quite famous for the pioneering work he did in developing breathing apparatus and extending the length of time divers could stay underwater and the depths to which they could go.'

A vague memory stirred in de Silva's brain. 'Ah yes, I think I do recall something about that. But what would his widow be doing here?'

'The article that I read in the paper was about how determined she is to continue her late husband's work. It mentioned she was coming to Ceylon. I suppose there are lots of places to dive in this area.'

'I'm sure of it.' He handed her the cocktail menu. 'There's a lot to choose from. What will you have? It's a whisky for me, but I expect you'll be more adventurous.'

'It does seem a shame not to try one of their cocktails.'

While she studied the list, de Silva surreptitiously watched the party at the table in the window. One of Elodie Renaud's companions produced a gold cigarette case and offered it around. The cigarettes looked to be an exotic brand with gold filters and black papers. When the party lit up, de Silva smelled a rich, nutty fragrance. The men started to engage in lively conversation while Elodie watched them with an expression of languid amusement. De Silva guessed that she expected to be entertained rather than entertaining others, but she must be a brave lady. From what he had heard of deep-sea diving, it was an activity that was not to be undertaken lightly.

His attention was diverted by Jane putting down the cocktail menu.

'I think I'll have a gin rickey.'

'What goes into that?'

'Gin, naturally, and some lime juice and soda.'

'It sounds very refreshing, but I still think I'll stick to whisky.'

He signalled to a waiter hovering nearby who came to take their order. While they waited for him to return, de Silva settled into the comfortable cane armchair and surveyed the room. It was very different from the bar at the Crown Hotel in Nuala. There, the atmosphere was similar to what he imagined it would be in a traditional British gentleman's club, all mellow wood panelling and baronial grandeur. In contrast, the decor in the Cinnamon Lodge's bar was much airier with pastel walls and large windows. He wondered if it had started life as an orangery. The generous size of the windows, with the addition of several skylights, suggested that it might have done. Ceiling fans rotated with a low hum, stirring the warm air. The blue and cream floor tiles were decorated with pictures of fantastical creatures, half human, and half fish. They had an antique patina, and de Silva wondered whether they dated from the days when the Dutch occupied Ceylon.

Apart from Elodie Renaud's party and the stout lady in puce, who had a much younger female companion with her, there were five other couples in the bar. One couple greeted a young man who had just arrived by himself. They summoned one of the bar staff and a chair was brought, so that he could join them at their table. From the snippets of conversation that drifted in his direction, de Silva guessed that all of these people were British. The table in the bay window overlooking the garden next to Elodie Renaud's was still empty.

'I wonder if there'll be any other special guests this evening,' remarked Jane, her eyes also resting on it.

'If there are any more celebrities, you're far more likely to recognise them than I am.'

Their drinks arrived and Jane took a sip of hers.

'It's delicious. Just the thing for a warm evening. I must say, even though we're by the sea, it seems hotter here than it is at home. One forgets how much difference the higher altitude of the hill country makes.'

'We'll just have to take life more slowly until we become acclimatised.'

'I'm sure that will be a very good thing.'

'What would you like to do tomorrow? Very slowly, of course.'

Jane laughed. 'It would be nice to drive into Galle and take a stroll around before the day gets too hot. I'd like to go to the fort and see the old town.'

'Very well, that's what we'll do.'

Once again the manager appeared at the door to the bar, this time ushering in a tall, dark-haired man who looked to be in his late twenties. His classically handsome features gave him an aristocratic air. He was accompanied by a lady dressed in fuchsia-pink satin who looked to be a few years younger than he was. The manager led them to the table next to Elodie Renaud's and held out a chair for the lady to sit down. For a moment, she turned to face the room and de Silva saw a pretty, vivacious face framed by stylishly crimped blonde hair.

'Are you going to tell me they're celebrities too?' he asked in a low voice.

'If they are,' whispered Jane, 'I don't recognise them, but they certainly make a very handsome couple.'

Eventually, the dinner gong sounded, and everyone went into the dining room. It was another light, airy room but this time the walls were painted a deep ochre and, as in the hall, the floor was tiled in black and white. A waiter showed them to a table on the left-hand side of the room and brought menus. It took de Silva no time at all to decide that he would sample some of the local dishes on offer. Jane studied the English section of the menu and chose soup followed by grilled fish.

Elodie Renaud's party had grown a little quieter than they had been in the bar. De Silva remembered reading somewhere that eating was a serious business with the French. Unlike the British who seemed happiest with plain food, they were fond of rich sauces and elaborate recipes and took a great deal of care over what they ate. The fact that two waiters, one of whom de Silva guessed was the head one, were kept busy attending to their table made him think that not only Elodie Renaud but also her companions were French. He began to feel rather sorry for the waiters. When they passed by his and Jane's table on one of their many errands, he noticed a sheen of sweat on their faces.

Meanwhile, the glamorous couple who had been in the bar and were once more sitting not far from Elodie Renaud and her party, seemed only to have eyes for each other. De Silva heard the chink of ice as a silver bucket containing a bottle of champagne was carried past on its way to their table. One of the waiters opened it with a ceremonial flourish and a little puff of vapour came out from the bottle's neck before the champagne was poured foaming into gold-rimmed glasses. Perhaps the couple were celebrating an anniversary, he thought.

Their meal arrived and they chatted as they ate. De Silva was glad to find that even if the hotel guests were mainly British, the hotel cooks knew how to make tasty local food. To him, Jane's grilled fish looked very plain, but he appreciated that she sometimes liked to eat the food she had grown up with in England.

Dinner came to an end and guests started to leave the dining room.

'I think coffee's being served in the lounge,' said Jane. 'But I'd be happy to save that for another night if you are. After the journey, I'm quite tired.'

De Silva nodded. It was no hardship to him. To his mind, the only hot drink worth having was tea.

They were just getting up from the table when the stout lady in puce and her companion passed by. 'I shall have to speak to the manager,' she was saying in a voice so like Florence Clutterbuck's that they might have been twins. 'The fish was terribly dry,' she went on loudly.

'My meal was very nice,' said her companion. She was a pleasant-looking young woman with auburn hair.

The puce lady gave an audible snort. De Silva noticed that despite her ample figure, she had small, neat hands that looked very soft. A thick layer of face powder had been applied to her smooth, plump cheeks and a strong scent of lilacs hung about her. 'That may be, but one *has* to be firm. Let the locals think they can get away with letting standards slip and where will we all be? From the moment your dear departed uncle and I came to Ceylon, I was always scrupulous about seeing to it that standards were kept up.'

With an inward shudder, de Silva was glad that Jane

hadn't wanted to go to the lounge for coffee. He didn't relish the thought of ending the evening listening to tactless remarks about his countrymen.

'What a silly woman,' said Jane as the pair vanished in the direction of the lounge. 'I'm sorry about her.'

'Don't be,' de Silva said. 'What's your British saying? Sticks and stones may break my bones, but words will never hurt me?'

She squeezed his arm. 'I'm glad you can say that. Well, I think I'll go up to our room. Are you ready to come?'

'If you don't mind, I'd like to take a stroll around the grounds first.'

She looked down at her shoes. 'I'd come with you, but these aren't really suitable, and the grass may be damp by now.'

'Don't worry, I won't be long.'

Outside, he saw that Elodie Renaud's party were a little way ahead of him. Presumably, they were on their way back to their guest bungalow. At a junction of paths, they turned onto the one that went to the left. At the far end of it, was the shadowy outline of a low building with lights glowing in its windows. De Silva set off along the path to the right, hoping it would lead him to the beach.

Soon, a salty breeze freshened the humid air along with the low rumble of waves breaking on the shore. Abruptly, the lush hotel lawn ended at a set of steps leading down to the beach. The ocean lay before him. The rocks that fringed the sandy shore glistened in the moonlight; palm trees loomed out of the darkness like gigantic ghostly apparitions from some ancient tale.

He descended the steps then bent to unlace his shoes, removed them, and took off his socks. Leaving them on the bottom step, he stepped onto the still-warm sand and felt his feet sink into it. He wriggled his toes and went a little further then stopped to admire the view once more. With the moonlight casting flecks of silver on its indigo waters, the ocean was a beautiful sight. It was so vast that if you sailed due south, there would be nothing but water until you reached the frozen wastes of Antarctica. In the face of such majesty, the puce lady and her opinions faded into insignificance.

He carried on walking and after a few minutes, rounded a rocky headland to find himself at another beach. If the tide hadn't been so low, he doubted it would have been accessible on foot. An old fishing boat lay in the shadow of a clump of palms. It seemed to have been painted red at some time in its existence but most of its paint had worn away. It didn't look very seaworthy either. Certainly, he wouldn't want to entrust his life to it for anything more than the shortest journey.

He went over to it, leant against the prow, and thought of the lives of the fishermen in the area. He'd heard that fish were plentiful in the waters around Galle, so no doubt the locals were able to feed their families and make a little money from selling their surplus catch. He wondered why this boat had been abandoned. It must have been a valuable asset at one time. He'd read that not all fishermen owned a boat; some stayed close to shore and cast their lines from the stilt-like wooden contraptions they set up in the shallow water.

A cloud drifted over the moon and a stiffer breeze made him shiver. It was time for bed. He returned to the place where he had left his shoes and socks, brushed the sand from his feet and put them back on, then out of curiosity decided to take a more roundabout path to the hotel.

A few minutes later, back on the level of the lawn, he found himself close to the guest bungalow he had seen Elodie Renaud's party heading for. The lights were on and there were people sitting on the verandah. Laughter and strains of music drifted towards him. He didn't recognise the tune, but he stopped for a few moments, enjoying listening to it.

When it came to an end, he was about to set off for the hotel but then he paused. In the trees close to the cottage, something was moving. The moon had disappeared behind a cloud. He strained his eyes, trying to see into the darkness. What if it was a wild animal on the prowl? Should he call out a warning to Elodie and her friends that they might be in danger? It wasn't unknown for animals to make a sudden attack.

But as he hesitated, the moon reappeared. If there had been something there, it was gone, or perhaps what he'd seen had been low trees and shrubs swaying in the breeze. Nevertheless, he thought he might wait a few more moments to be sure that he had just imagined an interloper.

He had almost decided that must have been the case, and it was time to go back to the hotel, when something emerged from the trees not far from where he stood. He stiffened, then to his relief he realised that the something had two legs not four and carried a torch. As its light came closer, he saw a man dressed in a uniform with the hotel's insignia on the pocket of the shirt. He raised a hand and saluted de Silva.

'Good evening, sahib. I am the nightwatchman. May I help you?'

'No, thank you, I was just taking a stroll before I turn in.'

'It is a fine night for it, sahib, but there are reports that a leopard has been seen in the grounds.'

De Silva frowned. 'I thought I might have seen something just now. Over there by that guest bungalow.'

'Ah no, sahib, that was me.' The man indicated his torch. 'I turn this off when I am close to the guests. I do not want to disturb them. But it is wise to be careful. If you wish, I will accompany you back to the hotel.'

De Silva smiled. 'Thank you, but I think I'll be safe on my own.'

'Then I wish you goodnight, sahib.'

* * *

Jane was already in bed when he reached their room.

'Did you have a nice walk?' she asked.

He nodded.

'Where did you go?'

'Along the beach. You can reach the adjoining one when the tide's low. I found an old fishing boat there.'

'I saw in the hotel information that guests can hire boats to take trips along the coast.'

'Not that boat, I trust,' said de Silva with a chuckle. 'I don't think you'd get very far. Did you come straight up here?'

'No, I decided to stay downstairs for a little while after all and do some exploring of my own. I discovered there's a library tucked away at the end of the corridor that goes past the lounge. It's only small but it might be useful if I run out of reading matter.'

De Silva smiled. 'Remembering how heavy that case of yours was, is that really likely?'

Jane laughed. 'Perhaps not, but another time I'd like a better look at what they have there. I stopped in the lobby to chat to the manager before I came upstairs. He told me that since the Cinnamon Lodge became a hotel, there have been many alterations, but the owners were keen to keep the library. They thought it was a nice feature.'

De Silva yawned. 'I agree. Oh, by the way, I saw Elodie Renaud and her friends too. They were going back to one of the guest bungalows. After that, I met a nightwatchman who seemed very concerned about my safety. He told me there'd been a report of a leopard in the grounds, and he wanted to guide me back here, but I told him there was no need.'

'Shanti, you really should listen to advice.'

'I'm safely back, aren't I? And anyway, I think he was really just after a tip. I first noticed him when he was near the bungalow, but I wasn't sure what I was seeing because it was too dark. As it turned out, he told me he turned his torch off when he was near the bungalow so as not to disturb the guests, but I'm sure he's aware that wandering around in the dark's not a good recipe for keeping safe if there's genuinely a predator about.'

'That's very cynical of you. His warning might have been well-intentioned. Promise me you'll be more careful in future. Our holiday has only just begun. I don't want it to end in disaster.'

He went over to the bed and put his arms around her. 'I certainly don't either. I promised you a proper holiday and that's what we'll have.'

CHAPTER 2

At breakfast the next morning, there was no sign of Elodie Renaud's party or of the celebrating couple.

'I expect they're staying at the other guest bungalow and the hotel will serve their breakfast there,' remarked Jane.

As the two of them walked to their table, de Silva saw that apart from a young man who sat at a table laid for one, deep in the book he was reading, the other occupants of the dining room had all been at dinner the previous evening. Like the husband of the celebrating couple, the young man was tall and dark-haired, but there the resemblance ended. No one would have called him glamorous. He was dressed in an ill-fitting linen jacket and a pair of baggy trousers that were both of a drab shade of brown. He wore wire-rimmed spectacles through which he was peering at his book, his eyes not leaving it as he conveyed forkfuls of omelette and gulps of coffee to his mouth. The savoury smell of the eggs and the coffee's rich aroma drifted towards de Silva's sensitive nose. What a pity such pleasures seemed to be wasted on this young man. He wondered why he had not been at dinner the previous evening. Perhaps he had arrived late at the hotel.

'Waiter! The water you brought for our tea is positively tepid!'

The stout lady's voice carried across the dining room and de Silva gave an involuntary start. Today she was garbed in a dress splashed with outsized pink flowers. Her young companion, looking embarrassed, murmured something to her, but she took no notice as she tapped her beringed fingers on the table and tutted. 'I really don't know what this place is coming to,' she said with a scowl.

A waiter scuttled over. From his resigned expression, de Silva guessed this was not the first time that morning that the stout lady had found something to complain about. He felt sorry for her young companion whose attempts to quieten her were clearly being unsuccessful.

'Good morning, sahib, memsahib.'

De Silva looked up to see that a waiter had arrived with their menus. They spent a few moments choosing what they would have then Jane ordered an omelette and toast and he asked for an egg hopper.

'And tea for me, please,' said Jane.

De Silva nodded. 'For me as well.'

The waiter glanced in the direction of the stout lady's table. She had quietened down now and was busy addressing a large plate of fried food. He permitted himself a ghost of a smile. 'I will make sure that the water for the tea is extremely hot, sahib.'

De Silva chuckled. 'See to it that you do.'

* * *

Breakfast over, they returned to their room and made ready to go out. Fifteen minutes later, they were ensconced in the Morris and motoring towards town. There wasn't a cloud in the cornflower blue sky, and it would be a few hours before the heat of the day built up. Plenty of time to enjoy a stroll through Galle's historic quarter and a walk around its walls before they returned to the hotel for lunch.

Jane put up a hand to hold her hat in place as they

bowled along, kicking up little clouds of dust in their wake.

'Would you prefer to have the top up?' asked de Silva, giving her a sideways glance.

'Not at all, I'm enjoying the breeze.'

He hooted as they came up behind a bullock cart loaded with vegetables and bundles of greenery. Its driver took his time moving to the side of the road, giving the Morris just enough room to pass. As he edged carefully through the gap, de Silva reflected that at home, there were advantages to being recognised as the local chief of police. Most other road users usually got out of the way a bit more smartly.

Stalls selling an assortment of fruit, vegetables, tin pots and pans, trays of snacks, and brightly coloured drinks were set up along the road. Presumably, their owners hoped to attract customers who didn't want to walk into town. Women haggled over the wares while groups of men loitered in the shade of palm trees gossiping and chewing betel. In some places, de Silva noticed beggars crouched on the ground, scrawny arms outstretched and hands holding battered tin cups. They were a less common sight in the hills where there was usually plenty of work on the tea plantations.

'Some people claim that Galle is the ancient city of Tarshish mentioned in the Bible,' he said, raising his voice to be heard over the wind. 'Ships following the old trading routes would have called in at her harbour. There are stories that merchants stopped here to collect cargoes for King Solomon – elephants, peacocks, ivory, and jewels.'

'It sounds romantic,' said Jane, 'but sadly, I'm sure the reality was far less so.'

'I'm afraid that's probably true.'

They lapsed into silence for a while. De Silva thought about all the twists and turns of history that Galle had seen. When the Portuguese came in the sixteenth century, they had built a fortress out of mud and palm trees, but it hadn't saved them when the Dutch arrived a hundred years later. The Dutch fortress, the one that still stood today, was a far more forbidding affair built of granite and coral and reinforced by massive bastions. When the British came to take control some fifty years after that, they had changed some Dutch street names to English ones and done a little building, but otherwise left the city much as they'd found it.

The long history of his country's subjugation to foreign powers, reflected de Silva. He wondered if he would be alive to see the British leave Ceylon. People whispered that the day was coming. He wondered if the war might bring about the change. The Indian National Congress was demanding a guarantee of independence in return for helping the British against Nazi Germany. If India left the Empire, surely it wouldn't be long before Ceylon followed.

Jane's voice brought him back to the present. He cupped a hand to his ear.

'Sorry, what did you say?'

'You seem very thoughtful. Is anything wrong?'

'Nothing at all.'

'I hope you're not worrying about what's happening at the station.'

'Goodness no. I'm sure Prasanna and Nadar are coping perfectly well. I have far more confidence in them than I would have done a few years ago. Anyway, if there's a prob-lem, we could be back in Nuala in a few hours.' He pulled out to pass a rickshaw. 'I'm far more worried about Billy and Bella. I hope they're being properly looked after. We've never left them before.'

Jane laughed. 'With four servants to watch over them, as well as Anif in the garden, I'm sure those little cats are having a wonderful time and hardly missing us at all.'

She shaded her eyes and pointed ahead. 'Look, not far to go now.'

The fort's walls gleamed in the sunshine and soon they

were driving through the main gate. De Silva parked the Morris and found a man to keep an eye on her. He gave him a tip, promising more if he looked after the car well until they returned.

Arm in arm, he and Jane set off through cobbled streets lined with small shops, and houses with cream or saffron-yellow walls and tiled roofs. Often, they were in a dilapidated state but the leafy trees that grew in front of many of them lent them charm. The old warehouses looked as if they had seen better days too. Once they would have been thriving and bustling with activity. Passers-by would have breathed in air fragrant with tea and spices. But Colombo had taken the shipping trade from Galle many years ago and the city had been relegated to a provincial backwater.

All the same there were still some fine buildings: the mansions and government offices that had been built by the British, the old Dutch hospital with its arcaded white frontage, and the splendid white wedding cake of a house that had once been the city governor's residence and was now the Eastern Orient Hotel. In the same square as the Dutch Hospital, black-robed lawyers hurried in and out of the courts and letter writers waited for clients.

In the centre of the square stood a small covered market building, and close by grew a vast banyan tree. From a distance its branches seemed to be hung with shaggy streamers, but de Silva knew they were aerial roots that if left unchecked would eventually reach the ground and grow into thick trunks independent of the original.

Jane fanned herself. 'I think I'd like to sit down for a little while. My feet are starting to feel sore from all these cobbles.'

They found a bench and sat contemplating the square. The courts must have been over for the morning for people were coming out. 'If we're to have time for a walk along the walls, we ought to be on our way soon,' said de Silva after ten minutes had passed.

Jane stood up. 'I'm as ready as I'll ever be.'

The stretch of the walls that they walked took them past the lighthouse and up to the tip of the peninsular. There they paused to look across the bay. Seabirds whirled and dived, and a few brightly coloured boats bobbed on the gently swelling waves.

'That's Rumassala,' said de Silva, pointing to a low, jungle-clad hill on the far side of the bay. 'When I was a child, my mother told me the legend of how it came to be there. In the battle between the army of Lord Rama and the army of the demon, Ravana, Lord Rama's brother Lakshman was badly wounded. It seemed he would die before sunrise, but his brother was determined to save him. The monkey god, Hanuman, was famous for his ability to jump great distances. Because of this skill, Lord Rama ordered him to go to a mountain in the Himalayas where a magical herb grew that would cure Lakshman. Hanuman set off, but when he reached the mountain, he wasn't sure which herb to bring back, so he pulled up the whole mountain and carried it on the palms of his hands back to Ceylon. On his way to the battlefield, he accidentally dropped a piece of it on Rumassala. The villagers say that is why rare herbs grow there.'

'What a lovely story. Was Lakshman cured?'

'Yes, and he went on to perform many wonderful deeds.' He glanced at his watch. 'Time we were getting back, or we'll be too late for lunch.'

Jane paused.

'What is it?' he asked.

'Oh, it's just that I noticed a pretty necklace in one of the shops in the bazaar that we passed. I think it's on the way back to the car. I'd just like to stop there for a minute and have a better look.'

He took her arm. 'Whatever you say.'

In the bazaar, Jane pointed out the necklace. It was a simple gold chain with the letter J hanging from it. 'Do you remember that I used to have one like it that I lost?' she asked.

He nodded. 'I do. You used to wear it quite often. Well, would you like this one to replace it?'

'It would be nice, as long as it isn't too expensive.'

He squeezed her arm. 'If you like it, we'll buy it anyway. It's not every day we're on holiday.'

The interior of the shop was small and dark. The shopkeeper hurried forward to greet them. Unable to resist bargaining, de Silva soon had him laying out several necklaces for display before working his way around to the one Jane wanted. Finally, they agreed a price and the necklace was wrapped up and paid for.

'Really, Shanti,' said Jane with an admonishing look when they were back in the street. 'That took far longer than I planned, or than it would have done if you'd left it to me.'

'Ah, but then we would have paid too much.'

She raised an eyebrow. 'A rupee or two perhaps.'

'But they might have been just the rupees that we need one day to spend on something else. What is that British saying: the devil is in the detail?'

'I don't think that's what the saying is meant to be about. You simply can't resist bargaining.'

He grinned. 'You may be right.'

The clatter of pots and pans and the aroma of spices drifted from open windows as they returned to the place where they had left the Morris. De Silva's stomach rumbled.

'This sightseeing business makes one hungry,' he remarked. 'And it's more energetic than I expected. After lunch, a leisurely afternoon with a book in the hotel gardens would suit me very well.'

'That sounds perfect.'

At the hotel, guests were already drifting into the dining room, so they hurried upstairs to freshen up before joining them. As he tucked into his meal, de Silva wondered whether he might have eaten something just as tasty in one of those humble houses in Galle but perhaps served on a tin plate or a banana leaf rather than bone china. Neither the French party, the celebrating couple, nor the young man with his book were having lunch, but the rest of the guests who had been at dinner the previous night were. De Silva was glad for the sake of the waiters that the stout lady seemed a little more subdued than she had at breakfast and was eating her lamb chops without complaint. She followed them with a large slice of treacle tart with custard, and de Silva decided to order the same. With his sweet tooth, he had always considered puddings by far the best thing about the food the British had brought to Ceylon.

'I'm on holiday,' he said cheerfully when Jane raised an eyebrow at the size of the portion. 'And I took plenty of exercise this morning. But if you insist, tomorrow we can walk twice around the walls.'

Jane laughed. 'I won't insist. As you say, we're on holiday.'

'I'll go and fetch our books,' he said when they had finished eating.

'Thank you, dear.'

The shutters had been closed in their room making it pleasantly cool. The air smelled of fresh linen and lavender-scented polish. He inhaled a deep breath and thought how pleasant this hotel life was. They should go away more often.

Downstairs, he was crossing the lobby in the direction of the garden when, through the open doors of the main entrance, he noticed a policeman in the uniform of a chief inspector standing at the top of the steps to the drive. With him was the manager, and de Silva observed that the urbane manner he had shown when they arrived had been replaced by one of anxiety. The policeman was doing all the talking, tapping his cane against a leather boot as he spoke. He was scowling.

The manager must have noticed de Silva watching them for he murmured something to the chief inspector and hurried over.

'Is there something I can help you with, sir?' he asked.

'No, I was just on my way to the garden, but I couldn't help noticing your visitor. Is anything wrong?'

'Oh, nothing at all. Merely a routine visit.' The manager smiled awkwardly. 'I hope lunch was to your liking.'

'Excellent, thank you.'

'And are you going into the city this afternoon?'

'No, we went this morning. My wife and I are looking forward to relaxing in the garden.'

'A wise plan.' The manager cast a glance over his shoulder towards the entrance. The chief inspector was already halfway down the steps.

'Please, excuse me,' he said hastily. 'I must have another word with Chief Inspector Lawrence before he leaves.'

'Of course, don't let me keep you.'

De Silva watched as the manager hurried away; he might almost have described him as scurrying, compared with his dignified bearing the previous day. *A routine matter, eh?* It was a strange way to behave if that was all it was. He wondered what was really going on, but then reminded himself that he was on holiday and before they left Nuala, he'd promised Jane that nothing would interfere with that.

* * *

In the garden, they found a quiet place to sit in the shade. A drowsy air hung over the afternoon. De Silva's attention wandered from his book and the next thing he knew Jane was tapping him on the arm.

'You've been asleep.'

'Have I? I hope I wasn't snoring.'

'Well, not very loudly.'

Yawning, he felt in his lap for his book and found it gone. Jane pointed to the small table between them. 'I put it there for you.'

'Thank you.' He stood up. 'I think I'll take a walk. It will wake me up. Would you like to join me?'

She flipped through the pages she had left to read. 'Not just now if you don't mind. I only have twenty pages to go and although I think I've worked out who did it, I want to know if I'm right.'

'Then I'll leave you to it.'

* * *

He set off to wander along the garden's winding paths. Many of the plants they grew here were very different to those he cultivated in his garden at home in Nuala. Away from the cooler air of the hill country, tougher, more leathery-leaved plants were clearly favoured: yuccas, aloes, and succulents whose plump leaves looked almost artificial. There were many cacti too and he examined their grotesque shapes with interest. Where they were blooming, the flowers that erupted from their spiny surfaces were startling shades of yellow and pink.

He was brought up short by a fence smothered in scarlet bougainvillaea and realised he must have reached the edge of the grounds. To his left, the path continued inside the fence and eventually meandered through a grove of cinnamon trees. He ran a hand over one of the trunks, found a loose piece of bark and broke it off then inhaled the sweet, spicy fragrance. Cinnamon was still a major export for Ceylon but hundreds of years ago, the island had supplied the needs of the whole of Europe. The Dutch and the Portuguese had fought wars over it and when the Dutch prevailed, they had even made it an offence punishable by death for anyone to compete with their plantations by selling wild cinnamon from the jungle.

'Good afternoon.'

A nearby voice startled him. He looked to see where it had come from and saw the stout lady's young companion smiling at him from a spot where she was half hidden in the shade of a pretty summerhouse. She sat on a small stool and had an easel set up with a painting propped on it.

'I'm sorry, I interrupted your thoughts,' she went on.

'There's no need to apologise. They were not important. I should apologise for interrupting your painting.'

The young lady laughed. 'Well, now that we have observed the formalities and apologised to each other in the approved British way, it's probably time I introduced myself. I'm Helen Morris.'

'Shanti de Silva, at your service, ma'am.'

'And how do you like the Cinnamon Lodge, Mr de Silva? Is it your first visit?'

'It is, and my wife Jane and I are enjoying it very much.'

'I'm so glad. I know it quite well as my aunt has made it her home. I live in Colombo, but I come to visit her several times a year. She always rests in the afternoon, so I decided to spend a few hours painting.'

'May I take a look?'

'You're welcome to, but I'm afraid it's far from being one of my best efforts. I haven't managed to catch the light as I wanted.'

As he approached, Helen Morris wiped the brush she

had been using on a piece of rag and turned her easel a little so that he could see the painting propped up on it.

'It looks very accomplished to me. You're clearly a perfectionist.'

'And you're very tactful,' she said with a smile. He noticed that when she smiled, she looked much prettier. In contrast to her rich auburn hair, she had pale skin, lightly dusted with freckles. Her eyes were amber, flecked with greyish green. He guessed that she was in her mid-twenties.

She hesitated. 'Speaking of tact, I must apologise for Aunt Edith's behaviour yesterday evening. She has a good heart but an unfortunate habit of not thinking before she speaks. I try to make her understand that her voice is more of a foghorn than a whisper, but she rarely takes any notice.'

De Silva chuckled. 'No offence was taken but thank you.'

'I'm glad to hear it. When my uncle was alive, they lived in the north of the island. The town wasn't large, but he held the senior official post there. I think she finds it hard to remember that she's no longer a big fish in a small pond.'

She glanced at her watch. 'It's time I was going back to the hotel. Tea will be ready soon and Aunt Edith hates to be kept waiting.'

'May I carry something for you?'

'That would be most kind. I usually pack up and one of the staff who brings everything down for me comes to collect it, but it would save them the trouble.'

'Of course.'

'We have an interesting guest at the hotel,' she remarked as she began to pack her tubes of paint, brushes, and other equipment into a wooden box. 'Elodie Renaud is quite a celebrity.'

'So my wife tells me.' He took the box from her and picked up the easel.

'I think it's splendid that she wants to carry on her late husband's work, although the first time I saw her, I found it impossible to imagine such a glamorous creature dressed in one of those ugly suits that divers wear.'

De Silva agreed it seemed incongruous.

'I know a few of the other guests slightly from previous visits,' Helen went on. 'Most of them are colonial officials and their wives.'

'Last night, I noticed a young man who seemed to arrive on his own, before he was invited to join a couple at a table.'

'Oh, I expect you mean George Blaine. This is the first time he's been to the hotel. He's on holiday from his work in the Department of Roads and Railways. He's an engineer there.' She gave de Silva an awkward little smile. 'He's nice and we've played a few games of tennis, but I wish my aunt wouldn't keep talking about how we should get together. It's very embarrassing.'

De Silva murmured something noncommittal. Jane would know much better than he did how to answer such a remark. He wondered if Helen was younger than he'd originally thought. She seemed rather disingenuous.

'It's also the first time I've seen the couple who were drinking champagne yesterday evening,' she went on quickly, as if to cover her embarrassment at saying too much. 'His name's Jocelyn Reeve, and his wife is called Pamela. Aunt Edith doesn't approve of them. She thinks that a man of his age ought to be involved in the war effort, not enjoying himself on holiday. She's convinced he has something to do with the black market and that's where his money comes from.'

'And what do you think?'

'I think one shouldn't jump to conclusions.'

'What about the other young man on his own? We saw him for the first time at breakfast. I wondered if he'd checked in late on the night we arrived.'

'Oh, Max Larsson. No, he's been here for a while. He doesn't always come down for meals. Sometimes he prefers to eat in his room. He seems pleasant but very shy. Even Aunt Edith hasn't managed to find out a great deal about him, although she says that he's already visited the hotel several times this year. She approves of him though because he's always very polite and respectful towards her. He's Swedish and a keen amateur naturalist. He's studying the flora and fauna along this coastline, but apparently he's less interested in the marine life as he's nervous of water. I believe his real job is something to do with the mines at Ratnapura.'

De Silva knew the name. The mines were famous as the place for Ceylon's prized sapphires.

With everything packed, they set off in the direction of the hotel. 'May I enquire what brought you to Ceylon?' he asked as they walked.

'I came out from England a few years ago after my parents died. I teach art and help out with games at a school for British girls in Colombo.'

'And are you happy there?'

'Oh yes. Everyone's very kind, and the girls are well behaved. Ceylon is so beautiful, and the weather is far better here than it is in England. If I'd stayed there, I might have been teaching in some dreary old place that was freezing cold in winter. I haven't forgotten my old convent school. The nuns believed that discomfort was good for the soul, and the food was horrible.'

De Silva laughed. 'I've never believed that discomfort is good for anything and I'm very fond of my food, so I'm glad I was spared a similar experience. I was educated at a day school in Colombo and didn't leave home until I went to police cadet college.'

'So you're a policeman?'

'Yes, I'm in charge of the police force in a town called Nuala in the hill country.' He reflected that it was perhaps a rather grand way to describe Prasanna and Nadar, then smiled to himself. He must be getting old if he wanted to impress an attractive lady who was young enough to be his daughter.

'I think I know it,' she said. 'It's a charming place and the countryside is lovely with all the hills and tea plantations.'

'Thank you. Jane and I are very fond of it. I spent the first twenty years or so of my career in Colombo, so it's quite a change.'

'Is Nuala where you met?'

'No, we met in Colombo. Jane was governess to a British family there.'

He wondered what Helen Morris thought about a Ceylonese man being married to a British woman, but he was aware that it wasn't the British way to put such thoughts into words. Unless, of course, you were of the stamp of Helen's Aunt Edith. From the easy way that Helen carried on chatting, however, he presumed that she was untroubled by the situation. Perhaps, like his friend Charlie Frobisher at the Residence, young Britishers who came to Ceylon were more open-minded than the older generation tended to be.

The easel and the box of equipment were more cumbersome than he'd expected, and Helen walked at a brisk pace. A little out of breath, he was reminded that he wasn't getting any younger. He was glad when they came in sight of the hotel and a servant hurried across the lawn to meet them. Apologising profusely, he took the easel and box from de Silva, and Helen told him to take them up to her room.

The man nodded. 'Tea is being served on the lawn, memsahib. Your aunt Memsahib Pargeter is asking when you are coming there.'

'Thank you, Ajith. Please tell her I'll be with her directly.'

She smiled at de Silva. 'It's been a pleasure meeting you. I hope we have the chance to talk again.'

'The pleasure has been all mine and I hope so too.'

'Now, I must go and find Aunt Edith. It doesn't do to keep her waiting, especially where tea is concerned.'

De Silva bade her goodbye and went to find Jane who was just closing her book.

'Were you right about who did it?' he asked.

'I was, although the author threw in a twist at the end that I hadn't expected.'

'It sounds like the kind of thing that causes a great deal of trouble in real life.' He sat down. 'I met the stout lady's companion on my walk. Her name is Helen Morris, and it turns out that she's a niece. A very pleasant young lady. She was kind enough to apologise for her aunt's behaviour yesterday evening. She was doing some painting, and she told me she teaches art at a school for British girls in Colombo.'

'It was kind of her to apologise,' said Jane. 'Although I think the apology should really come from her aunt.'

He shrugged. 'No matter. Perhaps, like Florence Clutterbuck, Edith Pargeter would be not so bad if you got to know her.'

'You're being very generous.'

He laughed. 'It must be the sea air. Anyway, I enjoyed my talk with her niece. She told me some interesting things about some of the other guests.' He proceeded to explain.

'And now,' he said when he'd finished, 'I believe that tea's being served on the lawn. Would you like to go and have some?'

'I've done very little to work up an appetite this afternoon, but I confess the idea's tempting.'

The lawn to one side of the house where tea was in progress was shaded by two venerable chestnut trees. Edith Pargeter and Helen Morris had already been served and as de Silva and Jane walked to a free table, Helen smiled and raised a hand in greeting. Her aunt looked up from spreading jam on her scone and made some remark to her. At a guess, thought de Silva, she was asking about them.

Their tea arrived, served with scones, little cakes, and finger sandwiches. He was happy to leave the latter to Jane. He had never understood the British fondness for sandwiches. They seemed to him an abomination. The scones and cakes were, however, delicious. 'I shall have to take many more walks while we are here,' he said ruefully as he tucked in.

CHAPTER 3

The rest of the day passed very pleasantly. After a sound sleep, de Silva woke early to see the first glimmer of light seeping through the bedroom shutters. He got out of bed and went to open them a fraction. The sky was still grey, but it was streaked with red in the east. A chorus of unseen birds twittered.

Jane stirred and sat up. 'Gracious, is it morning already? I must have slept very deeply. I'm sure the sea air makes one sleep well, and it's so peaceful here too.'

She looked at the clock on the bedside table. 'Two hours until breakfast time. I think I'll stay in bed for a while and then have a nice long bath before I dress.'

'You do that. I'm going to take a walk. I'd like to see the sun come up over the sea. It should be a splendid sight.'

* * *

He washed quickly, put on some clothes, and went quietly downstairs. The night porter saluted and let him out through the main doors to the drive. There was dew underfoot on the lawn leading to the beach, and his shoes left little indents in the spongy grass. He walked briskly; sunrise was swift in this part of the world, and he didn't want to miss it.

Down at the beach, he buttoned up his jacket to keep out the early morning chill. Over in the east, the sun was already almost clear of the horizon, and a warm golden glow was spreading across the water. Too far away for him to make out what they were, seabirds swooped low over the waves. He found a dry outcrop of rock and sat down to enjoy the scene. He might not tell Jane he had spent more time sitting than walking.

Soon the sun was fully risen, and the colour of the sky had turned from peach and pink to limpid blue. He was debating whether to set off again and retrace the route on which he'd met Helen Morris the previous afternoon, when a flash of movement caught his eye. A tall man was striding down the far side of the beach. He stopped short of the water and shed his trousers and shirt. Underneath them, he wore swimming trunks.

Leaving his clothes in a heap on the sand, he waded into the shallows. When the water came up to his waist, he launched himself in and struck out with a powerful crawl, rapidly leaving the beach far behind. Finally, he stopped swimming and de Silva saw his head bob up and down in the water, but he didn't rest for long and was soon on his way back, his arms carving a smooth path through the waves.

De Silva watched him with a touch of envy. How exhilarating it must feel to be so at home in another element. His own experience of swimming was limited to a few excursions to the beach in Colombo as a child and his father's efforts to teach him to swim. His memories of the occasions were not entirely happy ones, involving many mouthfuls of saltwater and fits of coughing in between his efforts to keep afloat. His father had been fond of swimming and good at it. Now de Silva appreciated how admirable his patience had been. He consoled himself that he was not alone in finding swimming a challenge. He had heard somewhere that even though Ceylon was an island and blessed with a hot climate, a large proportion of her population didn't know how to swim and apparently had no desire to learn.

The swimmer reached the shallows once more and stood up. He shook the water from his hair then stood still for a few moments looking out to sea. De Silva wondered whether he should call out a greeting, then hesitated. There was something about the man that suggested he wanted to be alone with his thoughts.

After a minute or two, he retrieved his clothes and pulled them on. For a white man, observed de Silva, his trousers were surprisingly loose and casual, as was the shirt he wore. He put on his sandals and turned in the direction of the hotel. As he did so, he noticed de Silva and acknowledged him with a perfunctory wave. De Silva nodded in return then realised that the swimmer was the man with the glamorous wife who had been drinking champagne on the evening he and Jane had arrived at the hotel. What had Helen Morris said his name was? Jocelyn Reeve: that was it.

Reeve left the beach, heading in the direction of the hotel. De Silva stood up to follow him but allowed himself a slower pace, then took the circuitous route past the summerhouse where he'd met Helen Morris the previous afternoon. As he walked, he enjoyed the early morning freshness of the gardens and inhaled the rich aromas of damp earth and burgeoning vegetation.

Back at the hotel, he looked into the dining room where waiters were busy putting the final touches to the tables laid for breakfast. Gleaming cutlery, the hotel's monogrammed plates, crisp linen napkins, and vases that each contained a single vivid flower presented an inviting prospect.

Upstairs, he found that Jane was dressed and applying her makeup. He went to the bathroom and washed his hands. The air was warm and steamy and smelled of floral bath salts. When he went back into the bedroom, Jane was surveying herself in the mirror.

'Will I do?'

'Of course. You look lovely.'

'Flatterer. This dress is years old.'

'Does that matter?'

She laughed. 'Not in the normal run of things, but with stylish guests like Elodie Renaud and the Reeves here, I feel the stakes are higher than they are at home.'

He squeezed her shoulder. 'And for me you win every time.'

'Thank you, dear.'

She rested her cheek against his hand for a moment then straightened up. 'Time for breakfast. You must be hungry after your long walk.'

'I certainly am.'

CHAPTER 4

'Well! I hope we aren't all going to be poisoned!'

Edith Pargeter's voice carried across the lobby as de Silva and Jane came down the stairs.

'I assure you, ma'am, everything has been done to ensure that this unfortunate incident doesn't occur again.' The manager's voice was plaintive, and de Silva felt sorry for him. It seemed the man was destined to have two bad days in a row. First the visit from Chief Inspector Lawrence that was, de Silva was convinced, not as routine as the manager claimed, and now this. 'The kitchens have been cleaned from top to bottom,' he went on. 'I have personally inspected all the supplies.'

'I expect nothing less,' snapped Edith Pargeter. 'I really don't know what the world is coming to.' She swept off in the direction of the dining room and breakfast, but her niece hung back.

'Good morning,' she said, coming over to where de Silva and Jane stood. 'I'm afraid my aunt isn't in the best of tempers this morning.' She held out a hand to Jane. 'How do you do, Mrs de Silva. I'm Helen Morris. Your husband may have mentioned that we met yesterday.'

Jane smiled. 'He did, and it's a pleasure to make your acquaintance.'

Helen glanced at the manager who had taken refuge behind the reception desk. 'Poor man. Just now Edith found out from one of the staff that Elodie Renaud and her companions were all taken ill yesterday. They were due to go out on her first dive and it had to be cancelled. They must have been so disappointed. Although they've been here for several days, up until the last day or so, the sea's been too rough. It can be dangerous out on the reef and apparently even after the weather's grown calm, it's best to wait a while until the sand stirred up from the ocean floor settles. Otherwise visibility under the surface is poor.'

'Good morning!'

The young man Helen had said was called George Blaine joined them. He appeared to be in his mid-twenties, tall with an athletic build and dark hair that looked as if it would be curly if it had been allowed to grow longer. He wasn't handsome like Jocelyn Reeve, but his amiable expression gave him an agreeable air.

'Good morning, George.' Helen Morris smiled at him. 'Have you met Inspector de Silva and his wife?'

'Don't believe I've had the pleasure.'

'We were just talking about this unfortunate business with Madame Renaud and her party.'

'Yes, damned shame. I understand they were all set to go out on a dive today and the plan had to be abandoned. As you might expect, the manager's in quite a state.' He lowered his voice. 'I'm afraid the grief your esteemed aunt's giving him hasn't helped, although I don't think there's any cause for her to be anxious. It's only the Renaud party who've suffered. I doubt it's anything to do with the hotel food. Just one of those unfortunate occurrences.'

De Silva wondered whether Helen's Aunt Edith was really worried. She had probably intended to enjoy a hearty breakfast all along. He suspected that she was simply constitutionally incapable of letting an opportunity to criticise pass her by.

'I don't think I'll start my next book yet,' said Jane when they had eaten breakfast.

'Would you like to go into town again, or perhaps just out for a drive?'

'I'd be happy to explore the hotel grounds a little more. If it won't bore you, that is. I feel you've already seen much more of them than I have.'

'Well, not all of them by any means. There's a whole area beyond the lawn where they served tea yesterday that I haven't seen at all.'

Jane went upstairs to fetch her sunhat then they set off. This part of the garden was more overgrown than the parts de Silva had already seen, and the paths not so well main-tained, but as they followed one that wound through groves of tall evergreen shrubs and tree ferns, they heard the sound of rackets hitting balls. When they emerged, they saw a tennis court where Helen Morris and George Blaine were playing a game. As they changed ends, they both noticed the de Silvas and waved.

'We meet again,' Blaine called out cheerfully. 'You're just in time to witness my humiliation! Helen's giving me her usual thrashing.'

Helen laughed. 'What nonsense, I'm only one set ahead. You'll probably beat me.'

'Do you mind if we watch?' asked Jane.

'Not at all, do we, Helen? She's worth watching even if I'm not,' added Blaine.

Helen had already taken up position at the service line. De Silva sat down next to Jane on a nearby bench and watched as she bounced the ball on the ground a few times then tossed it up to serve. He noticed that she had a very determined expression on her face. Clearly, she didn't intend to let her opponent win without a fight.

De Silva knew very little about tennis and, apart from on a few occasions at the garden parties that the Clutterbucks held at the Residence, had rarely watched anyone play, but as the game went on, it became apparent to him that although George Blaine had the advantage in height and strength, Helen was the better player. She was very fast on her feet and her shots were usually accurate, whereas George Blaine had more power than precision. After she'd won the second set, she and Blaine came up to the net and shook hands. He went to one side of the court and wound the net down a little way then he and Helen walked over to where the de Silvas sat.

'There, what did I say?' asked Blaine jovially. 'A thrashing! But in my own defence, I was up against an expert. She teaches tennis at that school of hers.'

'I *help* to teach the girls,' said Helen. 'I think luck was on my side this morning.'

He grinned. 'More than luck.'

However amiable George Blaine was, thought de Silva, no man really liked to be beaten at games by a woman. He suspected that Blaine was smitten with Helen Morris. He certainly seemed to be making a big effort to be personable. If she was keener on him than she had professed to be the previous afternoon, perhaps her Aunt Edith's plan would come to fruition after all.

'Goodness, it's almost a quarter to twelve,' said Helen, looking at her watch. 'If you'll excuse me, I ought to go and find my aunt. I don't want her to think I'm neglecting her, and it will be lunchtime soon.'

'Your aunt suggested I join you for lunch,' said Blaine. 'I hope you have no objection.'

'Of course not,' replied Helen, but de Silva thought she stiffened a little.

Blaine picked up their rackets and balls. 'I'll bring this lot, shall I?'

'Thank you.'

Jane looked up at the sun. It was almost overhead now. 'It's rather hot for any more walking. Shall we go back too, Shanti?'

'Very well.'

As they retraced their steps to the hotel, Jane and Helen walked in front chatting and de Silva fell into step with George Blaine.

'Have you heard any more news about Madame Renaud and her party?' Blaine asked.

'No, but I hope for the manager's sake as well their own that their indisposition is not serious.'

'Likewise, and hopefully it won't last for long. Even if it's not the fault of the hotel, it's bound to cause embarrassment.' Blaine lowered his voice. 'Just between the two of us, and I hope I can rely on you not to pass it on, the manager has more to worry about than the Renaud party being ill. One of the nightwatchmen went missing the night before last. Subsequently, he was found dead in the grounds, apparently killed by a wild animal.'

De Silva's mind went back to the warning he'd been given by the nightwatchman he'd met near Elodie Renaud and her party's bungalow. It sounded as if the man's concern had been well founded, and he'd had a lucky escape.

'Do you know exactly where the body was found?'

'I believe it wasn't far from the guest bungalow where Madame Renaud and her party are staying. Apparently, whatever got him made a very nasty mess of him. I had a word with the local chief inspector, Lawrence, when he was up here. He said the poor fellow was badly mauled. Lawrence had the body taken away immediately. As he said, the last thing one would want would be for a guest to see it.'

No wonder the manager had looked so uncomfortable, thought de Silva. Were it to come out, a death on the premises, particularly such a grim one, would do the hotel's reputation no good at all. He shuddered. It sounded like the dead man was the same nightwatchman he'd talked to on the evening he and Jane had arrived at the hotel. He might well have been killed not long after they spoke.

'Something the matter?' asked Blaine giving him a curious glance.

'I think I spoke to the man not long before he died. I'd gone for a stroll in the grounds after dinner and I met a nightwatchman near that guest bungalow. He warned me there might be a leopard on the prowl. I'm afraid I didn't take it too seriously. Sadly, I seem to have been proved wrong.'

'Unless the fellow was taken completely unawares, I'd be surprised if Elodie Renaud and her companions heard nothing. It's unfortunate that now's not the time to ask them, but apparently the police have questioned the waiter who was delivering coffee and after-dinner drinks from the bar to them. He saw a nightwatchman who told him there was a wild animal on the prowl. The waiter was nervous, and when the nightwatchman offered to take the trolley on to the guest bungalow so he could go back to the hotel, the waiter readily agreed. It looks as if the unfortunate nightwatchman met his end not long after his kind act to help a fellow employee.'

'Has the drinks trolley been found?'

'I don't know. Why do you ask?'

'Oh, no particular reason, but I'm a policeman myself. It's just habit.'

'Ah, I see. Going back to what you told me about the nightwatchman, perhaps you should mention to Lawrence that you met him not long before he was killed.'

'If the information could be of use to him, I'll be happy to oblige.'

'I must admit,' said Blaine after a moment's pause. 'I'm not too impressed with Lawrence.'

'Why do you say that?'

'I may be misjudging him, only time will tell, but I suspect he won't spend long investigating the death. Of course I'm no expert, but as a policeman yourself, wouldn't you say he ought to rule out any other possibilities before taking the firm view that this was an animal attack?'

De Silva couldn't argue with that. It was the approach that he had always chosen. 'What did you have in mind?'

Blaine shrugged. 'Oh, I don't know, you're the expert, but people make enemies, and for all sorts of reasons. Perhaps there was an issue of personal jealousy or revenge. Something like that. An animal could have mauled the body later.'

De Silva was impressed by Blaine's attitude to getting at the truth, but also surprised. In his experience, where the death of a local was concerned, plenty of Britishers would be satisfied with an easy answer. Even those who weren't, might be reluctant to express their doubts to anyone outside their community, particularly someone they'd only just met. Perhaps like Helen Morris and Charlie Frobisher, Blaine was more open-minded than the older generation of Britishers tended to be. Also, Helen had mentioned he was an engineer. It would make sense for him to be trained, in the same way that a policeman was, habitually to analyse and question everything.

'Anyway,' Blaine went on, 'when you've spoken to him, I'd be interested to hear what he has to say.'

'Of course.'

They had reached the hotel and after a few pleasantries, parted company.

'You were having a very serious conversation with George Blaine,' said Jane as they went to their room to tidy up for lunch.

'Do you know, sometimes I really believe that you have eyes in the back of your head.'

She laughed. 'So, what was it all about?'

De Silva told her about the nightwatchman's death.

'Oh, how dreadful,' she said. 'That poor man.' She gave de Silva a stern look. 'I hope you'll take warnings seriously in future. It might have been you that was killed.'

'I'm all too well aware of that, but the case may not be all it seems.'

'What do you mean?'

'Blaine was speculating as to whether this really was a case of an attack by an animal.'

Jane frowned. 'Does he think that the nightwatchman might have been murdered?'

'Well, he suggested it was a possibility that ought to be considered. I think that like me, he favours the belt and braces approach. I told him about my conversation with the nightwatchman and he suggested I report it to Lawrence, the local chief inspector. I saw him yesterday in the hotel lobby, talking with the manager.'

'Will you do that?'

'Certainly. If nothing else, it will help to establish what the nightwatchman's movements were that evening and possibly even provide a clue as to when he was killed.'

'I expect Chief Inspector Lawrence will be grateful for any help.'

'Hmm. I'm not sure, but I'll tell him anyway.'

'Why do you say that?'

'Blaine told me that he wasn't impressed by Lawrence. Blaine's not convinced that he'll take the trouble to investigate the case thoroughly.'

Jane frowned. 'That would be disgraceful, particularly if there's any room for doubt.'

'I agree.'

'If it is the case, couldn't you do something?'

He shrugged. 'I've no jurisdiction here, and anyway, he's senior to me.'

'But perhaps Archie might be persuaded to step in.'

De Silva raised a hand. 'Your concern does you credit, my love, but we mustn't lose sight of the possibility that Blaine has misjudged Lawrence. For the moment, I think it's best to see how matters progress.'

Jane sighed. 'I suppose you're right.'

De Silva thought, but didn't say, that the problem then would be that unless George Blaine happened to get any more information from Lawrence, it might be hard to find out what was going on. Briefly, he wondered why Lawrence had told Blaine as much as he'd already done. Whether it was murder or a tragic accident, the death was bad publicity for the hotel. Surely, the manager would have asked Lawrence not to talk about it with guests unless it was absolutely necessary to question them in the course of an investigation. But if Lawrence wasn't interested in investigating the case, that eventuality was ruled out. Perhaps Lawrence was just careless, but it would be interesting to know exactly why he'd divulged information to Blaine. Had Blaine needed to press him hard for it? De Silva couldn't help but wonder whether Blaine was merely the amiable fellow guest he'd seemed to be at first sight. Was there more to him than met the eye? There was no reason why he shouldn't take a holiday like anyone else, but the Cinnamon Lodge wasn't the most obvious choice for a young single man. Meeting an attractive girl like Helen Morris was hardly a foregone conclusion.

'My conversation with Helen Morris was a little odd,' Jane went on.

'In what way?'

'Well, I thought she was very relaxed at the tennis court, but when we walked back together, her mood seemed to have changed. It was as if something had annoyed her, although I can't think what.'

'Ah, I believe I can answer that one. When we met in

the garden yesterday afternoon, she mentioned something about her aunt embarrassing her with a lot of talk about how she should encourage George Blaine who obviously has a soft spot for her. I imagine she felt that her aunt should have asked her first before issuing the invitation to lunch.' He gave Jane a sideways glance. 'The perils of matchmaking.'

She made a face. 'I know you tease me about that, but you're perfectly well aware that I only do it in my mind. I'd never dream of really trying to interfere in other people's lives. One can so easily do more harm than good.'

He grinned. 'I know, and I'm only joking.'

'All the same, it would be a shame if Helen's aunt spoiled a budding romance. George Blaine seems a very nice young man and Helen Morris may find that her choices diminish as the years go by.'

'Goodness! What a gloomy turn this conversation's taking. Shall we go down to lunch?'

* * *

An excellent lunch that included sweet and sour fish and beetroot curries occupied de Silva's attention for a while, but eventually his mind strayed back to what George Blaine had told him. The story aroused his curiosity. When he'd met the nightwatchman, the fellow hadn't mentioned anything about delivering the coffee and drinks for the waiter. There was no particular reason why he should, although it would have given weight to his warning about the predatory animal, but why did he turn his torch off near the bungalow? He'd said it was to avoid disturbing the guests, but why be bothered about that if he'd recently delivered their drinks to them?

It would be interesting to know when he'd done that. If

it was close to the time when he and de Silva met, turning the torch off was odd, but if it was earlier, it was more understandable. He'd seen Elodie and her companions going back to the bungalow on his way to the beach. He doubted they would put up with being kept waiting long for their coffees and nightcaps, so probably he should assume the latter, but it would be good to be sure.

'You're very thoughtful,' said Jane. 'Have you decided what you'd like for dessert? Our waiter's coming over to clear the plates, so we could order. The kulfi ice cream looks nice. I think I'll have that.'

'Then I will too.'

'Now,' she said when the waiter had departed. 'I'd like to know what's on your mind. Is it something to do with this unfortunate nightwatchman?' She raised an eyebrow. 'If it is, holiday or not, it's not fair to leave me in suspense.'

He reached for her hand. 'I'm sorry, but it's hard not to be tempted to find out more. It's something the nightwatchman said that I'd like to take a bit further.' He explained about the torch then paused while the waiter brought their ice cream.

'What do you think?' he asked when the man had gone again.

'I agree it would be nice to clear up the point.' She smiled. 'And knowing you, you won't be happy until you have done.'

De Silva picked up his spoon and took a mouthful of ice cream. It was refreshing and sweet.

'Delicious,' he remarked.

'So, what do you plan to do?'

'If I can find out who he is, I'll have a word with this waiter. That's if you don't mind,' he added a little sheepishly.

'No, I don't mind, but then I think you should report to Chief Inspector Lawrence and leave everything to him.'

'You've changed your tune.'

'I suppose I have,' said Jane. 'But when we talked about it earlier, you were all for giving him the benefit of the doubt, and on reflection, I agree. You'd be very cross if a policeman from another force came to Nuala and started trying to meddle in one of your cases.'

'That's true. Very well, I'll see if I can speak to the waiter, then after that I'll mind my own business.'

CHAPTER 5

The bar was deserted apart from a barman who stood behind the counter polishing its already gleaming wood with a cloth. He looked up as de Silva approached.

'What can I get for you, sahib?'

De Silva thought there was a touch of weariness in his voice. In Ceylon's tropical climate, it was the time of day when most of the guests were likely to be enjoying a reviving rest, and the staff could reasonably expect to be left in peace.

'Nothing to drink, thank you. I'm hoping you'll be able to give me some information.'

A wary look came into the barman's eyes. 'If it is in my power, sahib,' he said cautiously. De Silva wondered how much the staff had been told about the death of the night-watchman and, if they knew about it, whether they'd been told not to answer any questions from guests. There was only one way to find out.

'Were you on duty here the evening before last?'

'Yes, sahib.'

'I believe that after dinner that evening, one of the waiters collected drinks for Madame Renaud and her party from the bar. I'd be interested in having a word with him. Do you know where I might find him?'

The barman looked relieved. Presumably he'd had no instructions to keep silent on that score, at least not yet.

'It was Carolus who came for the drinks,' he said. 'Cointreau for Madame Renaud and brandies for the gentlemen.' He glanced at the clock above the bar, framed by shelves of spirits and all manner of liqueurs. 'If he's still on duty, he's likely to be in the dining room.'

'Thank you.' De Silva produced a few coins from his pocket and put them on the counter. The barman smiled. 'Thank you, sahib.'

* * *

The appearance of the dining room was very different from what it had been an hour or so earlier. Several waiters were busy stripping tablecloths off tables that were revealed to be made of cheap wood. On a sideboard, the flower posies that had provided the centrepieces for the tables at lunchtime drooped in their vases. A waiter carrying a large tray of dirty glasses was backing out of the room through the green baize door to the kitchen. As it opened, de Silva heard loud voices and the clatter of washing up. He buttonholed the nearest waiter.

'I'm looking for Carolus.'

The waiter glanced around the room and pointed to one of the window tables. 'He's over there, sahib.' If he was curious as to why de Silva wanted to speak to his colleague, he didn't say anything. De Silva thanked him and went over to the table.

'Carolus?'

The waiter turned around from bundling up a crisp white cloth.

'Sahib? You have left something behind? I'm afraid nothing has been found yet, but if it is, I will take it to reception and ask for you to be notified.'

'No, it's not that. I have a few questions for you about the evening before last.'

A guarded expression came over the waiter's face. He didn't answer.

'I know you had the job of taking a trolley with coffee and drinks to one of the guest bungalows after dinner. The guests were Madame Elodie Renaud and her companions.'

'Everything was normal and perfectly healthy,' the waiter said quickly, a distinct note of anxiety in his voice. 'Our manager knows this. The coffee was prepared in the kitchen and the drinks came straight from the bar. I took them to the bungalow as I was told to do.'

De Silva raised a hand. 'I'm sure you did nothing wrong, but I understand that you met a nightwatchman on your way to the bungalow. He told you there were reports that a leopard was prowling in the hotel grounds and offered to take the trolley the rest of the way so you could go back to the hotel. Is that right?'

The waiter looked calmer. 'Yes, sahib.'

'Can you recall the time?'

Carolus thought for a moment. 'It must have been soon after ten o'clock.'

Then nearly an hour would have elapsed between then and the time when de Silva had met and spoken with the nightwatchman. There was nothing strange about his being careful not to disturb guests with the light of his torch.

'Thank you,' he said. 'That's all I wanted to know.'

Carolus lowered his voice. 'Do you work with Chief Inspector Lawrence, sahib?'

'In a manner of speaking. Why do you ask?'

'People are saying that Jai the nightwatchman, has been found dead in the grounds. Some people say an animal killed him, but others say not. Perhaps he is murdered. Maybe his wife's family do not like him, or maybe it is one of the other staff in the hotel who owes him money. If you work with Chief Inspector Lawrence, I thought you might know.'

De Silva was familiar with the way that rumours spread like wildfire after a sudden death. He assumed his most reassuring expression. 'Whoever or whatever the culprit, I'm sure Chief Inspector Lawrence will get to the bottom of it. I merely wanted to piece together the sequence of events that night. So, just to be sure I'm absolutely clear about what happened, you met Jai and he took the trolley from you at around ten o'clock?'

All at once, he noticed that Carolus was frowning. 'Jai, sahib? It wasn't Jai who took the trolley from me.'

De Silva's ears pricked up. 'Who was it then?'

'I didn't know him. I asked his name and why he was there, because it was usually Jai who watched that part of the grounds at night.'

'What was his answer?'

'I'm not sure what his name was. He muttered something hard to hear. He said he was new to the hotel and had been given Jai's place. I asked where Jai had gone to, but he didn't know.'

'Have you seen him since?'

Carolus shook his head.

'Did you tell Chief Inspector Lawrence this?'

'It was a young policeman who came to speak to me. He only asked when I saw the nightwatchman.'

De Silva sighed inwardly. It was a great pity the waiter hadn't thought to mention the new man, but then if he hadn't been asked the right questions, he wasn't really to blame. He reflected that he would be very disappointed if Prasanna or Nadar didn't do better when sent to interview a witness. He would also take some of the blame for not training them more thoroughly. Loath as he was to get a junior officer into trouble with his boss, if the interests of truth were to be served, it seemed he might have to. At least he had something worth reporting to Lawrence.

'Thank you,' he said. 'You've been a great help. There's

no need for you to speak of this to anyone else. I'll see that Chief Inspector Lawrence is put in the picture. But if you come across this man again, I'd like to know. You can leave a message for me at reception. My name is Inspector de Silva.'

* * *

His mind buzzed as he went to find Jane. She was still in the garden, sitting in the shade with her book in her lap. He sat down in the deckchair beside hers.

'You look pleased with yourself,' she said.

She listened as he gave her the gist of his conversation with the waiter. 'I'm sure that Chief Inspector Lawrence will be interested to hear what you've found out,' she said when he'd finished. 'Will you ask the manager who the nightwatchman that you saw was and why he was working in Jai's place?'

'No, I promised you that when I'd spoken to the waiter, I'd leave the rest to Lawrence. You're right about it being inappropriate for me to interfere as the case progresses.'

She patted his hand. 'Good. Now, if we go into town this afternoon, there should be time to visit the police station and take a longer walk around the walls afterwards when the day's cooling down. I'd love to watch the sunset from the lighthouse.'

'Then that's what we'll do. What do you say to rounding off the trip with a drink at the Galle Fort Hotel? I could drop you there anyway so you can have a cup of tea in comfort whilst I go and talk to Lawrence.'

'That sounds like a very good plan.'

CHAPTER 6

The police station in Galle was grander than Nuala's and had an imposing façade. The central section was gabled, and this was flanked by loggias with open balconies above them. A flight of steps led to a pillared entrance. Several police vans were parked in front of the building.

Inside, de Silva went up to the counter. There was only a desk sergeant in the public hall, but the hum of conversation and the clack of typewriters could be heard through the half-open doors of the rooms leading off it. One door was firmly shut and that had the words "Chief Inspector Lawrence" displayed on it in gold lettering.

'Can I help you?' The desk sergeant spoke in a manner which suggested that the prospect didn't please him.

'If he can spare the time, I'd like a word with Chief Inspector Lawrence.'

'The chief inspector doesn't usually see anyone without an appointment.'

'I appreciate that, but this is important.'

The desk sergeant still looked unimpressed. 'Without an appointment, it is difficult. Perhaps you would like to make one?' He reached for a ledger bound in brown leather, opened it, and began to turn over the pages. 'In three or four days he may have some time to spare.'

'My business can't wait that long.'

'What's it in connection with?'

'I'd rather tell that to the chief inspector myself.'

'Your name?'

'Inspector de Silva. I'm in charge of the police force in Nuala in the hill country.'

The sergeant looked slightly more accommodating. 'I'll tell him you're here.'

He went over to the door with the gold lettering, knocked and went in. Left alone, de Silva looked around the unwelcoming room. The walls were painted an institutional light green, broken up by posters printed with faded regulations and a few asking for information about stolen property or missing suspects. Despite being larger than the public room in Nuala, it had a similar smell. It was a smell that, no matter how hard he tried to banish it by telling Prasanna and Nadar to open windows to air the place, never really went away: a combination of sweat and stale tobacco given off by many of a police station's unwilling or complaining visitors, and the lingering odour of frequent brews of tea. He hoped, however, that Prasanna and Nadar cut better figures than the sullen desk sergeant.

A row of punitively hard chairs was ranged along the wall opposite the desk. He sat down on one of them and spent a few moments wondering whether it might be desirable to make a few changes to the station in Nuala, just to show that he and his men didn't automatically assume that everyone who came in was reprehensible, but then he decided that the size of the percentage that were, ruled the idea out.

The door opened and the sergeant reappeared.

'Chief Inspector Lawrence can spare you two minutes. Please come this way.'

Lawrence's office was larger than de Silva's own and his desk more orderly. In fact, apart from a blotter, In and Out trays with a few papers in them, and the impedimenta that showed he was a smoker, there was nothing on it. Either there was less crime in Galle than there was in Nuala, which seemed unlikely, or Lawrence dealt with it extremely efficiently, notwithstanding any failings his junior officers might have. At close quarters, de Silva saw that he had ice-blue eyes and a narrow face. Deep lines ran from the sides of his sharp nose to the corners of his thin-lipped mouth. De Silva guessed that he was several years younger than himself.

'Good afternoon, Inspector de Silva, I hear you want to see me on an urgent matter.' Lawrence indicated the chair on the opposite side of the desk from his own. 'Please take a seat.'

De Silva thanked him and sat down.

'What brings you to Galle?' asked Lawrence.

'My wife and I are on holiday, but I've not come about business of our own.'

Lawrence sat back in his chair, hands folded in his lap and thumbs pressed firmly together. 'Go on.'

'We're staying at the Cinnamon Lodge. I understand that a member of staff was found dead in the grounds yesterday.'

Lawrence frowned. 'Who told you that?'

'One of the British guests, a man called George Blaine.'

'Ah yes, Mr Blaine. He was asking questions and I saw no reason to keep the situation from him, although I had hoped that I'd impressed upon him that I didn't want the story to circulate.'

'As far as I'm aware, it's gone no further. Blaine asked me not to pass it on. I suspect he wouldn't have told me if he hadn't been aware that I was a policeman.'

'I'm glad to hear it. One doesn't want alarm spreading amongst the guests. Of course, the staff have been made aware of the need for extra caution, particularly at night, but in any case, the manager assures me that a thorough sweep of the grounds has been made and there were only a few places in the perimeter fence where a wild animal might enter. Those have been stopped up and an extra patrol has been arranged to keep an eye on the boundary with the beach.'

'Then you believe it was a wild animal that killed this man?'

'I certainly do. Has anyone suggested otherwise?' A slight look of puzzlement came over Lawrence's face.

'With respect, in my experience, it's early days to be sure of anything. I thought it might be useful to you to know that I happened to be taking a stroll in the grounds the previous evening. I ran into a nightwatchman near the guest bungalow where Madame Elodie Renaud and her party are staying. He mentioned that there'd been reports of a leopard on the prowl in the area and offered to escort me back to the hotel. I declined his offer—'

'It sounds as if you had a lucky escape,' interrupted Lawrence. 'I'm glad to hear it, but I assure you, you need have no concern now.'

'I appreciate that but there's something else. A waiter who was in the process of delivering a trolley of after-dinner coffees and drinks to the same guest bungalow that evening also met the nightwatchman. He warned the waiter about the danger and offered to take the trolley the rest of the way to the bungalow. The waiter accepted his offer.'

'Your point being?'

'I spoke to the waiter earlier today. He told me that although Jai, the man who was killed, is normally on duty in that area, the man he met wasn't Jai. The waiter hadn't seen him before and hasn't done since.'

Lawrence shifted in his chair and gave an audible sigh. 'Forgive me, Inspector, but I still fail to see your point. The indoor and outdoor staff are quite separate. It's not beyond the bounds of possibility that your waiter had never met this man before and hasn't seen him since. There could be all sorts of reasons why he was on duty in the area. Are you suggesting there are any sinister conclusions to be drawn?'

His tone was civil, and an uncomfortable feeling came over de Silva that he might be wasting this man's time. Nevertheless, he decided not to give up just yet.

'Not inevitably, however, in my experience, in the case of an unexplained death it's worth investigating anything out of the ordinary. A detail that might at first seem unimportant can sometimes lead to the solution to the case. I thought I should inform you of what the waiter told me. Particularly as I understand from him that the young officer sent to interview him didn't pick up the point. As I'm sure you're well aware, there have been times when what was initially viewed as a natural or accidental death has turned out to be murder. This other nightwatchman may have heard something that will help with the investigation.'

'I'm grateful for the information, and I'll have a word with my officer. He's usually reliable but perhaps he was devoting insufficient attention to the job that day. We can also check with the manager, but I expect there will be a simple explanation as to why the man you and the waiter saw was on duty in that area. The hotel probably put on extra security because of the rumour there was a predator about. When we know who the man is, naturally he'll be questioned, but as for murder, there's no indication of human agency and every indication of the killer being an animal. The unfortunate man's body was badly mauled.'

'May I ask what's been done with it?'

'It's already been cremated.'

Lawrence's voice had become a degree or two colder than before. He stood up. 'If there's nothing else, I have work to be getting on with, and I'm sure you're anxious to get back to your wife.'

As de Silva hauled himself out of his chair, a sudden smile lifted the corners of Lawrence's mouth and the deep lines softened. 'My sergeant tells me you're based in Nuala. A charming town. I've visited it a few times for the motor rally and the races. Sometimes I think I should ask for a transfer up country. The hill country air and the slower pace of life must be very beneficial to the health, especially as one nears retirement. Perhaps we'll be neighbouring colleagues one day.'

It was good to hear praise of his town but when it was coupled with the hint, however good-humoured, that he wasn't getting any younger, de Silva wasn't sure whether to be pleased or put out by Lawrence's remarks. He decided on the former and smiled. 'I'm sure that when the time comes, you would be warmly welcomed.'

Lawrence went to the door and held it open. 'Thank you again for coming.'

* * *

'How did it go?'

He had arrived at the Galle Fort Hotel to find Jane in the lounge.

'Well enough after I got past their desk sergeant. Lawrence was polite and very complimentary about Nuala. It seems he's visited a few times.'

'That was nice.' She gave him a closer look. 'What's wrong?'

He shrugged and sat down. 'Oh, just that he gave the impression he thought it was a bit of a backwater for policemen who are over the mountain.'

Jane smiled. 'Over the hill, dear, and I'm sure you're being far too sensitive. I don't expect he was thinking any such thing. Now, what did he have to say about the information you gave him?'

'He thanked me, and said he'd speak to the manager

about the nightwatchman I met but he's confident there'll be a simple explanation as to why he was on duty there. He'll question him to find out if he heard anything, but basically, I had the impression that he's convinced this man Jai was killed by an animal not a human and he won't treat his death as a potential murder investigation.'

She reached out a hand and placed it over his. 'You have to respect his judgement. Let's face it, he's in possession of more information than you are and aside from George Blaine's opinion, and that's purely personal, you've no reason to suppose that Lawrence won't carry out his duties properly.'

'I suppose so. And the fact that the body was mauled does carry great weight, although as Blaine suggested, that might have happened after death. Lawrence has put paid to any further investigation, however, as he's already had it cremated.'

'Shanti!'

'Oh, I know. I mustn't let his insinuations about my work affect my views on the thoroughness of his.'

'Quite right. Now, would you like some tea before we take our walk?'

He looked at his watch. 'No, I'll leave it until later. It's not long until dark. If we're to catch the sunset, we should be on our way.'

But as they left the hotel and strolled in the direction of the point, he resolved that if an opportunity arose, he would try to find out if there was some kind of history between George Blaine and Chief Inspector Lawrence.

CHAPTER 7

'What would you like to do today?' asked de Silva over a late breakfast the following day. 'We could go back into town or for a drive along the coast. Unless you'd rather just stay here.'

Jane considered for a few moments. 'It might be nice to visit the town again. I'm sure there are still plenty of nooks and crannies we haven't explored and comfortable as it is here, it would be a shame not to see them. We could make tomorrow a day to relax.'

'Good, a trip to town it is.'

'I'd like to finish the letter I was writing to Delisha first, though. There are few jobs I want her and Sria to do in the house that I forgot to mention before we came away. Then I can hand it in at reception and ask them to have it posted for me. I'll try not to be too long.'

'No need to rush. I'm happy to take one of my strolls.' He crumpled his napkin and put it on the table. 'I'll come back for you in half an hour or so, shall I?'

'That's fine.'

* * *

In the garden, he set off on what was becoming a familiar route in the direction of the guest bungalow where Elodie Renaud and her party were staying. He'd decided not to visit the beach that morning. However much care one took when replacing one's shoes and socks, sand had a way of making its presence felt for the rest of the day. Instead, he would carry on past the bungalow to the summerhouse where he'd met Helen Morris doing her painting.

The morning air was still pleasantly fresh and cool, and birds were singing in the trees. As he passed a grove of pomegranate trees, he noticed a pair of golden orioles feeding on the fruit. Disturbed by his approach, they swooped away with their shallow, dipping flight.

The guest bungalow was a couple of hundred yards ahead of him when he saw a short man carrying a black bag coming away from it. He was dressed in a dark three-piece suit and a black homburg hat and looked rather out of place in the lush surroundings. He nodded as their paths converged. De Silva suspected he would have carried on without stopping if he hadn't accosted him, but from the black bag he carried, he guessed the man was a doctor. He was curious to know how matters were progressing with Madame Renaud and her friends.

'I'm glad to say, there's been some improvement overnight,' said the doctor when de Silva asked him the question. 'Although I've advised them to rest for another day or two.' He looked at de Silva closely. 'Are you a friend of Madame Renaud's?'

'A fellow guest. I'm glad to hear that she and her companions are on the mend.'

The doctor looked at the watch on his waistcoat chain. 'I must be off. I came up here early so that I'd be back in town in plenty of time for my morning surgery, but time's running on.'

'Before you go, have you been able to identify a cause for the malady?'

A hint of suspicion came into the doctor's eyes. 'I'm not at liberty to discuss that.'

'Forgive me,' de Silva said quickly. 'I meant no harm in asking.'

'And you are?'

'Inspector Shanti de Silva from Nuala in the hill country.'

'Then I suppose I can entrust you with more information than I would the other guests,' said the doctor after a momentary pause. 'In confidence, you understand.'

'Naturally.'

'The fact is, it's hard to say. Their symptoms resemble a case of acute gastritis or dysentery. Food poisoning is an obvious conclusion, but the violence and duration of the attacks are unusual. I've enquired of the manager what the party ordered for their meals, and many of the other residents consumed food cooked in the same batch without any ill effects. Infection is also a possibility, but in the same way, no other guests have suffered. Frankly, I'm at a loss to find a satisfactory explanation, I'm simply glad that the malady, whatever it is, seems to have responded to rest and time, coupled with water and a very small amount of bland food. To the extent that they've barely been able to keep anything down at all, that is, because I have nothing significant in my armoury to help them.' He tapped his black bag.

'Thank you, that's most interesting.'

'If I was given to fanciful speculation,' the doctor added, 'I'd consider whether there has been a deliberate intervention. On the other hand, why would anyone wish Madame Renaud and her party any harm?'

De Silva frowned. 'Do you mean poison?'

The doctor shrugged. 'The idea is ridiculous, naturally.' He tipped his hat. 'I must be on my way. No doubt other patients are waiting for me to attend to their ailments. A pleasure meeting you, Inspector. I hope you enjoy the rest of your holiday.'

* * *

Jane was putting the finishing touches to her letter when he returned to their room. She looked up and smiled. 'I'm nearly ready. I just need to address the envelope and find my sunhat. Did you enjoy your stroll?'

'I met the doctor who's attending Madame Renaud and her party and had a very interesting chat with him. It seems that they have a bit of a mystery illness. He even hinted at poison, although he quickly ridiculed the suggestion.'

'Poison! Gracious, whoever would want to poison them?'

'A jealous rival?'

Jane shook her head. 'Really, dear, you promised we'd have a holiday. If you're missing having a crime to solve this much, perhaps we should give up the idea.'

He chuckled. 'I'm sorry. I'm not really missing it at all.'

'Good.' She addressed the envelope, put the folded letter inside and sealed it. 'There, give me two minutes. As we're going into town, I think I might take this to the post office after all. It will get home faster.'

The drive into town was slower than it had been on their first excursion, with many more carts and rickshaws to negotiate a way past.

'Perhaps there's a special market today,' remarked Jane. 'Still, we're in no rush and it's interesting to see so much going on.'

She seemed happily engrossed in doing that, so in between avoiding hazards, de Silva had ample time for his thoughts to stray back to his conversation with the doctor.

Poison. It was an outlandish idea, but stranger things had been known. But what would be anyone's motive? He ran over the substances he was familiar with. Which one caused symptoms that mimicked acute gastritis? Arsenic came to mind, but he wasn't sure. An idea had just occurred to him when he realised that Jane was speaking.

'I didn't hear that. It must be the wind.'

She raised an eyebrow. 'You were miles away. It's as well we're having to go so slowly.'

'Sorry.'

'I assume your mind's still on Elodie Renaud and her companions?'

He nodded, feeling a little guilty. 'As we're going to the post office, I might just see if I can telephone Henry Bruyn. I have my notebook with my list of important contacts with me.'

'So are you taking this idea of poison seriously?'

'Well,' he drew out the word. 'It would be interesting to have Doctor Bruyn's opinion. I'm sure the local doctor's a worthy fellow, but Bruyn is, after all, one of the most eminent medical men in Colombo. I appreciate he can do no more than make a conjecture, as he won't be able to see the patients or carry out tests, but I know he's very interested in the subject of poisons.'

'I suppose there's no harm in it, although Chief Inspector Lawrence may not see it that way.'

De Silva shrugged. 'I'm not even sure I'll tell him. This is for my satisfaction. I've already accepted that he has the right to be left alone to pursue the investigation in accordance with his own methods. In a similar situation, I would consult David Hebden and I expect Lawrence will do the same with his local doctor.'

'Would it be easier to consult David?'

'As I'm not officially involved in this case, I wouldn't want to put him in an awkward position.' He chuckled. 'Whereas Henry Bruyn is a law unto himself.'

The massive wall surrounding the old town rose up ahead of them, a patchwork of roughly hewn exposed stone, peeling plasterwork, and emerald lichen pierced by an archway. At its apex, a carved plaque displayed the heraldic device of the lion and the unicorn supporting a crown and a coat of arms. They drove through and parked the Morris at the spot where they had left it on their first visit.

The General Post Office was a long, low building with

a loggia supported by slender columns running across its frontage. Inside, the loud hum of people coming and going and transacting their business made de Silva feel as if he had entered a giant beehive. He left Jane queueing at a counter to purchase her stamp and went over to the line of telephone booths at one end of the cavernous room. Finding a free one, he dialled the operator and asked for the call to be placed. He listened as the number rang and when it was answered, put his money in the slot.

He gave his name to the receptionist and there was a short pause before Bruyn's familiar rumbling voice came on the line.

'This is a pleasant surprise. I understand you're calling from Galle. How's the weather down there?'

De Silva smiled to himself. He knew of old that Bruyn always gave the impression that nothing, and certainly not an unexpected call from the police, disturbed his habitual calm.

'Excellent.'

'I'm glad to hear it, but I imagine this isn't a social call.'

'I'm afraid not, I'd be grateful if you'd spare me a few minutes to answer some questions.'

Bruyn chuckled. 'My wife expects me home for lunch shortly, but as you usually bring me something of interest, I'm all ears.'

He listened as de Silva outlined the situation at Cinnamon Lodge, occasionally asking a question.

'I've heard of this lady,' he said when de Silva came to the end of his story. 'I won't ask what your interest in the case is. I'm satisfied you have a good reason for this enquiry, or you wouldn't be making it.'

De Silva felt relieved.

'Just to make sure I have all the facts,' Bruyn went on, 'I understand that the doctor didn't mention that any of his patients were exhibiting breathing difficulties. Nor was there any talk of convulsions or muscle spasms, mental confusion, loss of consciousness, or bleeding. Their symptoms have been confined to the digestive organs.'

'That's correct. It occurred to me that if poison was administered, it might be arsenic.'

Bruyn laughed. 'You could have saved yourself an expensive telephone call, my friend. That's precisely what I was going to suggest, although of course without an examination and proper tests, I can't be sure. What is the condition of the patients at the moment?'

The pips cut through their conversation. Hastily, de Silva pushed more coins into the slot.

'The local doctor told me they're on the mend,' he went on. 'He confessed there'd been nothing he could do for them except prescribe rest, water and a very bland diet if they were able to eat at all.'

'What was his view about what had caused the problem?'

'He suggested food poisoning or an infection but as none of the other guests at the hotel have been taken ill, he didn't venture either of those as a firm diagnosis.'

'Did he mention deliberate poisoning?'

'Yes, but he dismissed it in the next breath.'

'Hmm.' There was a pause before Bruyn spoke again. 'Naturally, if Madame Renaud and her companions had been given a large dose of arsenic, they would not have survived it and the situation would have been much more suspicious. It has happened in the past, however, that a succession of minute doses has been given to victims by their poisoners. Over time, the victim becomes increasingly ill. By the time the final dose is given, it's much more plausible that death has come about through natural causes. Of course, if we are dealing with poison, this assumes there is a poisoner who has set out to achieve such a result.'

De Silva frowned. 'What else would there be?'

'It might be a case of misadventure. No doubt you're

aware that in days gone by, arsenic was sometimes used in household wallpapers to obtain the strong colours that were popular. In damp climates, the glue that stuck the paper to the wall was an ideal medium for growing mould and this released arsenic into the air, occasionally with unfortunate results. That seems an unlikely explanation here, but significant amounts of arsenic are often present in soil and rocks. There have been modern cases where wells have produced contaminated water. Might the source of supply to the guest bungalow have changed recently?'

'I'm not sure.' *And finding out might be problematic*, thought de Silva. There were bound to be questions about why he was asking.

'There have even been instances where men seeking to build up their physiques and lung power, or ladies seeking a more curvaceous figure and a blooming complexion, have deliberately ingested grains of arsenic. I've read that used for short periods and in moderation, the treatment can be surprisingly effective.'

'Are you suggesting that Madame Renaud and her companions were trying this and mistook the amount they should eat?'

Bruyn laughed. 'Not seriously, but if they were, let's hope they never repeat the experiment.'

A man waiting outside the telephone booth looked pointedly at his watch then rapped on the glass. De Silva thanked Bruyn and hung up, then left the booth and went to find Jane.

'I think I could have walked with my letter to Nuala by now,' she joked.

'I'm sorry. When he gets on his subject, Henry Bruyn always has plenty to say. It was good of him to take my call at such short notice. It would have been uncivil to try to cut him short. Anyway, it was most interesting. I'll tell you about it as we go.'

* * *

They ate lunch at one of the many street stalls in the old town as he explained what Henry Bruyn had told him.

'How extraordinary these arsenic eaters sound,' said Jane. 'Poisoning oneself seems a very drastic way of achieving a peaches and cream complexion and a better figure. But then using dangerous substances in cosmetics has a long history. For hundreds of years, fashionable people painted their faces with lead to make their skin white and cover up scars if they'd suffered from smallpox.'

'If accidental poisoning seems very unlikely, it leaves us with the answer that someone wished them harm, but no explanation as to who and why.'

'Perhaps the manager was wrong when he insisted that it wasn't anything to do with a mistake the hotel had made,' said Jane. 'It is the easiest explanation.'

'I suppose it is.'

They finished their lunch and afterwards explored some of the places that they had missed on the previous day's visit, but the afternoon heat made the narrow streets unpleasantly stuffy.

'Would you like to walk a bit further, or shall we go back to the hotel?' asked de Silva after a while.

Jane deliberated for a moment. 'If it suits you, I think I'd rather go back. It really is very hot and I'm beginning to feel quite tired.'

Two days of walking around cobbled streets had begun to make de Silva footsore. 'It certainly suits me,' he said gratefully.

CHAPTER 8

Back at the Cinnamon Lodge, they stopped at the croquet lawn to watch two of the colonial couples having a game. It seemed to de Silva that they played indifferently and spent a great deal of time arguing over the rules.

'Until I knew you,' he said to Jane with a smile, 'I thought croquet was a civilised, genteel game. I remember the first time we played, you told me we would take it at a leisurely pace. Leisurely pace indeed! I was exhausted afterwards.'

'One of the families I was governess to in England had a passion for croquet. They played it all summer long and I was often asked to take part. I had to keep my end up to preserve my authority with my pupils.'

De Silva pulled out a handkerchief from his pocket and mopped his brow. 'I think that's enough of watching croquet for me. It's too early for tea but what do you say to going in search of a cold drink?'

They found a hammock in the shade and a servant brought them glasses of mango juice. The air hummed with the sound of the bees feeding on the purple flowers of a morning glory that scrambled up a sunny wall nearby. A little further off, a small pond glittered in the sunshine; iridescent-winged insects hovered over its surface.

De Silva took a sip of his mango juice and stretched his legs. 'This is very pleasant. I could get used to this kind of life.'

Jane laughed. 'I doubt that. Not long ago, you were all set to involve yourself in a new investigation.'

He shook his head. 'And you were right to caution me against it. Lawrence has every right to conduct his case in whatever manner he thinks fit.'

'I'm glad to hear it. A death is very sad, of course, but there's nothing we can do to help, and we only have a few more days of our holiday to enjoy.'

'I hope George Blaine sees it that way. I'll have to catch up with him and tell him what Lawrence said. I hope he won't try to push me into making more of a fuss.'

'If he does, I think he ought to show a good reason for not trusting Lawrence.'

He reached out and patted her hand. 'And that's the tone of voice I shall use if I have to tell him so.'

Jane laughed. 'He's only a young man, dear. What authority to take charge can he possibly have?'

'I suppose that's the right way to look at it. Anyway, I'm on holiday, so if George Blaine wants to clash with Lawrence, he can do so himself.'

They continued chatting comfortably and didn't notice that the tea hour had passed.

'It's probably just as well,' said Jane. 'All those delicious cakes are very fattening, and we'll enjoy our dinner all the more.'

Rather regretfully, de Silva thought of the array of cakes and tartlets that the kitchen had produced on previous days. To him, one of the best things about British food was the baking, but his waistband reminded him that Jane made a good point.

With its usual swiftness the tropical sun sank towards the horizon, suffusing the sky with vibrant washes of tangerine and crimson. As dusk softened the outlines of trees and bushes, they walked up to the hotel and were about to go to their room when George Blaine emerged from the lounge.

'I'd better get it over with and tell him about my talk with Lawrence,' said de Silva.

Jane nodded. 'I'll see you upstairs.'

To de Silva's consternation, a frown came over Blaine's face as he approached him. Wondering what had happened to disturb the young man's usually relaxed and friendly manner, he braced himself for what might be an awkward conversation.

'Good evening, Mr Blaine. I'm glad I saw you. I went into Galle yesterday and visited the police station as you suggested. I spoke to Chief Inspector Lawrence. He was grateful for what I had to tell him, but despite it, he remains satisfied that this man Jai was mauled by a predator. He won't be treating the matter as a murder investigation.' Deliberately, de Silva didn't mention his conversation with the waiter. Lawrence had said he would make further inquiries if they were needed, but as he'd implied, he'd probably read too much into it anyway.

Blaine gave him a blank look and shrugged. 'Lawrence knows his own business best,' he said tersely. Then perhaps he noticed de Silva's surprised expression for he gave a fleeting smile. 'Good of you to speak to him. Now, if you'll excuse me, I need to find someone urgently.'

De Silva paused to watch him go. George Blaine's interest in Jai's case seemed very short-lived. It was odd when only the previous day, he'd suggested that de Silva pass on his information to Lawrence. Perhaps Blaine wasn't really all that sympathetic to the locals, and his previous attitude was simply an instance of the British tendency to want to take charge and get things done. A tendency that, in de Silva's experience, sometimes produced the opposite result to the desired one. And what about his claim that he didn't have a high opinion of Lawrence? He'd certainly changed his tune there.

Whoever he was looking for, it appeared to be a matter

of considerable importance to him. De Silva wondered if it was Helen Morris. Had they had an argument? He hoped her aunt hadn't been causing more trouble. It would be sad if two such likeable young people were set at odds by her meddling.

He was halfway up the first flight of stairs when an unfamiliar voice behind him made him pause.

'I say there, would I be right in thinking you've been in town this afternoon?'

He turned to see a guest whose name he didn't know.

'Yes, my wife and I've not been back long. Is there some problem?'

The man came closer. 'I'm not sure,' he said in a low voice. 'Edith Pargeter's in a flap. Says her niece has gone missing. Something about going off this morning by boat to a beach to do some painting and not back yet. Apparently, she assured Edith that she'd return in time for tea but there's no sign of her. Did you see her in town by any chance?'

De Silva looked at his watch. Teatime was long past. 'I'm afraid not. Did she say exactly where she was going?'

'Edith wasn't sure.' The man rubbed a hand over his chin. 'Strikes me as not the wisest thing for a lady to do, but perhaps she intended to arrange for whoever took her out to stay on watch. I believe it's not the first time she's done something of the kind.'

'Are you sure no one here has seen her?'

'Absolutely. Blaine had no idea where she is and has gone off to look for her. I even asked that fellow whatsh-isname – the Swedish chap. He was very concerned and asked how he could help. Decent of him, I thought. Up until now I haven't been too sure about him. Seemed an odd sort of chap. No conversation. I visited Sweden when I was a young man, but I haven't even been able to draw him on that.'

'Is there anything my wife and I can do?'

'Just keep an eye out.' His voice sank lower. 'Mind you, if I was related to Edith Pargeter, I'd need to escape sometimes. Helen Morris seems a very pleasant young lady. I don't know how she puts up with it. With luck she'll turn up any time now and it will have been a storm in a teacup. Nevertheless, if you should see her first, it would be a kindness to send a message to her aunt.'

'Of course I will.'

'Good man. My name's Jenkinson, by the way. Harold Jenkinson.'

CHAPTER 9

Dinnertime came and there was still no sign of Helen Morris. The table where she and Edith Pargeter usually sat wasn't laid.

'I wonder if Mrs Pargeter has decided to have dinner in her room,' said Jane. 'I'm sure that in her situation, I'd prefer to eat quietly on my own.'

George Blaine, the Reeves, and Max Larsson were nowhere to be seen either, although in the case of the Reeves, thought de Silva, that wasn't unusual. He had noticed that they rarely appeared in the main building of the hotel.

After dinner, he and Jane went to the lounge to have their coffee. Previously, it had seemed an attractive room. Comfortable chairs, upholstered in floral cretonne and arranged in small groups around low tables, vases filled with flowers, and a variety of luxuriant ferns or fleshy-leaved evergreens planted in large copper pots, combined to make it a charming place to relax. Yet this evening the atmosphere was more like that of a spartan station waiting hall whose occupants wished they were anywhere but there.

Although it seemed that Edith Pargeter had eaten in her room, she was now downstairs at the centre of a circle of sympathetic guests. 'Mr Larsson has been so kind,' she was saying. 'He'd been out all day on one of his nature rambles, but as soon as he heard Helen was missing, he came to find me. He telephoned Chief Inspector Lawrence to alert him and now he's gone into town with George Blaine to join in the search for the boatman who took Helen out this morning. Until they find him, Lawrence says that it's impossible to make a sensible decision about where to start looking for Helen.'

'Have you heard anything from them?' asked one of the ladies. She was dressed in a drab shade of green that did nothing to flatter her pale complexion, but she had a pleasant open face and a no-nonsense air to her.

Edith Pargeter shook her head.

'You must try not to worry,' the lady in green said kindly. Harold Jenkinson stood behind her chair with his hand resting on the back of it. De Silva assumed she was his wife. The other men had also remained on their feet. With their grave faces and black dinner jackets, they reminded de Silva of a British expression Jane had told him: a parliament of rooks.

Edith Pargeter dabbed at her eyes with a small handkerchief. 'It's very hard not to be anxious.' There was a murmur of sympathy from the other guests.

'My advice is to get some rest,' the lady in green continued. There was another murmur, this time of assent. 'As soon as there's news, one of us will make sure that you're woken. Worrying about how to find Helen won't help. That's the job of the police.'

'I suppose you're right. I'll go up to my room, although I doubt that I'll sleep much.'

After some of the ladies in the group had hugged her with a display of feeling that de Silva had rarely observed amongst the British, and even a few of the men had patted her awkwardly on the shoulder, Edith started for the door. As she reached the place where de Silva and Jane sat, he stood up. She paused, and he noticed the scent of Parma violets.

'We're so sorry to hear that your niece is missing, Mrs Pargeter,' said Jane.

'Thank you.' She sighed and suddenly looked far more human and vulnerable than de Silva had ever seen her. 'My friends have persuaded me to go to bed. As they rightly point out, no amount of fretting will find Helen.'

'It's good advice,' said Jane gently. 'I hope you manage to get some rest.'

Edith gave her a shaky smile. 'I'll do my best. Goodnight to you both.'

A servant hurried to hold the door open for her and she left the lounge. With her departure, the other guests also began to drift away.

'Poor Mrs Pargeter,' said Jane. 'I remember an occasion when one of the children of a family I worked for in Colombo vanished. I don't think I've ever told you about it. He was too young to be my responsibility and his ayah was in charge of him, but I still felt very anxious.'

'I take it he was found eventually.'

'Yes, after a couple of hours, but they were very long ones. It felt as if time stood still, and normal life couldn't resume until he was back safe and sound. In fact, he wasn't really in any danger. He'd gone off to play with some local children who had a tame monkey.'

'What happened to the ayah?'

'Luckily for her, the family were so relieved that they excused her lapse. I was glad, for her sake. I was sure she'd be extra careful in future and in her defence, he was a very wilful child.'

'Let's hope Helen's story has an equally happy ending. I wonder if I should go to town and offer my services.'

Jane shook her head. 'Chief Inspector Lawrence has his own men and extra helpers. I'm sure everything possible is being done. Isn't it better to wait and offer assistance when we hear where Helen was last seen?'

De Silva thought for a moment then nodded. 'You're right.'

She looked around the now-deserted lounge.

'It's almost eleven o'clock. Perhaps we should get off to bed and let the staff clear up.'

In their room, she was soon asleep, but it took de Silva longer to settle. She was probably right about Lawrence. It was a sad fact of life that he would no doubt be particularly scrupulous in performing his duties now that a British lady rather than a local servant was involved.

All the same, being away from the action felt alien and uncomfortable. In situations like this, he was used to being in the thick of it, not waiting on the sidelines. The only benefit was the insight he gained into how people in that position felt when, frustrated and anxious, they had little to do except wait for the news he would bring them.

He wasn't sure what time he fell asleep but in the early hours of the morning, the sound of footsteps and low voices roused him. He slipped out of bed, put on his dressing gown, and went out into the corridor. George Blaine and Max Larsson were outside the door to the room on his left. Larsson was putting his key in the lock. Both men looked weary and dejected.

'Sorry to disturb you, de Silva,' said Blaine. 'We've just got back from town.'

'What's the news?'

'No sign of Helen yet, but Lawrence has managed to track down the boatman. He claims he left her painting at the beach next door to the hotel's. She said he didn't need to stay so he arranged to come back for her later. He'd have to fetch her by boat because the tide is too high to allow anyone to walk back from there to the hotel until well after sunset. He's adamant he returned as agreed, but there was no sign of her.'

'Didn't he think to mention to anyone that she wasn't at the beach as expected?'

Larsson shook his head. 'He had a tale about how another boat must have come along and taken her back to the hotel. I think this is a strange story,' he added in his heavily accented voice. 'Did he not want to be paid?'

'Unless she paid him in advance,' said Blaine. 'But I agree it seems unlikely she'd have paid the full amount, and, anyway, the fellow might have been hoping for a tip when he finished the job. Lawrence seems pretty sure there was something suspicious going on. He told me he has nothing concrete against the man, but there's reason to suspect that he's untrustworthy.'

'Did he give any particulars?'

Blaine scowled. 'I didn't ask,' he said in a sharp tone. 'I was more concerned with finding Helen. Larsson here came with me to the beach. Tonight the tide was out, so the water was low enough for us to walk from the hotel, but we didn't find her. If she's still in the area, she must have gone deeper into the jungle. After a preliminary search, we realised it was hopeless to carry on in the dark. We've come back to get a few hours' shut-eye and we'll start again as soon as it gets light.'

'I'd like to help if I may.'

'That's good of you. The tide will be high by dawn. Lawrence is sending a boat to pick us up so we can meet him at the beach. Jenkinson's already arranged to accompany us but with luck, there'll be room for you as well.'

'I'll be ready.'

CHAPTER 10

It was barely light when the boat came to collect them. It turned out to be roomy enough to fit everyone in, including Jane, who had insisted on coming to help.

'I wondered if that fellow Reeve would offer his services,' remarked Jenkinson as the two men who had brought the boat rowed them out into open water and set off for the adjacent beach to meet Lawrence. The air was crisp and cold. De Silva was glad of the extra layers he wore.

Max Larsson raised an eyebrow. 'No, he did not offer. I think it did not please the aunt of Miss Morris. She already does not have a good opinion of him.'

'Don't know anything about him myself,' said Blaine. He peered towards the east where a low bank of cloud lay like a long smudge of ink on the horizon. Above it, the sky was rapidly turning from pearl grey to soft pink. As the boat rounded the outcrop of rocks that divided the two beaches, the sun rose through the cloud like a ball of fire; the pink of the sky deepened.

The beach came into sight. Foam-edged wavelets gleamed at the edge of the sand, and seawater nosed and frothed its way into the crevices between the dark rocks that bordered it. The sun's rays illuminated their contours.

A few moments later, one of the crew got up and went to the prow of the boat. De Silva felt the bump of the hull on wet sand. There was a scraping noise followed by a splash as the crewman jumped into the shallows, the rope that had been coiled up in the prow slung over his shoulder. He brought the boat a little further up onto the beach, then de Silva and the others disembarked.

The beach was about the same size as the hotel's one but much wilder in aspect. Beyond the rocks that formed a horseshoe around it, jungle stretched as far as the eye could see. In the sunlight, the old boat with the remnants of red paint on its hull that de Silva had seen on his earlier visit looked even more dilapidated than it had by moonlight, but it added a picturesque touch to the scene. De Silva understood why Helen Morris had wanted to paint there, but if she'd left by land, it must have been by a route that would be an extremely difficult one to travel, and virtually impossible at night. If, on the other hand, she had left the beach by sea, why hadn't she simply returned to the hotel? A chill came over him. Had she planned an assignation that had ended badly? Or had she been the victim of a predator as Lawrence claimed that the nightwatchman Jai had been?

'No sign of Lawrence and his men yet,' said George Blaine. 'If they're not here in the next ten minutes, we'd better make a start.' He shaded his eyes against the sun's rays. 'As far as I can tell, there are only a few places where someone would be able to penetrate the tree cover. None of them look easy. I'm afraid we have a challenging task on our hands, gentlemen.'

A few minutes passed and still there was no sign of another boat.

'We can't wait any longer,' said Blaine. 'I suggest we get a move on. Will you go that way, Larsson?' He pointed to the left. 'If you go in this direction, de Silva,' he pointed again, 'Jenkinson and I will cover the rest. Mrs de Silva, would you be prepared to wait here on the beach to tell them where we've gone?'

'Certainly.'

'If anything alarms you, shout and we'll get back here as soon as we can.'

De Silva frowned. 'I'm not sure staying here is a good idea.'

'I'm not afraid,' said Jane calmly.

'I'm sure you're not.' Blaine smiled at her. 'In any case, Lawrence and his men will probably be here any minute.'

With a lingering feeling of unease, de Silva gave in. He knew that it was hard to get Jane to budge when she'd made up her mind. He set off with the others towards the trees.

The first part of the track was very narrow. From the droppings that he noticed amongst the leaf litter on the ground, he guessed that it had been made by small deer of some kind. He broke off a length of the straightest branch he could find and used it to beat away the undergrowth that encroached on either side. With increasing faintness, he heard the other men's voices calling out Helen's name. From time to time he shouted it too, but there was no answer, only the incessant hum of insects and the croak of frogs.

As he went deeper into the trees, even that ceased, leaving only the crackle of dry leaves under his feet to break the eerie stillness. The tree canopy grew denser, reducing the sun's rays to a pale, sickly light. Surely Helen Morris wouldn't have come this way? Unless, and the thought came to him with chilling clarity, she had been running from something or someone, in fear of her life.

The track had been following an upward path with jungle on either side, but suddenly it began to skirt the lip of a ravine. For a few yards, a narrow verge overgrown with ferns and cycads separated the ravine from the path but then the verge ended. To his right, the ground fell away steeply. Dizziness overwhelmed him as he looked down and saw the bottom of the ravine hundreds of feet below. The stream that ran through it shone like quicksilver as it meandered between rocks and fallen trees. He stepped sideways and nearly stumbled on the rough ground at the other side of the path. His breath clotted in his throat and his vision fogged. With a huge effort, he fought down panic then peered cautiously into the ravine once more, imagining the events of the previous night. If in the darkness Helen had come this way, she might not have realised the ravine was there until it was too late. He shuddered. No one could survive such a fall. The grim fact must be faced that her broken body might be lying down there amongst the rocks and trees, and if that was the case, finding it would be a herculean task.

The section of path ahead of him looked even more treacherous than the one he was on. Even a sure-footed deer might have turned back or gone another way. He decided to retrace his steps and try to find some other path Helen might have taken that he had missed on the way up, although had she come this way, his confidence that she was still alive was rapidly ebbing.

By the time he reached flatter ground, he'd seen no openings in the vegetation bordering the path that anything but the smallest of creatures might have pushed through. Then suddenly, the sound of police whistles came from the direction of the beach. Alarm seized him. For the last few minutes, he had forgotten Jane would still be there. Berating himself, he headed back as fast as he could. There were shouts now. His heart pounded as he broke into a run, stumbling over roots and kicking free of the tangle of low plants that threatened to pull his feet from under him. Sweat poured into his eyes and his clothes stuck clammily to his skin.

It seemed like an eternity before he emerged onto the beach. The sunshine hit him like a hammer blow. He stopped abruptly to let his eyes adjust and his breath return, then to his relief, he saw Harold Jenkinson and Jane standing together. Lawrence was about a hundred yards away from them near the tree line, supervising two of his men who were digging something out of the sand. A sinking feeling in his stomach, de Silva went over to them.

'What have you found?' he asked.

'Some broken pieces of wood. Looks like the remains of a painter's easel.'

One of the men stopped digging. 'There's something else here, sir.'

'Give me that.' Lawrence took the shovel and started to scrape away at the sand. After a few moments, he straightened up and handed the shovel back to his officer. He reached into the pocket of his jacket and produced some gloves, put them on, and bent down. De Silva watched as he brushed away sand to reveal a box. It looked very like the one de Silva had carried back to the hotel for Helen Morris.

Lawrence picked it up and opened the lid. 'And here's the rest of Miss Morris's equipment, I believe.'

He pointed to a large, flat stone that lay nearby on a piece of cloth. 'There's blood on that stone and a few strands of hair. Auburn hair. The boatman who brought Helen Morris out here is already in custody. I have no doubt his fingerprints will be all over this box and the broken easel, left there after he made his clumsy attempt to bury the evidence of his crime. Combined with the evidence we already have, we can prove his guilt.'

'What other evidence?' asked de Silva.

'His boat was searched early this morning. We found a necklace with a pendant in the shape of a letter H concealed in one of the lockers along with a considerable amount of money. He's been charged with robbing and killing Helen Morris. In the absence of a body, I conclude that he dumped it at sea then returned to harbour, pretending she was missing when he went back to the beach to collect her.'

He turned to one of his men. 'Get me some bags from

the boat. We need to pack all this up and take it back to the station. It'll be wanted as evidence.'

'What did the boatman have to say?' asked de Silva.

'As you'd expect, he denied everything and insisted he returned to the harbour after he left Helen. He said that several people saw him there.'

'Have they been questioned?'

Lawrence scowled. 'I hope you're not telling me how to do my job, Inspector,' he said sourly. 'Naturally, they will be, but the word of local fishermen isn't worth much. In any case, in addition to a motive, the boatman had ample time and opportunity to commit his crime before he left the beach for the first time. He may not even have made the second journey, merely set out in this direction to cover his tracks.' He lowered his voice. 'There may have been another heinous crime committed − a lone white woman would be greatly at risk in such a situation − but I'm sure you agree that it would be inappropriate to mention it in your wife's presence.'

Smarting at the slur on his countrymen, de Silva still had to admit to himself that Lawrence had some justification for being annoyed that his handling of the case was being questioned. He might have the same reaction himself, although he hoped there would be less need for it.

It was a subdued party that waited for the crews to ready the boats and drag them back to the shallows. As he waited, de Silva noticed a dead seagull that lay in the broiling sun near a piece of driftwood. Its grey and white plumage was soiled and bedraggled, its head twisted at an unnatural angle, and its only visible eye dulled by death. Ants infested one broken wing, turning it black. He wondered if it had died where it lay, or whether it had been washed in on an earlier tide. Perhaps it had been attacked by other gulls; they could be vicious birds. He remembered how they used to fight in Colombo harbour, shrieking like quarrelsome children and mobbing each other with jabbing beaks and flapping wings as they squabbled over the scraps left by the fishermen.

The violent image brought him back to Helen Morris. He thought sadly of their first conversation at the summerhouse in the hotel garden. All premature deaths were tragic, but it was hard not to be more deeply affected by some than others. Youth, warmth, humour, and a talented artist: Helen Morris had possessed all those qualities and, if Lawrence was right, they had been cruelly snatched away. It was only the fact that they hadn't found her body that gave Shanti any hope she was still alive.

Jane touched his arm. 'Shanti! Everyone else is on board. We're the last.'

'We'd better get on then,' he said quickly. 'Here, let me help you.'

When he had handed her into the boat and clambered over the side to join her, he cast a glance at George Blaine. The young man sat in the prow, silent and withdrawn, an aura of sadness hanging over him. De Silva pitied him. He might not have succeeded in winning Helen's heart, but now he would never know if he would have done so in the end.

The boat carrying Lawrence and his men made better speed than the one that de Silva and his companions were in. By the time they reached the hotel beach, Lawrence was already there, waiting for them to catch up.

'I now have the unpleasant duty of informing Mrs Pargeter of her niece's death,' he said when they had disembarked. 'In these situations, it can be a help if someone is with the bereaved person.'

'My wife has become friendly with the lady. I'm sure she would oblige,' said Jenkinson. 'Shall I go up to the hotel and find her?'

'Thank you. I'll come to the lobby shortly and wait for you there.'

Jenkinson went into the hotel leaving Lawrence and his men with de Silva and the others.

'I don't suppose I can be of much help,' said Blaine. 'I'm sure Jenkinson's wife will do a much better job of comforting Helen's aunt than I could. If you'll excuse me, I'll be on my way.'

As Blaine walked away, Lawrence turned to his men. 'Wait for me at the cars and take the evidence bags with you.' He jerked a thumb towards the waiting boats. 'Tell the skippers to return to the harbour. If they come to the police station later, they'll be paid for their trouble. Inspector de Silva, it was very good of you and your wife to help out this morning. I'm sure you'll be glad to carry on with your holiday and put this sad episode behind you.'

'We were acquainted with the young lady,' said Jane, 'and we won't easily forget her, but of course our feelings are nothing compared to the grief her aunt is bound to suffer.'

'Regrettably, I'm sure you're right, Mrs de Silva.'

CHAPTER 11

The rest of the day passed slowly for de Silva. After a lunch that he had little heart to eat had been served in the dining room, he and Jane collected their books from their room and found a shady place to sit in the garden.

He wondered if he'd made a bad choice when he'd chosen the one he was currently reading. At school where lessons had been conducted in English, English literature had been the rule rather than the colourful tales of his own culture. He remembered not much enjoying the books they had read in those days, but now he suspected that he had been too young to appreciate them. Over the years he'd lived in Nuala, he'd grown to share Jane's love of reading and decided it was time to try again. Unfortunately, Thomas Hardy's *Far from the Madding Crowd* was not the most cheerful of reads. The wit and wisdom of, say, Jane Austen would have been far more effective in raising his spirits. But as Jane was engrossed in her book, he tried once more to immerse himself in Hardy's harsh world of rural toil, suffering, and dark passions, until after ten minutes he gave up.

Jane looked up from her book. 'You're very restless.'

He scratched his head. 'I'm sorry.'

She sighed. 'I feel the same. I'm not really taking this in. I can't stop thinking about Edith Pargeter. I expect she knows by now, poor lady.'

De Silva stood up. 'Would you like to walk for a while?'

'I think so.'

They walked in silence, keeping to the shade. In the heat of the afternoon, the birds were silent. Even the trees and flowers seemed to droop, as if they too mourned Helen Morris.

'Do you really think Chief Inspector Lawrence is right about this case?' asked Jane eventually. 'I'm sure he has a great deal of experience, and it's probably wrong of me to question his judgment, but...'

'But?'

'There are things about it that put doubts in my mind.'

'For example?'

'Well, the necklace with the pendant for one thing. It sounds very like the one you bought for me in the bazaar. Helen admired it when we were walking back from the tennis court yesterday, but she didn't say anything about owning a similar one. In fact, she said she might go to the bazaar before she left and see if they had one with her initial on, but as she went off on her boat trip early the following morning, how would she have had time?'

'That's true. Anything else?'

'Lawrence said a considerable amount of money was found in the boat, but why would Helen be carrying that on a painting expedition? Anyway, it does seem a huge risk for the boatman to take anything at all. He was always going to be a major suspect.'

De Silva nodded. 'It's occurred to me that unless her body is found, there's always the possibility, even though a remote one, that she's alive and trapped somewhere.'

Jane looked troubled. 'I hadn't thought about that, but you're right.' She was silent for a few moments before she continued. 'There's something I noticed while I was waiting for you all at the beach. I didn't say anything at the time but on reflection, it might be important.'

'What was it?'

'Blue paint. There were some flakes of it on the rocks I was sitting on. The rocks were dry, and from the seaweed that lay on the sand near them, my guess is that the water tends not to reach them unless the tide's very high. If someone was dragging a boat up onto the beach, particularly if they were on their own and it was awkward, they might have caught the side of the boat on them. It would be interesting to know what colour the boat that took Helen to the beach was. Neither of the boats that took our or Lawrence's party out were blue, and the old one already on the beach was red, not that it looked as if it had been used for a very long time. If Helen's boat wasn't blue either, it would show that someone else had landed on the beach, possibly on the day she was there.'

'You make some good observations. But even if we do find out that there was another boat, it wouldn't automatically prove anything, you know.'

'Oh, I realise that, but you always say one should leave no stone unturned.'

He smiled. 'I can't deny it. So, we need another visit to town to have a look around the harbour in case there was another boat and it's still there.'

* * *

They left the hotel an hour later but were only halfway to the car when Jane realised that she had forgotten her hat. As he waited on the drive, de Silva noticed Jocelyn Reeve coming down the steps from the hotel. He looked to be in a hurry, and his handsome face took on an irritable expression as he went over to a member of staff who had just parked a dark blue Lagonda on the drive.

Reeve grabbed the keys from him, but the staff member

didn't seem in a hurry to go. They exchanged a few words then Reeve's expression became even more irritable. De Silva was too far away to hear exactly what was being said, but he managed to make out a few snatches of the Sinhalese they were speaking in. It sounded like the man was asking for a tip. Finally, Reeve reached into the breast pocket of his jacket. He tossed a few coins at him then got into his car and drove away at such speed that if the man hadn't moved quickly, he might have been knocked down.

De Silva frowned. A strange encounter. It was very odd for a member staff to importune a guest, especially in full view of the hotel where one of his superiors might see him.

'Goodness!' Jane arrived at his side, her sunhat in her hand. 'I wonder what that was all about. He nearly ran that poor man over.'

'He certainly seemed very annoyed about something.'

'Perhaps Edith Pargeter's assessment of him as an unpleasant character isn't so very far off the mark.'

* * *

In Galle, they took the road leading to the harbour. Whereas the predominant odours in the old town had been of spicy cooking and drains, down at the harbour the smell of fish overwhelmed everything else. Most of the catch that the fishermen had landed that morning had already been sold. Apart from a few baskets of oysters and clams, only herring and mackerel too small to interest buyers remained, the silvery sheen of their scales now dulled by the heat. In places the ground was slippery with blood. Raiding parties of gulls with darting malicious eyes and sharp beaks squabbled over fish heads and guts. De Silva thought back to the dead gull on the beach. Not long ago, it might have been joining in the fun.

Small groups of fishermen sat cross-legged mending nets, the sun beating down on their leathery skin. Every so often, the hum of their talk rose to a crescendo and there were harsh bursts of laughter, but when de Silva and Jane went over to the nearest group, the talk and laughter ceased.

For the moment, de Silva decided not to let on that he knew the boatman had been arrested. 'We're looking for the man who took a young British lady out to the beach near the Cinnamon Lodge hotel yesterday morning,' he said. 'Do you know where we might find him?'

The fishermen regarded them warily. De Silva wondered whether it was because they already knew what had happened to the boatman, although it was possible that it was simply that the sight of a local man and a white woman together was strange to them. At first no one answered then one of the older ones spoke up.

'The police have taken him. People say he robbed the British lady and killed her.'

'Do you believe that?'

Several of the younger men shook their heads. 'He is married to my cousin,' one of them said. 'He is a good man. When he went back to the beach to fetch her, the British lady was gone. He thought she had been collected by someone else.'

'But what about payment? Had she already given him the money for taking her out to the beach?'

'No, but he said he would go up to the hotel later and ask to be paid.'

'Did he do that?'

'No, because his son is sick. He had promised his wife he would go home after he fetched the British lady. If the police had not come to arrest him, he would have gone to the hotel this morning.'

'Were you here when his boat was searched?'

The man shook his head. 'We were out at sea all night,

but he wasn't with us. Because he expected that the British lady would give him the money she owed him, and with his son's sickness, he stayed at home. After we brought the catch in early this morning, we heard that the police had already searched the boat and gone to his home to arrest him.'

'Which one of the boats is his?'

The men pointed to one that was moored a little way off from all the others, its landward side blocked off by a makeshift wooden fence. It was still possible, however, to see that it was painted green.

De Silva thanked them, and he and Jane started to walk around the rest of the area where the local fishing boats were tied up.

'What did they say?' asked Jane. 'I didn't understand all of it.' De Silva and the fishermen had spoken in Sinhalese and their accents were not always easy to follow.

'The story sounds plausible enough,' she said when he had explained the parts she had missed. 'Don't you think so?'

'I do, but someone had to put that necklace and the money on the boat. If the fishermen were out at sea all night, whoever it was probably had ample opportunity to do so unobserved.'

They carried on walking and spoke with several other groups of fishermen, but de Silva received much the same answers to his questions. Amongst the fishing boats, they only found three that were painted blue. The first one was turned upside down like a turtle, and its owner was scraping barnacles from its hull with a blunt-edged knife. He shook his head when de Silva asked if he had hired his boat out in the past week.

'I fish. I never hire my boat out.'

'What about the owner of that one over there?' De Silva gestured in the direction of the second blue boat.

'He is the same.'

De Silva pointed to the third boat. 'And that one?'

The fisherman scowled then hawked up a gobbet of phlegm and spat it out on the ground. He grunted something inaudible and went back to scraping barnacles.

De Silva sighed inwardly. This was like getting blood out of a stone. 'Did the owner hire it out this week?' he asked, trying to remain patient.

'So he said.' The fisherman rolled his eyes. 'He told anyone who would listen how much money he made.'

'When was it returned?'

'It was back here when we came in from fishing this morning.'

'What's this owner called?'

'Mohen,' the fisherman said flatly.

'Can you tell me where we'll find him?'

The fisherman gestured with his knife towards a tin-roofed shack a short distance away. 'In the bar.'

CHAPTER 12

In a valiant attempt at decoration, a few strings of ti-
ger-striped and mottled brown and cream seashells had
been looped around the entrance to the bar. De Silva
stopped outside and turned to Jane. 'Are you sure you want
to come in with me? I don't think it will be a very salubrious
place.'

'That won't worry me. Anyway, I'd rather come in than
stay outside on my own.'

'Very well, we'd better get on with it.'

The stench of fish pursued them as they crossed the
threshold, but now it competed with the odours of sweat,
alcohol, and rancid tallow. Presumably, the candles that
gave off the smell were only lit at night, for apart from the
few rays of sunshine that penetrated the door and the gaps
in the tin roof, the room was shrouded in gloom. Sand was
scattered over a floor of beaten earth, and apart from a few
posters, the putty-coloured walls were bare. One of the
posters showed a bottle of India Pale Ale with its green and
red label. In the background, two smiling couples dressed
in tennis whites were being served with tall glasses topped
with thick froth. The scene seemed a world away. The bar
itself consisted of a plank balanced on two oil drums. There
were a couple of crates of local beer on the floor beside it
and on top of the bar, some bottles of arrack and a cluster
of cloudy glasses.

The bartender gave them a guarded look, but his only customer, a man who was slouching against the bar leaning on one elbow, stared at them with a more confident expression on his face. He had bare feet and was dressed only in a loincloth like the fishermen outside, but he was plumper than most of them, with a broad, flat nose, thick eyebrows, and pockmarked skin.

'I'm looking for Mohen,' said de Silva.

The man straightened up and put down his glass. 'I'm Mohen. How can I help you, sahib?'

'I'm told you've been hiring out your boat for the past few days.'

Mohen looked uncomprehending and de Silva repeated the question in Sinhalese. Presumably, Mohen's command of English was limited.

'I have it back now. If you want to hire it, I give you good price. Take you anywhere you want to go. The beaches, the reef, anywhere you like to see.'

'No, I don't want to hire it. But I would like to know something about the last person who did.'

A more cautious expression came over Mohen's face. 'Why do you want to know?'

'I'd like to find him.'

Mohen's eyes narrowed. 'What's it worth?'

De Silva bit back the reply he would have made in Nuala. He wasn't in uniform so the fellow could have no idea he was talking to a policeman. 'That depends on what you have to tell me,' he replied calmly. 'Where did you take him to?'

'He took the boat out on his own.'

Mohen grinned and de Silva saw the flash of a gold tooth. 'But I made sure he left money with me in case it was damaged or didn't come back. A lot of money. I know how to make good bargain.' He waved a hand towards the door. 'Not like the fools out there.'

If that was his attitude, de Silva wasn't surprised that the other fisherman didn't like him.

'Tell me what this man looked like.'

'Tall with dark hair. Younger than you.'

That description could apply to many people, thought de Silva.

Mohen's eyes drifted to one of the bottles of arrack on the bar. De Silva saw that his glass was empty. He nodded to the barman who refilled it.

'I need more of a description than that. Was he good-looking, plain, ugly? Did he have any features that would make him stand out in a crowd?'

Mohen shrugged. 'All Britishers look alike.'

'You're sure he was British?'

'He was white.'

De Silva sighed. So, this mystery man wasn't necessarily British.

'I don't think this is getting us very far,' he muttered to Jane.

'I've understood most of it, but have you asked if he found out why this man wanted to hire the boat? That might help us.'

Mohen shrugged when the question was put to him. 'I asked him, but he told me it wasn't my business.'

De Silva raised an eyebrow. 'And you were still content to hire the boat out to him?'

'The money was good.' Mohen took a swig of arrack. When he put the glass down, there was a defensive look on his face. 'If he planned to do anything bad, it wasn't my fault.'

'I'm not suggesting it was.'

Mohen's eyes went once more to the bottle of arrack. The bartender looked at de Silva, who shook his head.

'No more questions,' he said. 'But if you see the man again, I'd like to know. You can send a message for de Silva at the Cinnamon Lodge hotel. There might be a few more drinks in it,' he added.

He paid for the arrack and he and Jane went back into the sunshine. 'That fellow isn't such a sharp operator as he thinks he is,' he said with a chuckle. 'We got the information we wanted, at least as far as he appeared to have it, for the price of a glass of arrack. If he's telling the truth though, it seems that whoever hired the boat was prepared to lay out a good deal of money to ensure that whatever he was up to remained secret, and he expected to be obeyed without question. Someone wealthy and overbearing with it.'

'Does anyone come to mind?'

'Maybe. Do you remember that we saw Jocelyn Reeve leaving the hotel in a great hurry?'

'Yes.'

'Whilst I was waiting for you at the car, he was talking to one of the staff in a way that I would describe as overbearing and we know he's wealthy. I'm pretty sure he was speaking in Sinhalese too, so he could have communicated with Mohen who clearly doesn't speak much English.'

'But plenty of white people speak some Sinhalese, and I'm afraid it's not unusual for them to treat locals in an overbearing fashion.'

'I'll admit the link is rather tenuous, but it's a place to start.'

'How do you plan to take it further? Ideally, we want Mohen to identify Reeve, but I very much doubt Chief Inspector Lawrence would agree to arrest him on a hunch.'

De Silva frowned. 'My camera's hardly been out of its case since we arrived but even if I managed to take a photograph of Reeve without his noticing, it would take days to develop the film. No, I think we need to find a way of bringing Mohen to the hotel and letting him see Reeve without Reeve being aware of it.'

'That might be a tall order.'

'Can you think of a better idea?'

Jane smiled. 'I confess that I can't. Do you want to talk to Lawrence about all this?'

'I'd rather not mention my suspicions about Reeve just yet.' He grinned. 'You know how you Britishers stick together. If I introduce the idea too early on, I might lose his cooperation entirely. I'll start by telling him about the blue boat and Mohen's hiring it out then see how he reacts.'

'Good idea.'

* * *

They had left the harbour behind and were walking through the centre of the old town. By the time they reached the police station, it was nearly half past four. The sergeant who had been on duty on de Silva's first visit was behind the counter in the public room reading a newspaper, which he quickly tucked away when de Silva and Jane walked in. He crammed the last bite of something flaky into his mouth, swallowed quickly and wiped his lips.

'Can I help you, sahib?' he asked in a tone that was considerably less perfunctory than the one he had used on the earlier occasion.

'I'd like to see Chief Inspector Lawrence, please.'

'The chief inspector is out.'

'When do you expect him back?'

The desk sergeant spread his hands, an apologetic expression on his chubby face.

'I'm not sure. He is a very busy man. Shall I take a message for him?'

'Just tell him that Inspector de Silva would like to speak to him. I have information that may be important in a case he's investigating. I'm going to the Cinnamon Lodge now. If he comes back this afternoon, he can telephone there and ask reception to fetch me.'

'I will tell him, sahib.'

'Is the boatman who was arrested this morning still here?'

'No, sahib. He has been taken to Colombo to the jail there. There is nowhere suitable to hold him in Galle. He is a dangerous criminal.'

Unless the boatman had confessed, Lawrence seemed to have judged him rather prematurely, thought de Silva.

'Very busy man, my foot,' he muttered as he and Jane descended the steps. 'Lawrence has probably gone home for the day. I shouldn't think his desk sergeant would risk stuffing his face and reading the newspaper if his boss was likely to come in at any moment. I didn't hear sounds from the offices off the public room either.'

'Are you surprised that the boatman has already been sent down to Colombo?'

'A little. Lawrence certainly doesn't waste any time, but the man may have confessed.'

'If he has done, I hope it wasn't because he was under duress,' said Jane worriedly.

'We've no reason to suspect that Lawrence has abused his position.'

'I suppose not, but for him to solve the crime so quickly does seem rather convenient.'

CHAPTER 13

Conversation in the bar and at dinner was hushed that evening. Edith Pargeter didn't come down from her room, and Jocelyn Reeve and his wife were also absent, but George Blaine, Max Larsson, and Harold Jenkinson were sharing a table. Whilst they waited for their meal to be served, Blaine got up and came over to speak to the de Silvas. He still looked very disconsolate.

'Larsson and I thought we'd keep each other company this evening,' he said. 'Pretty grim eating dinner on one's own after the day we've had. We suggested that Jenkinson join us as his wife's volunteered to sit with Edith Pargeter. The doctor's given her a sedative but he recommended that she wasn't left alone tonight.'

'I'm sure that's good advice,' said Jane. 'She must be terribly distressed. I believe she was very fond of her niece.'

A spasm of pain crossed George Blaine's face. 'With good reason. I was due to stay on for a few more days,' he went on, 'but I may leave earlier now. Larsson's saying the same. I don't suppose you've heard anything more about the boatman, have you?'

De Silva squashed down his conscience and shook his head.

'The manager's not a happy man. At this rate, his hotel will soon be half empty. I hear that Madame Renaud and her party are leaving in the morning. They've recovered sufficiently to travel, and they've decided against trying to set up their dive again.'

'Where will they go on to?' asked Jane.

'I'm not sure. After such an unpleasant experience, I expect they're eager to shake the dust of this place off their shoes. But with the situation in Europe, I think one can assume that whatever they do, they won't be going home to France.'

Their meal arrived and Blaine left them to return to his table.

'Since this sad business with poor Helen Morris, I'd almost forgotten about Madame Renaud and her companions,' said Jane. 'I wonder what they'll do when they leave here. I'm sure George Blaine's right about them not returning to France.'

She looked sad, and not for the first time, de Silva reflected that feeling the same way she did about the situation in Europe didn't come naturally to him. Britain might rule Ceylon, but he would never look on himself as British, although as anyone who loved freedom would, he had been dismayed when the Nazi armies had swept down, compelling the British forces in northern France to retreat. By summer the Nazis had marched into Paris, and a few months later their dominance in Western Europe was complete. Only Britain stood against them now, her cities suffering nightly bombardments by the Luftwaffe as the Nazis tried to crush her into submission.

'Perhaps they'll stay somewhere else in Ceylon or head for India,' he said. 'I've never been there, but I'm told that the beaches in the south are very beautiful. Perhaps Madame Renaud could organise her diving there.' He forked up a mouthful of beetroot curry and rice. It almost seemed sacrilegious to be enjoying his food on an evening like this, but it was excellent.

He looked across at George Blaine and Max Larsson

who, like Jane, had chosen from the British menu. Larsson was making short work of his leg of lamb and boiled vegetables, but Blaine, who he'd noticed usually had the good appetite one would expect from a young, athletic man, seemed mainly to be pushing his food around the plate.

Jane's eyes followed his. 'Poor George Blaine. I'm sure he was very fond of Helen. How sad that it ended this way. I suspect she wasn't as impervious to him as she made out and it was an act to stop her aunt interfering. Once they were back in Colombo, things would probably have been quite different.'

'Do you know that Blaine works in Colombo then?'

'We were chatting once before all this happened and he mentioned something about being based there although he sometimes has to travel for his work.'

'I suppose that if it's to do with roads and railways that would make sense. Presumably he holds a fairly senior position.'

'Why do you say that?'

'Well otherwise, in the same way as Jocelyn Reeve, one might wonder why he's still a civilian.'

* * *

After dinner, they took coffee in the lounge then decided on a stroll before retiring to bed. At the place where the hotel gardens stopped at the beach, they paused and looked out over the ocean. The day's events gave its ebony waters a sinister aspect. It was easy to see why people used to believe that there were monsters and magical creatures in the depths. In the Hindu religion, there was the sea monster Makara who carried Varana, the god of the ocean, on his back. Makara was half mammal and half amphibian, often depicted with the head of an elephant and the tail of a fish.

Then there were the Ketea, monsters that were half human and half fish, some of them with thick, coiled tails of immense length. They lived under the sea but came out to graze on the shore. They were particularly fond of dates and would wrap their tails around the trunks of palm trees and shake them to bring the fruit down. These monsters were harmless if you kept a respectful distance, but there were also tales of malicious ones like the sirens who used their beauty and their celestial voices to lure sailors onto rocks where they would meet their death. But all these were only creatures of legend. Perhaps a few of the older fishermen still believed in them but he doubted that nowadays there were many other locals who did. There were certainly no supernatural forces at work where Helen Morris was concerned. But if she was dead, was it really the boatman who had killed her?

Jane shivered and he put his arm around her. 'Are you starting to feel cold?'

'Not really. It's just that I can't get poor Helen Morris out of my mind. It's dreadful to think of how she must have suffered or might still be suffering.'

'Yes, it is.'

What more could he say? Neither of them spoke as they walked back up to the hotel and went sadly to bed.

CHAPTER 14

'I'll go into town and hope that Lawrence is at the police station,' said de Silva at breakfast the next morning.

'Would you mind if I don't come with you?' asked Jane. 'I woke up with rather a headache. I think I had too much sun yesterday.'

'Of course not. I'd like a stroll around the garden and then I'll be off. With luck I'll be back in plenty of time for lunch.'

He didn't like to admit it to Jane, but he wasn't anticipating that the visit would be very productive in any case. Overnight, doubts had crept into his mind. When set against the evidence Lawrence had, was he going to accept that a few scrapes of paint on some rocks and a mystery man who had hired a boat that he could have taken anywhere were worth taking seriously? Somehow, he doubted it, even if only because the chief inspector might well resent any interference, particularly from a policeman who was junior to him in rank. He would deliver his information, but he was prepared for it to fall on deaf ears. If that was the case, short of taking the risk of going over Lawrence's head, he was at a loss to think of anything more he could do.

Breakfast over, he left Jane reading in the hotel garden and set off on his morning stroll. First, he headed for the steps leading down to the beach. The tide was coming in fast, and waves dashed sea spray against the rocky headland that separated it from the beach Helen had disappeared from. Until low tide late tonight, it would once again only be possible to reach it by boat.

De Silva gazed out over the ocean. It looked far less forbidding in the daylight. Was poor Helen Morris at peace in its silent depths? Some lines from Shakespeare's play *The Tempest* drifted into his head.

Full fathoms five thy father lies,
Of his bones are coral made,
Those are pearls that were his eyes...

It was easier to believe in Shakespeare's romantic vision when one stood here, looking out over the ocean in a place largely unspoiled by man. The scene that met one's eyes in Colombo was very different. There, every kind of vessel from merchantmen to fishing boats came in and out of the port. Oil scum and rubbish sullied the water, and ships' funnels belched gritty, coal-black smoke into the sky. Instead of this quiet beach, there were docks where restless activity hardly ever ceased. Even at night, sailors could still be found drinking in the waterfront bars or sleeping off the after-effects. Packs of feral cats roamed the cobbled alleyways, hunting for the rats that plagued the warehouses, or stripping the remains of rotting fish from abandoned scraps.

He took a last look at the view then curiosity pulled him in the direction of the guest bungalow. If George Blaine was right that Elodie and her companions had decided to leave, it would be interesting to see if any preparations for doing so were being made.

* * *

When he reached the path that led from the lawn to the bungalow, he had to step smartly aside to avoid colliding with the large trolley loaded with expensive-looking luggage that rumbled towards him. Two servants moved it along, one pushing from behind and the other guiding from the front.

Bundles of laundry were heaped on the verandah. He walked up the steps and went inside. A small army of housekeeping staff had already descended on the place. On the table in the main room, flower arrangements waited to be thrown away and there was a smell of water that had begun to stagnate. Servants were busy sweeping floors and polishing furniture. In the bedrooms, beds were being stripped, pillows fluffed, and rugs shaken. It made de Silva think of a flock of egrets lifting from a lake.

He stopped at the door of the largest and grandest bedroom, presumably the one where Elodie had slept. It was light and charmingly furnished but his nose wrinkled at the lingering, antiseptic smell of the sickroom that it gave off.

He heard a movement and turned to see that one of the hotel staff was watching him from a few yards away. 'Can I help you, sahib?'

'Are you in charge here?'

'Yes,' said the woman. 'I am the head housekeeper.'

'I take it that Madame Renaud and her party have left?'

'They went an hour ago. I hear they had a long journey today. I'm afraid that if you wished to speak with them, you're too late.'

'It's no matter.'

'Is there anything else I can help you with?'

'Thank you, there's nothing.'

If the housekeeper was curious about what he was doing there, she didn't show it. Instead, she beckoned to a cleaner who was coming across the hall with a large pail and a mop.

'Have all the drawers and cupboards been checked?'

The woman nodded. 'Nothing has been left behind.'

'And all dusted out?'

Another nod.

De Silva sighed inwardly. If Elodie and her companions had been poisoned, any evidence that might have been in the bungalow was very likely gone.

* * *

After de Silva left her, Jane had been reading for half an hour when a shadow fell across the page of her book. She looked up to find Max Larsson standing a few feet away. He was so tall, she thought, that the way he towered over her would have been intimidating if he hadn't had a smile on his face.

'Forgive me for disturbing you, Mrs de Silva. A fine day, is it not?'

Jane smiled back. 'It certainly is, but then don't you find that every day in Ceylon is beautiful? Except during the monsoon season, of course.'

'Yes, the rain then is' – he searched for a word – 'astonishing.'

Jane laughed. 'That's a good description for it. When I first came to the island, I remember being amazed by how hard rain could come down. It rains a lot in England, but in a different way.'

'In Sweden it is also different. Where I come from in the north, the winters are long and cold and we have much snow, but they are mainly dry. In summer it is warm and even at night the sun shines, but the air is not humid as it is here.'

There was a pause. It must be the first time she and Max Larsson had exchanged more than a brief greeting, thought Jane. Since they seemed to have exhausted the topic of the weather, she wondered what was coming next, then felt uncharitable. Apart from having dinner with

George Blaine and Harold Jenkinson last night, Larsson didn't seem to talk much to anyone. He was probably shy. What a shame he was on his own. She hadn't studied him closely before, but with his blue eyes and dark hair he was really rather a pleasant-looking young man. To keep the conversation going, she asked, 'Are you planning to go on any more of your plant hunting expeditions before you leave, Mr Larsson?'

'Max, please. No, I think not.' A sad look came over his face. 'The death of Miss Morris is most tragic. It would be hard to enjoy them now. Tomorrow I go back to Ratnapura and my work there.'

It crossed Jane's mind that this shy young man might also have been one of Helen's admirers.

'I'm sure we all feel the same. My husband and I plan to spend the rest of our time here quietly.'

'He is not with you this morning?'

Jane thought quickly. She could hardly tell Larsson the real reason for Shanti's absence. 'He's gone into town. He wanted to visit someone.'

'Does he have business in Galle?'

'An old friend to see.'

'But you do not accompany him?'

'No, I think I had a little too much sun yesterday. I decided to have a quiet morning.'

'The sun is very strong. I myself am most careful to avoid spending too much time in it.'

There was another pause. Jane searched for something to say but Larsson spoke first.

'I'm sure you agree it is an excellent thing that the murderer has been caught so soon. A fine result for the police here.'

Jane wondered if she imagined that he was studying her closely. Perhaps it was just that his slow, precise way of speaking made him seem intense.

'Oh yes,' she said quickly.

'I believe your husband is a police inspector. He will have experience of such matters.'

'He does, but of course he's not involved in Helen Morris's case. We're merely here on holiday.'

Larsson smiled again. 'And I have disturbed your reading.'

'Not at all. I've enjoyed our chat.'

'I too have enjoyed it. Now, I will leave you in peace, Mrs de Silva.' He gave a little bow.

Jane watched him as he walked away in the direction of the hotel then picked up her book again. She read a few pages, but it no longer held her interest. She wasn't sure whether it was due to the plot, which she had come across in several other books, or because of her conversation with Larsson. She had to admit that it had both intrigued and unsettled her.

With a glance at her watch, she saw that it was mid-morning. A cold drink might be pleasant. She was gathering herself together when a new voice hailed her.

'Good morning, Mrs de Silva!' Harold Jenkinson was coming in her direction. 'On your own?'

Jane smiled but underneath she felt a glimmer of suspicion. The remark might be innocent, but it was rather odd that two of the hotel guests were going out of their way to talk to her and ask about where Shanti was this morning.

'Yes, my husband has an appointment in town, but he'll be back for lunch.'

'I saw you managed to have a conversation with young Larsson,' Jenkinson went on jovially. 'As I said to your husband, can't get more than two words out of him m'self. I used to be a bit of an expert on plants and so forth but pretty quickly drew a blank with him there, and on the subject of his home country too.'

'He does seem rather shy.'

'Ah well, never mind. Changing the subject, my wife, Muriel, is hoping to persuade Edith Pargeter to get a bit of fresh air this afternoon. She's not left her room since this terrible business with her niece. At least the culprit's been arrested. Lawrence put on a good show there.'

A woman's voice called out and he looked over his shoulder. 'Ah, that's Muriel now. I'd better see what she wants. Good day to you, Mrs de Silva.'

CHAPTER 15

The drive from the hotel to Galle was becoming familiar. De Silva even recognised some of the stallholders that he passed. When he drew up outside the police station, he almost felt guilty not to be employing the services of the man who had kept an eye on the Morris for him on his previous visits to town with Jane, but he reckoned that the car should be safe as he was leaving it right outside the station entrance.

The desk sergeant looked a little more alert this morning and his uniform tunic was free of crumbs, but his worried frown told de Silva that there was going to be a problem.

'Is your chief here?' he asked.

'I am sorry, sahib, he is not available. There has been a nasty business he has had to attend to. I expect him to be out for many hours.'

De Silva sighed inwardly. He didn't want to spend all morning in Galle waiting for the chief inspector to return, but on the other hand he would rather not make a second trip.

The desk sergeant puffed out his chest and assumed a solemn expression. 'It is a very serious matter. A body has been found at the fishing harbour.' With a podgy hand, he made a slicing gesture across his throat. 'A murder,' he said with relish.

A germ of suspicion flickered through de Silva's mind.

Maybe he would go down to the harbour and see what was going on. He decided it would be quicker to drive than walk, so he thanked the sergeant and returned to the Morris.

At the harbour he saw a police car at the bottom of a roughly surfaced lane that led away from the ocean front. He parked the Morris, got out and went over to a nearby fisherman.

'Do you know where the policeman who arrived in that car has gone?' he asked.

With a calloused finger, the man pointed up the lane. De Silva thanked him and set off.

Shacks built from an assortment of mud bricks, palm fronds, canvas, and sheets of rusty metal mushroomed along either side of the lane. It didn't take de Silva long to work out where the chief inspector was likely to be. Outside a shack that was slightly larger and more substantial than the rest, a crowd had gathered. He made his way through it and pushed aside the curtain that served as a door. A young constable stepped forward to bar his path.

'No one is allowed in. Orders of Chief Inspector Lawrence,' he said briskly.

De Silva stood his ground. 'I'm Inspector de Silva, chief of police in Nuala. I believe I have important information for him.'

Someone shouted from inside the shack. 'What's going on, Constable? Didn't I tell you to keep everyone out?'

'Sorry, sir. The sahib says he is a chief of police and has important information.'

A moment passed then Lawrence emerged from the gloom of an inner room.

'Good morning, Chief Inspector Lawrence. Forgive the intrusion, but I have information that may be of use to you. Can we speak privately?'

Grudgingly, Lawrence nodded. 'But I haven't much time to spare, you understand.'

'Of course.'

Lawrence turned to his constable and pointed to the crowd outside. The men at the front were watching what was going on with great interest. 'Make that lot clear off,' he said sharply.

The constable went outside, pulling the curtain across behind him. Immediately, the air in the shack grew even hotter and the smell of unwashed bodies more pungent.

'Has the victim been identified?' asked de Silva.

Lawrence nodded. 'There aren't many rogues around here who aren't known to me.'

For a moment, de Silva hesitated. He would feel foolish if he was barking up the wrong tree, but then he would look foolish if he backed down now. 'May I ask his name?'

'Mohen.'

The name gave de Silva a jolt.

'I've just come from the police station,' he said. 'Mohen's the man I wanted to talk to you about. I spoke to him yesterday. He told me he'd hired his boat out to a man who wouldn't say what he wanted to use it for, but I believe he may have been at the beach where Helen Morris was on the day of her disappearance.'

Lawrence was silent for a moment then nodded and gave de Silva a perfunctory smile. 'Good of you to interest yourself in my case. May I ask if Mohen expected payment for his information?'

With some reluctance, de Silva nodded. 'He didn't know I was a police officer.'

'I see, but in any case, I would never have relied on a word he said. The man was a well-known liar. Always coming to the station with trumped-up stories about wrongs his neighbours had done him. I learnt not to give them any credence. If you were hoping for reliable information that would help to shed light on who killed Miss Morris, you were wasting your time, and if you're suggesting Mohen was silenced for not keeping his mouth shut, you're wrong.'

'So what is your theory about who killed him?'

'Easy enough. It will have been a neighbour that he got on the wrong side of once too often. His throat was cut and from the look of it, the knife used was of the kind the local men use to gut fish. I have my suspects and I've already made two arrests.'

He put his hand on the curtain that covered the entrance and twitched it aside. 'Now, if there's nothing else, Inspector, I'll bid you good day. Enjoy your holiday, and have no fear, everything is under control.'

* * *

At the hotel de Silva found Jane in the garden and told her about Mohen's fate and the meeting with Lawrence.

Jane shivered. 'Poor man. Even if he was unpopular, no one deserves to die because of that.'

'I'm afraid it happens. I just hope that in his eagerness to solve the case, Chief Inspector Lawrence isn't being too hasty. I may have been wrong about his handling of Jai the nightwatchman's death, but to be so quick in reaching a conclusion about a case twice in one week could indicate he's lazy.'

Jane raised an eyebrow.

'I agree that it would be wrong to criticise the man just because I haven't taken to him,' de Silva went on, 'and if I were in his shoes, I wouldn't welcome interference on my patch, but to me, the theory of the disgruntled neighbour doesn't ring true. Mohen was murdered less than a day after we spoke to him. What if our visit had come to the ears of the man that he hired out the boat to?'

'You mean he might have wanted to silence Mohen?'

'Lawrence dismissed the idea, but I still think it may be the truth.'

Jane looked distressed. 'Then we could be responsible for his death.'

'But his involvement may not have been as innocent as he claimed it was.' He glanced at his watch. 'Half past four. We may as well get back to the hotel. I think we could both do with a cup of tea.'

CHAPTER 16

They had finished their tea and were walking through the lobby when one of the staff behind the reception desk hurried over to them.

'A message has been left for you, sahib.' Gingerly, the man handed over a grimy sheet of folded paper secured with a kind of pin made from a sharpened splinter of wood. De Silva's name was written on the front in pencil.

'When was it delivered?'

The man looked apologetic. 'I'm not sure, sahib. It was in the pigeonhole for your room when I came on duty. But I can ask if anyone remembers when it was brought in.'

'No matter.'

'It certainly wouldn't have come with the post,' said Jane as they went upstairs. 'There's no stamp on it and the stationery is most odd.'

In their room, he carefully removed the makeshift pin and unfolded the paper. 'It seems to have been torn from a small book. Even though it's dirty and damp, it looks as if originally, it was of good quality.'

'It's very thick,' said Jane. 'Not really like normal letter-writing paper at all. More like paper you would have in a sketch pad.'

De Silva scanned the pencilled words with mounting surprise and relief. He didn't recognise the writing and some of it had been smudged by damp, but the name that was written at the bottom of the page was only too familiar: Helen Morris.

'Shanti? What is it?'

'It's from Helen Morris. She says she's been forced to hide in a village in the jungle and needs help.' He read the rest of the letter out loud: '*It's very important that no one except you and your wife know, not even Aunt Edith. When she can be told, I hope she'll forgive me and understand why I've asked you to keep my secret. The villager who brought this letter will be waiting for you at the summerhouse where I was painting when we met on that first afternoon. He'll show you the way.*'

Jane beamed. 'She isn't dead! Oh Shanti, isn't that marvellous. But how odd that she doesn't want her aunt to be told that she's alive. Why do you think that is?'

De Silva shrugged. 'I've no idea, but we should respect her wishes and let her have the opportunity to explain what this is all about before we tell anyone. I'd better go and find this villager she mentions.'

'I wish I could come with you, but there'll be no room for me once you have Helen in the car. Are you thinking to bring her back here? It might be hard to stop people seeing her, and she's obviously very frightened of anyone knowing she's still alive.'

'I think it would be best to find somewhere else she can stay for a few days until we sort out what to do. I'd better get down to the summerhouse. I don't want the man who brought the letter giving up on me. These jungle villages are virtually impossible to find without a guide. At least there are a couple of hours of daylight left. I might be gone for some time though. Will you be alright?'

Jane nodded. 'Of course I will. Now hurry along and good luck.'

* * *

126

When de Silva reached the summerhouse, there was no one in sight, then something moved in the bushes. He glimpsed a brown face amongst the leaves, but it quickly vanished.

He looked over his shoulder. There was no one coming. 'I'm Inspector de Silva,' he said in Sinhalese. 'I'm alone. You're safe to come out. I have the letter you delivered.' He hoped that whoever this villager was, he didn't only speak a local dialect. If that was the case, it might not be easy to understand each other.

A moment passed and de Silva was about to try again in Tamil when there was a fresh shaking and rustling in the middle of a clump of oleanders. The brown face reappeared followed by the rest of a young man. He had black, bushy hair and wore a faded red loincloth. He regarded de Silva nervously.

De Silva held up the letter that he'd brought with him. 'This says you're to take me to the British lady, Helen Morris. Can we travel some of the way by road?'

There was a pause then to de Silva's relief, the young man answered in halting Sinhalese.

'Yes, but we must walk too.'

'How long will it take to get there?'

The young man looked blank, and de Silva realised that he had no watch. He would just have to hope that it wasn't too far and if the sun had gone down by the time they got there, not too difficult a walk in the dark.

'Is the British lady injured?'

The villager clawed at his arms and legs with dirt-rimmed fingernails. De Silva hoped that all he was trying to show was that Helen was badly scratched, but it might be worse than that. His mind flashed back to the nightwatchman Jai.

'Has an animal hurt her?' he asked.

The villager frowned.

'An animal,' de Silva repeated. He did his best to mime a leopard on the prowl and saw a fleeting smile cross the young man's face. He shook his head. 'No.'

'Good. Well, we'd better be going.' Quickly, de Silva decided that he ought not to be seen with this young man. It would be unwise to do anything that might give rise to curiosity, particularly as Helen was so anxious to hide the fact that she was alive from everyone except him and Jane. 'I'll fetch my car,' he added. 'Wait for me at the gate where the hotel drive meets the road.'

Back at the hotel, he paid a brief visit to Jane to tell her that he had found the messenger then drove down to the gate. On the way, he turned the situation over in his mind. It was flattering to be trusted. He assumed that his being a policeman might have something to do with it, but if Helen needed police help, and it certainly sounded as if she did, he was surprised that she hadn't sent her message to Lawrence. He might be lazy and inclined to take the easy way out, but surely finding a missing Britisher, and a lady at that, would be a coup that he would be only too happy to take the credit for. On the other hand, perhaps she'd thought that the villager might be afraid to go to the police station.

The young man's eyes lit up when he saw the Morris. De Silva leant across the passenger seat and opened the door. 'Hop in.'

After a moment's hesitation, the young man did so, settling himself tentatively into the leather seat. His hands gripped its sides as de Silva set off but after a few moments he relaxed and began to inspect the dashboard with great interest. De Silva realised that he had probably never been in a car before. Despite the seriousness of their mission, he was unable to resist putting his foot down harder. The young man tilted his face up to the wind and laughed.

Soon, however, de Silva was forced to go more slowly. It was growing dark, and the road was much rougher than the one between the Cinnamon Lodge and town. Deep pot-holes threatened, that his headlights only picked out when the Morris was perilously close to them. The last thing he wanted was to have a puncture delay Helen's rescue. From painful experience, he knew that changing a tyre on a lonely road at night wasn't a pleasant job. If this young man had never been in a car before he was unlikely to be a great deal of help either.

But he was obviously skilled in his own way. When he suddenly tapped de Silva on the arm and pointed to the side of the road, de Silva had no idea how he'd known that this was where they needed to stop. He pulled the Morris in as close as he could to the tree line, offering up a quick prayer to any gods who might be the protectors of four-wheeled creations that if another vehicle came past while they were fetching Helen, the driver wouldn't run into the back of her.

As the young man led the way into the trees, de Silva was glad that Jane had insisted he change into the sturdiest shoes he had with him. Even through their thick soles, he felt the sharp stones and sticks underfoot. He was amazed that the young man seemed to be so sure of where he was going and untroubled by the rough ground or the branches and creepers that they had to push through as they plunged deeper into the trees. He must have the eyes of an owl and the skin of a rhinoceros, or maybe he was just more practised at ducking and weaving about than de Silva. More than once, he had to call out that he needed to slow down. Soon, every inch of him was covered in a clammy film of sweat, and wiping the moisture off his forehead and out of his eyes had reduced his pocket handkerchief to a soggy, useless ball of cotton. Fervently, he hoped there wasn't much farther to go.

At last, he saw lights flickering amongst the trees and heard voices. They came out into a clearing dotted with a few huts. The smell of roasting meat drifted towards him. He saw that in the centre of the ring of huts, a fire had been lit. Two long forked sticks had been driven into the ground on either side of it with another balanced horizontally across them. It formed a spit for the plump bodies of three plucked jungle fowl. On one side, the horizontal pole extended a little way beyond the circle of the fire. Palms fronds were wrapped around it and a boy was slowly turning the carcasses over flames that hissed and sputtered as the fat dripped onto them.

In the dim light, it was hard to see exactly how many villagers were there, but de Silva guessed they numbered about twenty adults as well as numerous children. The children watched curiously as he and his companion came closer, covering their mouths with their hands and giggling and whispering amongst themselves. A group of women who had been chopping roots and herbs stopped what they were doing and stared. De Silva took a few more steps towards them, then suddenly a figure flew at him out of the shadows. He staggered as he caught the person in his arms. It was Helen Morris.

CHAPTER 17

'I can't tell you how grateful I am that you've come,' said Helen when she had recovered her composure. 'I'm sorry, I didn't mean to behave so foolishly when I saw you. I thought that I was managing to cope, but—'

'There's no need to apologise. You've clearly had a terrible experience. It's often after the worst is over that people find it hard to control their emotions.'

She smiled. 'Thank you for being so understanding. I was afraid that you might be angry about being dragged out here, but I thought I could trust you to be discreet.'

'I'm glad to be able to help and it's a great relief to find that you're safe. I'm afraid that in most people's minds, you were given up for dead. I know you asked for secrecy, but I'd like to tell your aunt the news as soon as possible. She's very distressed. If you'll allow me, I promise I'll be careful how I do it.'

Helen's brow furrowed. 'Poor Aunt Edith. Perhaps it was unkind not to trust her, but I felt I had no choice.' She gave him a sideways glance. 'I'm sure you're wondering why I didn't send my message to her rather than you. The fact is, although I'm extremely fond of her, I didn't think she would know what to do in a situation like this. I was afraid that she would turn to the wrong person for help.'

'Who would that be?'

'I don't know. That's the trouble.'

'Well, when you're ready to tell me what happened, perhaps between us we can work out who mustn't realise you're alive.'

One of the village women had brought each of them a piece of one of the cooked fowls. They ate with their fingers using dried palm leaves for plates. The meat was sinewy and had a strong gamey flavour, but it was good; crisp skin crackled as de Silva bit into it. It was generous of the villagers to share their food, he thought. They probably had little enough for themselves. Jungle fowl might be a comparatively rare treat they'd been lucky to find on a hunting expedition.

'The village women have been so kind,' said Helen. She looked down at her bruised arms, bound in places with rags. 'They cleaned my wounds for me and put wild honey on them. Most of my clothes were badly torn, so they loaned me lengths of cloth to wrap around myself whilst they mended them as best as they could.'

De Silva made a mental note to give the women whatever money he had on him before he took Helen back.

'The boatman I hired took me along the coast for a time,' said Helen when he gently prompted her to begin her story. 'I'd already done several paintings of the hotel gardens and the beach there, so I wanted to find somewhere new. I'd planned to ask him to stay with me when I found the place I wanted, but when I eventually decided on stopping at the beach next to the hotel's one, it seemed silly to keep him waiting for hours. I told him he could leave me there and come back later in the afternoon.

'I'd set my easel up in some shade and was painting when I saw a boat coming towards the beach. I was sure it wasn't my boatman because his boat was green and this one was blue. The helmsman beached it on the far side to where I was painting. I'd set everything up in the shade and I don't think he noticed me at first. He seemed to be having trouble with his boat. I think he may have scraped it against some rocks. Perhaps he'd not been to that beach before.'

That was probably where the blue marks on the rocks came from, thought de Silva. He chewed the last bit of flesh off the jungle fowl leg and licked his greasy fingers. Helen had stopped eating and the hand holding her piece of fowl trembled.

'Take your time,' he said quietly.

She drew in a deep breath then let it out slowly.

'There was something strange about him. It made me think I didn't want to call out and draw attention to myself. Eventually, he anchored the boat and after he'd done that, he reached into it and brought out a small bag and what looked like a metal cylinder. The kind of thing that might contain rolled up documents. The next thing he got out of the boat was a spade, then he took everything over to some rocks. From its colour, the sand seemed dry there. He started to dig, but it didn't look easy. The sand kept flowing back into the hole. He straightened up after a while and rested on his spade. It was then that a flock of parrots flew out of the jungle and landed on one of the trees close to where I was. It was a mango tree, and they must have been after the fruit. They were making a terrible commotion and he looked over at them. That was when he saw me.'

'Can you describe him?'

'He wore a tight black swimming costume that came down to his wrists and ankles, and he had a diving mask perched on his head. I'm afraid I'm a little short-sighted so I couldn't see his face clearly, but he was tall and athletic looking, and definitely white. I think his hair was dark although it's hard to be absolutely sure as it was wet. He picked up his spade again and started to come towards me. I decided that it was probably silly to be nervous of him, so I called out good afternoon, but he didn't answer, just pulled the mask down over his face.'

She shivered. 'I started to be really afraid then. He kept walking towards me, and I saw he had a long knife stuck in his belt. He began to speed up—'

Helen had gone very pale, and de Silva saw that tears glistened on her cheeks. He wished he had something to offer her apart from a soggy handkerchief. Some of the village women nearby gave her sympathetic looks. De Silva wasn't sure how much of the conversation they understood but they were clearly sorry for her distress. She wiped the tears away with the back of her hand.

'I left everything where it was and ran,' she continued. 'I wasn't at all sure I'd be able to get away from him, but by then I realised there was nothing else to be done. I managed to keep a little way ahead for a while although my heart was pumping like mad, and I was getting short of breath. Branches whipped into my face and made it sting. When I touched it, it felt sticky, and my fingers came away with blood on them. When I stopped to catch my breath, I heard him pushing his way through the undergrowth behind me, so I didn't dare stop for more than a few moments. The ground was sloping upwards, and it looked even steeper ahead. Soon, I had to pull myself up using the tree roots that stuck out from the earth. My arms ached, and I started to panic. It sounded as if he was getting closer all the time. Then I heard a loud chattering noise. A big monkey came out of the bushes a little way ahead of me, baring its teeth. I was afraid it would bite me, so I did the only thing I could think of, I tried to get around it. That was when I felt myself sliding downhill.'

She paused as one of the women put a small clay bowl beside her, containing something that de Silva guessed was herbal tea.

'Good for healing,' the woman said. Helen thanked her and took a sip. The woman smiled and went back to her friends.

'The hillside there was even steeper than the route I'd been on,' Helen resumed. 'At first, I tried to slow myself down by digging my feet into the soil, but it was baked so hard I soon realised it wouldn't help. I gave up and just kept sliding down for what seemed like for ever until I reached a level spot.

'I felt as if all the breath had been knocked out of me, so even if it had been safe to stand up, I don't think I could have done. I craned my neck to look up at the rim of the slope I'd come down. There was no one there, but I did see one of my shoes caught in a bush a little way below it. It must have come off when I was trying to slow myself down.'

She took another drink of the herbal tea and suppressed a grimace. 'Goodness, how bitter this is.' She glanced at the women. 'I must drink it though. I don't want them to think I'm ungrateful.' She swallowed some more and wiped her lips with the back of her hand. 'Where was I?'

'You'd come to a stop at the bottom of the slope.'

Helen nodded. 'I looked around for somewhere to hide in case the man worked out where I'd gone and came that way. There was a fallen tree not too far off, so I crawled behind it and lay there, I'm not sure for how long.' She gave a shaky laugh. 'There were all sorts of insects crawling about in the bark. It's lucky I'm not afraid of spiders and snakes, but I was very glad there were no stinging ants. Every so often I took the risk of peering out to look at the rim of the slope again, but when I'd done so several times, I'd still seen no one. I began to hope that the man had given up, thinking I'd escaped him or fallen to my death.'

De Silva admired her courage. He wouldn't have been so sanguine about the danger of meeting snakes.

'When I thought it was safe, I started to walk again. The tree canopy was too dense for me to see where the sun was, but I guessed the beach was behind me. I was afraid to go back there in case he was waiting for me, so I took the opposite direction, hoping to find help or at least a road I might be able to follow.'

'You did well. Finding the way in the jungle is very hard.'

Helen smiled. 'Thank you, but I'm afraid that by the time it was dark, I had no idea where I was or what direction I was going in. There were a lot more noises than there'd been in the day. They seemed louder and stranger than they had in the daylight, and I started to feel frightened.'

De Silva felt for her. Over his career, there had been a few occasions when he'd found himself alone in jungle country at night. He remembered the struggle to control his fears, the eerie cries of unseen creatures, and the hisses and rustles that might mean snakes or other poisonous reptiles were nearby. He flinched as he remembered how the soft, mossy lichen that hung from the trees brushed one's face like ghostly fingers.

'I dreaded having to spend the night on my own,' Helen went on. 'But I was trying to steel myself to make the best of it when a party of hunters from this village found me. It was difficult to communicate with them at first, but once they'd brought me back here, I found that a few of the younger women speak a little English. They tell me they've picked it up when they take the herbal remedies that they make into Galle to sell in the market. Sahan who came to fetch you also speaks some English. For a while, he worked in Galle in one of the hotels until he became too homesick to stay on and came back to the village.'

'How did you manage to write the letter?' asked de Silva. It would be unusual for villagers like these to know how to write or have any use for paper.

'As luck would have it, I had my little sketchbook and pencil with me. I usually have it in the pocket of my skirt in case I see something I want to draw.' She frowned. 'You said that people thought I was dead. Why did they think that? Was there a search for me?'

'There was and we would have gone on with it if it hadn't been for the fact that Chief Inspector Lawrence called the search off.'

'I don't understand.'

'He arrested the boatman who brought you to the beach. The boatman claimed that when he returned to collect you as you'd asked him to do, you were nowhere to be seen. He assumed that someone else had come along and you'd gone back to the hotel with them. Lawrence didn't believe him. He had the man's boat searched, and a necklace with a pendant in the shape of an H was found there, along with some money.'

Helen looked puzzled. 'I've never had a necklace like that. As for money, I had a little with me, but I still have it. If you'll take me to Chief Inspector Lawrence, I'll tell him so myself.'

De Silva hesitated. It was still troubling him that Mohen had been killed so soon after they'd spoken. It had also occurred to him that it was shortly after he'd told Lawrence's desk sergeant that he had more information that might be relevant to Helen's disappearance. As he'd done with Jai's death and Helen's assumed one, Lawrence seemed to have found a solution to Mohen's murder remarkably quickly. Did he have a magic touch or was something else going on? He'd recently given thought to the idea that Lawrence was simply lazy, but now he was not so sure that was all there was to it. Might he know something he didn't want revealed about the mysterious man who had hired Mohen's boat?

'I'd prefer to wait a little while before speaking to Lawrence.'

'Why do you say that?'

'Because I'd like to find out who that man on the beach was before I give him any more information.'

'But won't he want to help us find out?'

De Silva hesitated. How much should he tell her? By failing to trust Lawrence, he might be doing him a serious wrong.

But Helen's sharp mind hadn't been blunted by her alarming experience.

'I think I understand,' she said slowly. 'The necklace wasn't mine, but someone had to put it and the money on that boat. If the boatman had stolen them from someone else, why would he take the risk of leaving them on his boat? There must have been other places he could have hidden them. He might even have had time to sell the necklace before he took me out yesterday.'

'Exactly.'

'So, you think that Lawrence, or someone working for him, might have planted everything on the boat?'

'I can't be sure of it, but I think it's possible. It disturbs me that Lawrence seems to have made up his mind about your case so quickly and this isn't the first time he's done something similar.' He explained about Jai and Mohen. 'I think it's advisable that we tread very carefully. Lawrence may be lazy rather than culpable, but I'd like to know more, and for the moment, I'd rather you stayed here.'

Helen looked troubled. 'If you think that's best,' she said hesitantly. 'But even though the villagers are very kind, I hope I don't have to stay for much longer.'

De Silva understood her reservations. The meal of roasted jungle fowl was likely to be followed by plain dal for several days. Englishwomen were used to sleeping on comfortable beds too, not thin mats rolled out on the hard ground.

'But I'd like you to tell Aunt Edith now that I'm safe,' Helen went on.

'Of course, and I'll do my best to make sure she understands the need for secrecy.'

'In case you have difficulty,' Helen said awkwardly, 'I'll

write a note for you to give her. I want her to agree to your handling everything in whatever way you think appropriate.'

Although she didn't say it in so many words, de Silva guessed she meant that her aunt might treat a local policeman in a dismissive manner that she wouldn't adopt towards one of the British members of the force, but he decided there was no point taking offence. 'You mentioned that you were afraid she would tell the wrong person if you sent her the message first. What did you mean by that?'

'I wasn't being entirely truthful when I said I didn't know who that would be. The man I saw was tall with dark hair. The boat he used was a small one. I doubt it would have come from any further away than Galle. I suppose he might have found the beach by chance, but he might have already known about it if he was staying at the hotel.'

'And if this man is a guest at the hotel, who do you have in mind?'

'It's crossed my mind he might be Jocelyn Reeve—'

She faltered then rallied. 'Oh, I know I've made fun of my aunt for her sweeping assumptions about people, but whoever he was, the man was obviously burying something he wanted kept secret. I think he wanted that so badly that if he'd caught me, he would have killed me. My aunt may be right that Jocelyn Reeve is involved in some nefarious activities. I think he could be the man who chased me.'

De Silva thought of the morning when he'd seen Reeve swimming. He had certainly shown himself to be fearless in the water. The man Helen saw had worn a diving mask, so presumably he'd been in deep water some way from the shore. There were, however, other guests at the hotel who would fit the same description as Reeve. Max Larsson for one, although he had no apparent motive. And was it too soon to discount George Blaine? If de Silva were a betting man, he would hesitate to put money on Blaine being the guilty party, but the young man was also tall and dark with an athletic build.

He filed the thoughts away and decided that his immediate concern must be to ensure that Helen stayed safe. He should also return to Cinnamon Lodge. Jane would be anxious to know what had been happening and she might be having difficulty fending off the enquiries of other guests. Those might purely be motivated by curiosity, but there could be more sinister reasons. He pressed his lips together. Apart from telling her aunt, the news about Helen definitely had to be kept under wraps for the moment.

Before he left, he spoke with the headman and explained that Helen needed to stay in the village, perhaps even for a few more days. He seemed happy to accept it, especially when de Silva handed over some money by way of thanks for the villagers' help. Sahan, the young man who had brought him to the village, led him back to the place where he'd left the Morris. As he eased himself into the seat and started the engine, he felt a wave of relief that she'd not suffered any mishaps while he'd been away. He took careful note of where he was and in case he ever needed to find the place again on his own, committed it to memory before starting the engine. He turned the Morris around and set off for the hotel.

CHAPTER 18

When de Silva reached the hotel and found Jane in their room but still up, it took him some time to explain to her everything that had happened.

'It's such a huge relief that Helen's safe,' she said when he finally came to an end. 'But what a horrible experience she's had to go through. It says a lot for her strength of character that she managed as well as she did.'

'Yes, she's a most courageous young lady.'

Jane sat down at the dressing table, unpinned her hair, and began to brush it. 'We must do our best to ensure that she suffers no further misfortunes. When will you tell her aunt that you've found her?'

He made a face. 'I ought to do it soon, although it's far too late tonight, of course. But it's a delicate matter. I want to avoid anyone else getting wind of it.'

'Even the Jenkinsons? Muriel Jenkinson has gone out of her way to support Edith and spends a lot of time with her. She seems to be a good woman. If Edith's upset that she wasn't the first to know that her niece is alive, it might help to have her with you.'

'I'm sure Muriel Jenkinson is an admirable lady, but in my experience, the way to keep secrets is to tell them only when absolutely necessary. Even the best of people can let something slip, often unintentionally.'

'Would you like me to come with you instead? I don't know if I can make a difference but I'm happy to try.'

He smiled. 'Thank you.'

'We'll have to find a time when Edith's alone. A meal-time might be best. As far as I know, she's taking all her meals in her suite, but Muriel and Harold Jenkinson usually eat in the dining room.'

'Good. I think we should get some sleep now, but first thing in the morning, we need to find out what time Edith's breakfast is served and have a note delivered with it asking her to see us.'

He pulled off his shoes and socks and rubbed the arch of one foot. 'I'm getting too old for all this running around in the jungle. I'm not sure what aches most, my feet or my knees. I could have done with having Prasanna and Nadar and their young legs.'

Jane smiled. 'At least when this is over, you'll only have one more journey to make to fetch Helen home.'

'We have to catch the culprit yet,' he said gloomily, transferring his attention to the other foot. 'I fear that may not be all that easy. If it is Jocelyn Reeve, he's well protected by his wealth and status. And I'm not confident that I'll be able to rely on Chief Inspector Lawrence for help.'

'You really don't trust him, do you?'

'No. Once we've spoken to Edith, I'd like to find a boatman to take us round to the beach where Helen was attacked. It may be a forlorn hope, but if we can find out what her attacker was burying, there might be a clue there that leads to Reeve. Otherwise, short of a miracle, we have to hope that somehow he'll give himself away.'

'Are you convinced it was Reeve that Helen saw?'

'I'm not absolutely sure, but remember that time when we saw him arguing with the staff member outside the hotel? We thought then that Edith Pargeter might be right about him being involved in some kind of shady activity. I don't think I mentioned it to you at the time, but I also saw him one morning when I went down early to the hotel beach. He was swimming and obviously very good at it. The man Helen saw must have been good too if he'd been out to dive or swim in deep water.'

'I agree, but let's suppose for a moment that Helen's wrong about Reeve. There are two other young men staying here who are tall and dark.'

'Max Larsson?'

'Yes, and George Blaine.'

'The thought had crossed my mind, but I didn't say anything to Helen, particularly about George Blaine.'

'Quite right. She's had enough to deal without having to face the idea that a young man she thought of as a friend is capable of such villainy.'

'She may yet have to face it, although I think Reeve is the more likely candidate.'

He finished rubbing his foot and leant back against the pillows with a sigh. The guilty thought of what Helen Morris had to sleep on tonight went through his head. Still, she was safe and not alone.

'What do you think about Larsson?' asked Jane. 'He seems so mild and unassuming, but he did behave rather strangely today after you'd gone. I stayed in the garden reading, and he came up of his own accord and started talking to me when we've hardly exchanged a word until now.'

'What did you talk about?'

Jane laughed. 'The weather mostly, but he also asked about where you were. The way he did it made me think there might be more than idle curiosity involved.'

De Silva yawned once more and rubbed a hand over his chin. His palm prickled; he'd better have a shave before he and Jane ventured into Edith Pargeter's lair, even if it was with good news.

'Something Harold Jenkinson said about him has stuck in my mind too,' Jane added.

'What was that?'

'He said he'd mentioned it to you as well.'

'Oh yes, he told me he'd tried talking to Larsson about his interest in the plants and animals here, and about Sweden, but he didn't get much of a response.'

'I know that might be because Larsson's shy but taken together—'

'It raises the question of whether it's just shyness, or whether he wants to avoid the subjects for some other reason. Is that what you mean?' asked de Silva.

'Yes. Might he be afraid that if he gets drawn into conversation with someone who has a bit more knowledge than the average person, he'll trip himself up?'

'It's something to consider. For the moment, though, I think we should concentrate on making the arrangements to visit Edith and letting her know that Helen's safe.'

He brought out of his pocket the letter Helen had written. 'Helen wanted me to hand this to her aunt. I think she's perceptive enough to realise that Edith might need some encouragement if she's to be persuaded to accept advice from a local policeman.'

CHAPTER 19

The drawing room of Edith Pargeter's suite was spacious and bright, equipped with comfortable-looking sofas and chairs upholstered in jewel-coloured fabrics, and other delicate pieces of furniture, many of them carved and inlaid with ebony and brass in the Ceylonese style. De Silva was surprised to see it. Rather than associating Edith with such a fresh, attractive room, he had expected one that exuded old-fashioned formality. The remains of her breakfast lay on a small table that had been set up in the window embrasure. He smelled the tangy aroma of orange peel and the fragrance of Earl Grey tea.

Edith dabbed her lips with her napkin and rose to her feet. She crossed to one of the chairs and sat down. Despite her composure, she looked drawn and haggard. De Silva was glad they had good news for her. He only hoped that he and Jane would be able to allay any resentment she might feel that Helen had turned to him first, and convince her to listen to their advice.

'I won't pretend I wasn't surprised to receive your request,' said Edith. 'Since I lost my poor niece, I've found it intolerable to be in company, but your message said that you had important news for me.'

De Silva took a deep breath. 'I'm happy to tell you it's good news, ma'am.'

Edith Pargeter smiled wanly. 'I fail to see how anything could be, but please go on.'

'You niece is alive, ma'am.'

He saw Edith's hands grip the arms of her chair; her knuckles blanched. 'Is this some kind of tasteless joke?' she snapped, but her eyes filled with tears.

'No,' said Jane quickly. 'It's the truth. She's safe in a village in the jungle. My husband saw her there last night.'

Edith Pargeter stared at them, a bewildered expression on her face. She opened her mouth, but nothing came out.

'Shanti,' said Jane in a low voice. 'Give Mrs Pargeter Helen's letter.'

He handed it over and Edith took it tentatively. Her hands trembling, she unfolded the paper and began to read. For a few moments, her expression veered between hope and uncertainty then it cleared. When she raised her eyes to meet theirs, she looked as if years had fallen from her shoulders. She clutched the letter to her as if it was a talisman.

'I don't understand everything yet, but Helen says you'll enlighten me.' She raised an eyebrow. 'She also tells me that I have to trust you and take your advice. I'll do my best, but I hope you'll forgive an old lady who's set in her ways.'

'There's no need to apologise, ma'am,' said Jane. 'We understand.'

Edith tilted her head to one side and looked at Jane thoughtfully. 'Yes,' she said at last, 'I think you do.'

She listened without interrupting as de Silva went through the events of the previous night. When he had finished, she was silent for a moment before she spoke.

'Inspector de Silva, it's clear to me that my niece has had a very lucky escape and this man is extremely dangerous. Shouldn't we inform Chief Inspector Lawrence as soon as possible? The boatman who's been taken into custody may be an accomplice. Questioning him could be the way to discover this man's identity.'

'With respect, ma'am, for the moment at least, I strongly advise keeping Chief Inspector Lawrence out of this.'

Edith looked surprised then de Silva saw her natural inclination to be obeyed rise to the surface.

'Whatever for? I'm very grateful to you, Inspector, but surely, the chief inspector is the proper person to deal with matters from now on. My niece must be brought home and he can supply men to protect her until this man is found and arrested.' There was a note of impatience in her voice.

'There's more I haven't told you, ma'am. Please hear me out.'

Once more she listened as he explained about why he suspected Lawrence of being a villain. 'If this is true,' she said when he was done, 'the man is a monster.'

'And that's precisely why we don't want to arouse his suspicion.'

'But is Helen safe where she is? I want to be absolutely sure of that.' Edith frowned. 'What if you're right that Lawrence is corrupt, and he's involved with this man who attacked my niece? They might still be looking for her.'

'I think we can be fairly sure they believe she's dead, but in any case, she's safer where she is than she would be here. It would be difficult, perhaps impossible, to keep her presence a secret.'

She looked at him closely. 'Am I right that you think this man may be one of the guests at the hotel? The proximity of the beach suggests it. I know he wore a mask, but was she able to give you any description of him?'

'Just that he was tall and athletic looking with dark hair.'

Her eyes hardened. 'A fair description of Jocelyn Reeve. I've suspected from the moment I saw him that he's not to be trusted.'

'I'm afraid it's also a fair description of Max Larsson and George Blaine.'

'I hardly think we need seriously to consider either of them.' Edith's implacable expression reminded de Silva of what Helen had told him on their first meeting in the garden: that once her aunt had made up her mind, it was a herculean task to change it. While they had her cooperation, however tenuous, it was probably easier not to argue.

'You may be right, ma'am,' he confined himself to saying, 'but we'll need convincing evidence to arrest Mr Reeve.'

Edith's expression darkened, and the image of Florence Clutterbuck flashed through his mind. He reminded himself, however, that under her imperious manner, Florence possessed plenty of good sense. Hopefully, the same was true of Edith Pargeter.

To his relief, after a brief pause, she nodded. 'I'm forced to agree with you, Inspector, but whoever this man is I want him found, and found quickly. When you have your evidence, what will you do?'

'If Lawrence is one of the people who needs to be arrested, I'll have to report to the assistant government agent in Nuala to obtain his authority, and possibly call for backup as well before I take any action.'

Edith nodded. 'I understand, but please hurry. I want my niece back with me.'

* * *

'All things considered, I thought that went off satisfactorily,' said Jane when they had returned to their room. 'You handled Edith very well.'

De Silva chuckled. 'I'm glad you thought so, my love. I suppose I've had plenty of practice with Florence.'

'True. So, what do we do now?'

'I'd like to go back to the beach and see if whatever this man was burying is still there. I know it doesn't seem very likely he would leave it behind, even if he thought Helen was never going to tell any tales, but you know me. I like to be thorough.'

'If we're to go in daylight, and it doesn't seem practical to search at any other time, we'll need to get there by boat.'

He nodded. 'I propose we go to the harbour in Galle. With luck there'll be someone who's prepared to take us.'

CHAPTER 20

The boat turned towards the deserted beach and when it was in shallow water, the boatman who had agreed to ferry them out from Galle shipped the oars. They drifted in and de Silva felt a slight jolt as the hull touched sand. It was early afternoon and despite the sea breeze, the heat was intense. He wondered how their boatman, who was only wearing a loincloth and a piece of fabric wound turban fashion around his head, managed to walk on the burning sand with bare feet. He must have skin like leather.

De Silva shaded his eyes with one hand and studied the layout of the beach. From Helen's description, there were several places where her attacker might have been digging. He beckoned the boatman to follow him with the spades they'd brought with them. He'd chosen the man because he looked strong, but more importantly, in return for good pay, he'd promised to be discreet. They would have to hope he kept his word, thought de Silva.

At the first place they tried, water oozed up through the sand as the boatman lifted the first spadeful. When he dumped it down, it landed with a splat. Immediately, the hole left behind filled with water. Clearly, until the tide ebbed, further digging was only practical higher up the beach. De Silva pointed to another spot, and this time picked up the other spade and helped to dig. In a few minutes, they had created a hole a couple of feet deep and twice as wide.

De Silva straightened up and rested on his spade. Reeve, Larsson, and Blaine all appeared to be in good shape. No doubt they would manage to dig further down than this. The boatman had stopped digging too and was looking at him. He lifted the spade once more. 'Deeper,' he said.

A sweltering hour later, after they had dug holes in all the likely places, he leant his spade against a rock and mopped his face with his handkerchief. A flock of parrots, perhaps the same ones that had alerted Helen's attacker to her presence, squawked and jostled in the mango tree nearby.

'Don't you think that's enough?' asked Jane. 'If there was anything here, I'm sure you would have found it by now.'

De Silva puffed out his cheeks and exhaled a long breath. 'I'm ready to accept that now. You can stop,' he said to the boatman in Sinhalese. The man dropped his spade and went to crouch by the water, scooping it up in his hands and pouring it over his head so that it ran in gleaming rivulets down his body. De Silva followed him but satisfied himself with splashing his face.

'When the tide comes in, it will cover some of our tracks,' he said as he wiped the saltwater from his cooling skin. 'But we'd better fill in most of these holes before we set off.'

Another twenty minutes completed the job. The boatman stowed the spades in the boat and with de Silva's help, pushed it to where the rising water lapped the sand. They climbed onboard and set out for Galle and the harbour. Overhead, seagulls wheeled in the cloudless azure sky. De Silva's mind went back to the dead gull he'd seen on the beach. He hadn't noticed it today, so presumably a predator had taken it, or it had been washed out to sea.

'What are you thinking about?' asked Jane.

'A seagull I saw on the beach when we came to search for Helen. You remember that there was blood on her equipment.'

'Yes.'

'Well, she was badly scratched and bruised when I found her, but she said it was from escaping through the jungle. Her attacker never actually touched her. My guess is he wanted us to think she was killed on the beach.'

'Do you think he would have cut himself and used his own blood?'

'It's possible, and if so, there should be signs of a wound, but if he made use of the dead gull, or even killed it himself, that wouldn't be the case. Still, it might be worth trying to spot any recent wounds on our three suspects.'

* * *

By the time they reached the harbour, the sun was going down. The boatman stood up as the boat drifted in, ready to jump ashore. Before their eyes, the golden light that bathed the waterfront buildings turned to burnt orange.

De Silva licked his dry lips and tasted salt. He'd be glad to get back to the hotel and a proper wash, to say nothing of a cold drink. He paid the boatman the rest of the money he had promised and thanked him.

'And don't forget,' he added. 'You're to say nothing about where we've been. If someone asks, you took us along the coast for a sightseeing trip.'

The boatman grinned. 'Yes, boss.'

'Do you think he'll keep his word?' asked Jane as they returned to the Morris.

'Who knows? I hope he will for long enough to give us a chance to find out who the guilty parties are.'

He thought of Mohen's suspicious end. For the boatman's own sake, he would probably be wise to keep quiet. Careless talk seemed to be dangerous in this town.

* * *

'I've been thinking about Max Larsson,' said Jane as they drove back to the hotel.

'Mm?'

'I've had an idea. The hotel library has quite a few books about the plants and wildlife of Ceylon. It must have been a subject that interested someone who lived in the house before it became a hotel. I suddenly thought of the famous Swedish scientist Linnaeus. I think I've told you about him before.'

De Silva grinned. 'I expect you have, but you know I'm not always the most attentive of pupils.'

Jane shook her head and made a tutting sound. 'He's credited with founding the modern system of classification of plants, animals and minerals. No less a person than the poet Goethe said he was as important to science as Shakespeare was to literature. If Max Larsson is the keen naturalist he claims to be, he ought to know all about his famous compatriot.'

De Silva frowned. 'What are you suggesting?'

'Linnaeus's system was universal, and I believe he travelled widely, but I'm not sure if he visited Ceylon. If there's a book in the library that helps me, I'll try to strike up another conversation with Larsson and bring it around to his hobby. If Linnaeus came to the island, I'll say he didn't and vice versa, then see if Larsson corrects me.' She smiled. 'I'm sure that if he's genuine, he's the sort of serious young man who would.'

De Silva mulled the proposal over. It was one of Jane's more far-fetched strategies. 'It might work.'

'You don't sound very optimistic.'

'If he is hiding something, I don't want to make him suspicious.'

'Don't worry, I'll be very careful and if I think it might be at all awkward, I won't raise the topic.'

He took a hand from the steering wheel and placed it over hers. 'I know you will. I'm sorry to doubt you. It's just that with Edith Pargeter breathing down our necks, I don't want us to make any mistakes.'

The Morris turned into the hotel drive, and they were soon parked.

'Well, no time like the present,' said Jane briskly. 'I'll go to the library and see what I can find. If I have any luck, there may even be an opportunity to talk to Larsson this evening.'

'I'll come with you.'

There was no one in the library, so they were able to search in peace. The lighting in the room was dim but, as well as some armchairs, there was a large table topped with worn, bottle-green leather that had two brass reading lamps on it, one at each end.

It took some time for de Silva and Jane to select the books that might be relevant from the rows of cracked and faded spines on the shelves. When they'd done so, they carried them over to the table and switched on the lamps. Pools of light fell on the green leather.

De Silva opened the book on the top of his pile. The pages were thin and spotted with brown stains. He smelled mildew. An island where the air was usually hot and moist wasn't the best place for preserving old books. Afraid he might do more damage, he turned the pages carefully. The book had been published in the early nineteenth century; no wonder it was fragile. He tilted the curved neck of the brass lamp to throw a better light on it and turned a few more pages, admiring the engravings of flowers and trees that illustrated the text. Unfortunately, there were about five hundred more pages to go, and it was only the first book he had to deal with.

'There should be an index at the back,' said Jane. 'That ought to make the job a bit easier.'

He nodded. 'But I fear this book won't stand much more handling.'

'Neither will most of mine, and I hate to damage books, but it can't be helped.'

For a while, they continued in silence then Jane tapped him on the arm.

'I think I've found what we need. It says here that Linnaeus wrote extensively about Ceylon, but he based his writings on drawings and reports other people had brought back. He never visited the island. In fact he never travelled beyond Europe.'

De Silva closed the book he had been studying. 'So, you have your ammunition,' he said with a smile.

Jane smiled back. 'Now all I need is the opportunity to use it. Hopefully tonight.' She looked at the domed brass clock on the mantelpiece. 'I think it's time we changed for dinner.'

CHAPTER 21

As he opened the door to their room, de Silva noticed that an envelope had been slipped under it. He picked it up and took out the message.

'Who's it from?' asked Jane, closing the door behind her.

'Edith Pargeter, she asks if we'd spare her a few moments. She'll be in her suite.'

'I hope nothing's wrong.'

'There's only one way to find out. If you don't mind, I'd like to go now and change afterwards.'

'Of course.'

De Silva's knock was answered by Edith's voice telling them to come in. Immediately he saw her, he feared something was wrong.

'I hope there's no cause for alarm,' she said when they were all sitting down. 'But there's something I thought I ought to tell you.'

De Silva nodded, his feeling of uneasiness increasing. Although Edith's bearing was as imposing as ever, there was more than a hint of anxiety in her tone of voice.

'This afternoon, I decided to go down and take tea in the garden with the Jenkinsons. They've been so kind, particularly Muriel, that I couldn't resist telling them Helen's safe. I hadn't intended to, but somehow it just slipped out. Of course, I quickly made it clear that I didn't want them to share the news with anyone, not even the police, and I'm sure I can rely on their discretion, but a few people saw us together.'

She paused and de Silva noticed that she was twisting the large diamond ring on the fourth finger of her left hand. The skin around it was reddened. 'I'm afraid I may have looked more cheerful than would be expected in the circumstances.'

'Please tell me who these people were, ma'am,' he prompted gently.

'Jocelyn Reeve and his wife came to offer their condolences. That wretched man said it was nice to see me getting some fresh air. It looked as if it was doing me good. Max Larsson and George Blaine were on their way back from a game of tennis and came to offer condolences too. I pretended Harold had just told an amusing story that had taken my mind off poor Helen for a few moments.' A flush had risen to her cheeks.

'Do you think all of them were convinced?' asked de Silva.

'I hope so,' Edith said in a small voice, 'but I'm not sure.'

* * *

'Well,' said de Silva grimly as he and Jane returned to their room. 'If any damage has been done, there's not much we can do about it now.'

'It was kind of you not to criticise her.'

He shrugged. 'What would be the point? It was clear to me that the poor lady deeply regretted her mistake. I'm sure she rarely, if ever, admits to one. It made her seem positively human.'

'Do you think it will cause a problem?'

'I'm afraid we can't rule that out. If Reeve, Larsson, or Blaine are up to something, they may decide to make their move tonight rather than waiting. We need to be prepared.'

'What are you going to do?'

'I'd like a bit of time to think about that.'

* * *

That evening, the atmosphere in the hotel was still gloomy. De Silva imagined that by now, all the guests would have heard that Helen was presumed dead.

Jane's hopes of striking up a casual conversation with Max Larsson were soon dashed. When she and de Silva came in for dinner, he was sitting with George Blaine, and they were already eating their first course.

'What a nuisance,' she murmured in an undertone when they'd sat down at their table. 'I was hoping he might be on his own and we could have invited him to sit with us.'

'Better luck tomorrow, perhaps,' said de Silva, picking up the menu in front of him. 'Ah, mulligatawny soup. I think I'll have that.'

'Shanti, how can you be so calm? Especially when tomorrow may be too late.'

'On the contrary, my mind is like a whirlpool,' he said glumly. 'But an empty stomach won't help.'

The soup came: a creamy concoction of chicken, vegetables, and apples, spiced with chillis, tamarind, and fenugreek. As he ate, de Silva's spirits revived a little, but the effect didn't last. He wished Edith Pargeter had managed to keep her mouth shut. And could he be sure that the Jenkinsons would keep their word? They must think it odd that Edith hadn't wanted them even to talk to the police.

There was a stir over by the entrance door and he saw Jocelyn Reeve and his wife come in. Perhaps in deference to the subdued atmosphere, she was more plainly dressed than she had been on previous evenings, wearing only a simple gold necklace by way of jewellery. De Silva wondered what the pair were thinking. If Reeve was guilty, was Pamela implicated or was she, like Helen Morris, just an innocent bystander?

'You're staring, Shanti,' whispered Jane. 'They might notice.'

Quickly, he turned his attention back to his meal. By this time, a plate of grilled sole with English-style vegetables – in other words, plain, rather too enthusiastically boiled ones – but he had decided on a light meal. If something was going to happen tonight, he wanted to be ready.

* * *

As usual, coffee was served after dinner in the main lounge. Neither of the Reeves, George Blaine, nor Max Larsson appeared. It wasn't unusual in the case of the Reeves or Larsson but out of the ordinary for George Blaine who normally spent time chatting to other guests.

Jane finished her coffee and put down her cup. 'It's been a long day. I'm happy to go to our room and read if you are.'

De Silva nodded and stood up. His muscles reminded him that he had done a considerable amount of digging that afternoon.

In the lobby, they saw George Blaine coming through the main entrance from the direction of the drive.

'Been out for a stroll before I turn in,' he said when he came over to speak to them. 'There's not much light down here to spoil the view. The stars are a fine sight.'

They chatted for a few moments, but Blaine's smiles seemed forced, and de Silva sensed that underneath there was tension. Eventually, he left them saying he was off to the bar for a nightcap.

'There's something I want to do too before I come

upstairs,' de Silva said quietly to Jane. 'Don't ask me what it is right now. I'll explain when I join you.'

Later as he walked down the corridor leading to their room, he saw a faint band of light under the door of the one before it where Max Larsson was staying. Presumably, he had already retired for the night.

'Well, what was that all about?' asked Jane when they were in their own room with the door closed.

'In case our villain tries to leave the hotel tonight, I wanted to make sure I know which doors guests can get out by unnoticed and see if they're locked or just bolted from the inside. I think I managed to find them all without anyone wondering what I was up to.'

'What about using the main entrance?'

'Unlikely. There's a night porter who would see them.'

'George Blaine wasn't his usual cheerful self this evening.'

'I thought so too. I'm wondering if he was telling the truth about only being out for an evening stroll.'

Jane sighed. 'The more I think about it, the more my instincts tell me he's not our villain. The simple explanation is probably that the poor man is missing Helen and was trying to clear his head. It's such a shame he has to be kept out of the secret. I'd like to think that when it can be revealed that she's safe, the two of them will have the chance to get to know each other better.'

De Silva didn't argue with her, but he wasn't so sure. He wasn't ready to cross George Blaine off his list of suspects yet.

* * *

He had only just got ready for bed and Jane was still putting night cream on her face when they heard footsteps in the corridor. They grew louder as they passed the de Silvas' door then stopped. There was a rattle of keys and the sound

161

of the door to the room beyond theirs opening and closing.

'It sounds like Blaine's come to bed,' said de Silva. 'The nightcap didn't take long.'

He climbed into bed and reached over to the bedside table for his book. He hoped the digging at the beach wouldn't result in his sleeping too deeply.

* * *

The hands on the bedside clock showed that it was almost two in the morning when muffled noises from Larsson's room roused de Silva from a fitful sleep. He got up and reached for the clothes he'd left on a chair. Jane turned over and propped herself up on one elbow.

'What's happening?' she whispered.

He put a finger to his lips. 'Larsson,' he mouthed.

They heard a low cough then the sound of the Swede's door opening and closing. A moment later, there was the soft swish of the green baize door leading from the corridor to the landing outside.

'The nearest way out of the hotel from here is the door to the garden from that small lounge immediately below us,' said de Silva quietly. 'You can reach it without needing to use the main staircase and it's only bolted from the inside.' He pointed to the window. 'Will you keep watch while I get dressed?'

Quickly, he took off his pyjamas and started to pull on his clothes. Jane grabbed a skirt and blouse then hurried to the window and twitched the curtain aside a fraction. 'If you're going to follow him, I'm coming with you,' she said as she started to dress too.

Halfway through lacing up one shoe, de Silva glanced at her with a frown. She shook her head. 'It's no use arguing,' she whispered.

He sighed and started on the other shoe then froze. There were more footsteps in the corridor and again the swish of the green baize door opening and closing.

'Someone's out in the garden,' said Jane in a low voice. Briefly, the man turned and looked behind him and she caught a glimpse of his face. 'It's Larsson. He's heading in the direction of the steps down to the beach.'

'I heard someone else pass our room. It might be George Blaine. I'm going after them.'

Hastily, Jane found her shoes and slipped them on. They crept along the corridor and through the green baize door, waiting at the top of the stairs to make sure they weren't in sight of whoever was in front of them. At the bottom, they took the passage to the small lounge, looking in carefully before entering. If Blaine or someone else was following Larsson, they didn't want to alert them to their presence.

There was no one in the lounge and the door was shut, but the brass bolts at the top and bottom weren't pulled across. As quietly as possible, de Silva opened the door and peered out into the darkness. Even if he'd had a torch with him, he wouldn't have risked turning it on. They would have to hope that the light of the moon and the stars was adequate to see by. A sweet smell reached his nostrils from the jasmine that scrambled over the small porch outside the door. Cautiously, he stepped onto the terrace. The garden was full of shapes and shadows but none of them resembled a man.

Jane looked over his shoulder. 'I can't see anyone.'

'Nor can I. If Blaine or someone else is following Larsson, they must be close behind him.'

The lawn was already damp with dew. They kept to its edge, staying in the shadow of the trees bordering it until they reached the steps that led to the beach. Larsson was alone on the sands. He walked fast and had soon reached the rocky outcrop dividing the hotel beach from the adjacent one. There, he began to scramble across the rocks and was soon lost from sight. Was he after the bag and canister that Helen Morris had seen? If he was her attacker, he would have known she'd seen him burying them the first time, so had he taken the precaution of moving them to a completely different spot when he gave up chasing her?

De Silva and Jane reached the outcrop. At close quarters, the rocks looked far more treacherous than they had at a distance, wet and slimy, bristling with sharp edges, and riddled with narrow fissures where one could twist an ankle or trap a foot. He wished they could have walked on the sands, but that way was deep in water. The tide must have turned. 'Let's take this slowly,' he muttered. 'We can't afford any accidents.'

They set off, trying to keep low so as not to be visible from the other beach. Ropes and mats of seaweed gave off a greenish glow in the pale light, and shellfish and other sea creatures left stranded by a bygone tide floated in shallow rockpools. There was a powerful smell of salt and decay. Ahead of them, a beam of light flashed three times from out in the dark waters of the ocean. Moments later, three flashes from the direction of the adjacent beach answered.

'Larsson must be exchanging signals with a boat out there,' said Jane.

Intermittently, the flashes continued, the ones from the sea growing brighter all the time. De Silva slithered off the last of the hazardous jumble of rocks and held out a hand to Jane to help her down. He was glad to feel sand under his feet again. Both of them a little out of breath, they hung back in the shadow of a tall rock that jutted from the sand like some ancient megalith.

There was no sign of Larsson, but the red boat was still on the beach. Only now it was upright and had been moved down to the water's edge. De Silva presumed that the boat coming for Larsson was too large to land at the beach and he planned to use the red boat to go out to meet it. As long as he didn't have to go far, he might make it.

The sound of a low cough nearby made de Silva jump, and Jane clutched his arm. A figure stepped out of the shadows.

'Good evening, Inspector.'

Larsson's torch beam swung into de Silva's eyes, dazzling him. The Swede had a rucksack slung over one shoulder and a gun in his other hand. De Silva pushed Jane behind him, wishing his own gun was not back in Nuala.

'It's a great pity you chose to interfere,' Larsson said. 'But then I suppose it is an occupational hazard. I have no grudge against you. I would far rather let you and your wife go unharmed. Unfortunately, that choice is no longer open to me.'

Larsson paused and glanced out to sea. Again, the light flashed. Larsson responded, switching his torch on and off three times.

'My friends will be here soon. I'm afraid that when they find you, I can't answer for what they'll decide to do with you. Perhaps they'll be content to tie you up and leave you here.' Larsson shrugged. 'Or maybe they will have other plans. Forgive me if I don't try to plead your case.'

Despite his fears for Jane, de Silva took a step towards him. Larsson cocked the trigger of his gun and shook his head. 'I advise you not to test my goodwill, Inspector.' His eyes narrowed. 'On second thoughts, I think it will be best if you come with me to meet my friends.' He beckoned to Jane. 'Please come to the boat, Mrs de Silva.'

De Silva took a step back. 'Let my wife go, Larsson. Whatever it is you're up to, let me take her place.'

'And have her run for help? I'm not a fool, Inspector. Please, Mrs de Silva. I would dislike having to shoot you both.'

'Alright,' Jane said and started to walk towards the boat.

As she passed close to Larsson, he reached out and grabbed her by the wrist, swinging the torch beam into Shanti's eyes. 'Stay right where you are, Inspector. Try anything and I will shoot your dear wife.'

At the boat, still keeping hold of his gun, Larsson produced a short length of rope. 'Your hands behind your back, if you please, Mrs de Silva.'

'What if I refuse?'

'Then I'll shoot you right now.'

Glowering, Jane submitted.

Larsson put his gun down just out of her reach on one of the boat's slatted seats. With practised deftness, he bound her wrists together. De Silva's eyes measured the distance from where he stood to the boat. It was too much of a risk to try to get to the gun before Larsson was able to retrieve it and shoot.

Larsson picked up the gun again. 'Into the boat, please.'

Hampered by having her hands tied behind her back, Jane stumbled in and fell heavily against the nearest seat, letting out a cry that made Shanti's blood boil.

'We must launch the boat now,' Larsson said as he beckoned Shanti over, 'drag the boat into the water.'

De Silva's stomach churned. The boat was barely seaworthy. They would probably make it out to meet Larsson's accomplices but what then? Suppose he and Jane were cast adrift and the boat sank before they had the chance to get back to shore? He wasn't a strong enough swimmer to help her, and it was dark.

A hollow feeling overcame him as he went to the prow of the boat, the cold water seeping into his shoes. Jane had managed to right herself on the seat. He could sense her moods well enough to know that she was afraid, but her expression was defiant. She glared at Larsson. 'You won't get away with this.'

He laughed. 'I beg to differ.'

'Please, I implore you to see sense and let us go.'

'Shut up!' Larsson pointed his torch at the sea, flicking it on and off.

De Silva looked down into the boat and noticed that water was already pooling around Jane's feet. There was an oar on either side of the seat she was on, and in the bottom of the boat, a ferocious-looking spiked metal pole of the kind used to harpoon large fish. It would easily be sharp enough to drive through the rotting hull and speed up the boat's descent to the bottom of the ocean.

'Get a move on, Inspector,' Larsson said.

As he started to manhandle the boat towards the waterline, his mind raced and a plan took shape. 'When I shout "down",' he muttered to Jane, 'get as far down as you can in the bottom of the boat.'

'What was that?' snapped Larsson.

'I said my back is painful. You'll have to help me.'

In the torchlight, he saw suspicion written all over the Swede's face, but he came and added his weight to the task. Soon, the boat was floating in a couple of feet of water. Larsson stood back and at that moment, de Silva lunged for the oar nearest him, brought it up to shoulder height and swung it wildly, catching Larsson across the chest. Larsson stumbled back but quickly recovered. Taller than de Silva, he seized the oar and slammed it against de Silva's throat, forcing him back against the boat.

Fireworks exploded in front of de Silva's eyes. His breath coming in ragged gasps, he mustered all his strength and threw Larsson off. Larsson lost his balance and fell, grabbing de Silva as he did so and dragging him down. Sand and saltwater filled de Silva's mouth and nose as Larsson rolled on top of him, pushing his head under the water. His lungs bursting, he tried to fight his way up for air, but his strength was failing fast. Larsson was younger and stronger than he was. He held his breath, images of Jane flashing through his mind. *Jane in the garden. Jane playing with Billy and Bella. Jane laughing in the Morris, the wind blowing her hair…*

De Silva's lungs burned. His strength waned until he could hold on no more and his mouth opened to accept the inevitable.

But Larsson suddenly let go and fell to one side, splashing into the water as de Silva pushed himself up, gasping for air.

He staggered to his feet, spewing out water and shaking it from his eyes. Jane stood a few feet away, clutching the other oar. 'Oh, Shanti,' she said shakily. 'What if I've killed him?'

His heartbeat steadying, de Silva limped over to where Larsson's gun had fallen on the sand and picked it up then went back to Jane and put his arms around her. 'I expect he has a thick skull,' he said comfortingly. 'The question is, what do we do now?'

'I can answer that,' said a suave voice. De Silva swung around. As his eyes alighted on Jocelyn Reeve and George Blaine, his heartbeat started to race once more.

CHAPTER 22

'I believe it's time we introduced ourselves properly,' said Reeve. 'Lieutenant Commander Reeve, Royal Navy Intelligence, at your service. Blaine here has been working with me.'

He paused and looked out to sea. De Silva realised that he hadn't noticed any flashes of light for some time, although he had been rather distracted.

'It seems that Herr Larsson's friends have decided not to join the party. Just as well, as we've had very little time to prepare a suitable reception for them.'

Larsson moaned and struggled up to a sitting position then put his head in his hands. 'Keep an eye on him, will you, Blaine,' said Reeve.

'With pleasure.'

George Blaine pulled out a gun and went over to where Larsson sat. He prodded him with his foot. 'Up!' he said roughly.

Larsson scowled but after a few moments and another prod that was somewhat more forceful than the first one, he stumbled to his feet.

'Bring him along,' said Reeve. 'I suggest we continue our conversation in more comfortable surroundings.'

* * *

The Reeves' guest bungalow had an elegant lounge with tall windows and cream walls decorated with embroidered hangings. Several doors, de Silva assumed to bedrooms and bathrooms, led off it. He was even more painfully aware of his bedraggled state than he would have been in humbler surroundings.

Reeve's wife had stood up when they entered. He gestured to the windows. 'Close the curtains, would you, Hendry?'

He must have noticed the surprised look on de Silva's and Jane's faces, for he smiled. 'May I introduce Second Officer Pamela Hendry, Women's Royal Navy. I'm sure you'll agree she's done an excellent job of deflecting suspicion by posing as my wife.'

Pamela Hendry smiled. 'Thank you, sir.'

Briefly, de Silva wondered how far the pose had gone, then reprimanded himself. It was really none of his business.

'I expect you and your husband would like the chance to tidy up, Mrs de Silva,' Reeve went on, as casually as if they had just arrived for a house party, rather than having escaped a brush with death. 'Find them whatever they need, Hendry. I think Mrs de Silva's arm needs some attention too.'

De Silva looked at Jane's arm and saw that blood oozed from a raw patch on one of her wrists.

'It's nothing much,' she said. 'I caught myself on the spike that was in the boat. I had to use it to cut through the rope that Larsson had tied my hands with. I managed to get most of the way then I pulled them free.'

'Nevertheless, we don't want an infection setting in,' said Reeve. 'Hendry can help you to dress it while Blaine and I find somewhere for Larsson until we decide what to do with him in the longer term.'

De Silva glanced at Larsson. George Blaine had gagged him and tied his arms behind his back before they left the beach. He doubted the Swede would be given such hospitable treatment as he and Jane were being offered.

Pamela Hendry went to one of the doors and opened it. 'Please follow me,' she said.

Twenty minutes later, washed and tidied as far as possible and with Jane's injured wrist bandaged, they returned to the lounge. There was no sign of Larsson.

'I'd say drinks all round are called for,' said Reeve. 'I think we can regard ourselves as off duty.'

'Whisky, sir?' asked Hendry.

Reeve nodded. 'And don't drown it. What about you, Mrs de Silva? I hope we can find something you like.'

Jane accepted a small sherry and de Silva a whisky. He couldn't deny that after all the excitement, it hit the spot.

'I'm sure you appreciate that nothing of what you've seen tonight, or that I'm about to tell you, is to be spoken of outside this room,' said Reeve when they had made themselves comfortable. 'I must ask you both to swear to that. Lives may depend upon it.'

De Silva and Jane assured him of their discretion.

'Good. First of all, I'm interested to know what you were doing at the beach.'

A jolt went through de Silva. Was Reeve being charming in the hope they would drop their guard? Was it possible that he suspected them of having something to do with Larsson's activities?

As if he had read de Silva's mind, Reeve smiled. 'There's no need to be alarmed. If I didn't think you were in the clear, you wouldn't be here in the first place.'

He drank some of his whisky. 'That's why I'm prepared to explain a little about what's going on, but first I'd like you to tell me what you already know.'

As de Silva explained about finding Helen Morris and how he suspected Lawrence of arresting the boatman as a scapegoat for her supposed murder, Reeve listened attentively, his whisky glass cradled in his hand.

'Thank you,' he said when de Silva had finished. 'Splendid news that Miss Morris is alive and well, but I have to admit that earlier tonight we were far less sure than she was that you were to be trusted. When Blaine left his room to follow Larsson, he was pretty sure there was someone behind him. Once he was out in the garden, he concealed himself and waited to find out if he was right. He saw you and Mrs de Silva follow Larsson in the direction of the steps leading to the beach, then came to fetch me. That took a few minutes. When we caught up with you at the beach, you were all at the boat, and the darkness made it hard to see exactly what was going on. We had to consider the possibility that the three of you were accomplices. It was only when the fight started – and I commend you for your resourcefulness, Mrs de Silva – that we became confident you were on the right side.' He paused to drink more of his whisky. 'Now, do you have anything else to tell me about Lawrence?'

'I had my doubts about him early on in our stay here after one of the nightwatchmen, a man named Jai, was found dead in the grounds.'

Reeve nodded. 'I remember.'

'On our first evening here, the night before Jai's body was found, I was taking a stroll in the grounds after dinner. I met a nightwatchman patrolling the area around the guest bungalow where Madame Elodie Renaud and her party were staying. The following day, as I'm sure you're aware, they were all taken seriously ill and had to postpone a dive they had planned out at the reef.'

'Go on.'

'Lawrence came up to the hotel to see the manager, but I was concerned that his investigation of the case would be perfunctory.' He nodded to George Blaine. 'I recall that you thought the same.'

'So, you decided to become involved,' said Reeve. He frowned but de Silva didn't let himself waver. 'I felt it was important to get at the truth.'

'Very laudable.'

'Later, I learnt from Mr Blaine that the waiter taking after-dinner drinks to the Renaud party had met a night-watchman on his way to the guest bungalow. The night-watchman told him there had been rumours of a leopard on the prowl and offered to deliver the drinks trolley the rest of the way. An offer which the waiter later told me he gratefully accepted.

'From the timing of when I passed the bungalow on my return from my walk, I estimated that the nightwatchman would have delivered the drinks fairly recently. However, when I first saw him, he had his torch turned off and claimed it was because he didn't want to disturb the guests. I thought it was strange when he had very likely been to the bungalow not long before I saw him, but I might have been wrong about the timing. To satisfy my curiosity. I tracked down the waiter, who goes by the name of Carolus, and asked him what time he and the nightwatchman had met. It was from him I learned that the nightwatchman he'd met wasn't Jai, although Jai was normally the person on duty in that area. The waiter had never seen the new man before and hadn't seen him since. Jane and I considered the possibility that there might be a connection between the unidentified man and the sudden illness of Elodie Renaud and her party that brought about the cancellation of their dive, but we agreed that any further investigation ought to be left up to Chief Inspector Lawrence.'

De Silva decided not to mention his conversation with Henry Bruyn. Reeve might already be of the opinion that he had exceeded what little authority he had. It was unwise to risk making matters worse.

'When I gave him the information, Lawrence was polite, but I had the feeling he didn't plan to review his initial finding that Jai was killed by a wild animal.'

Reeve nodded. 'The thought also occurred to us that

the Renaud party's sudden illness was too convenient to be mere coincidence. We were pretty certain that for reasons that weren't yet clear, someone wanted to make sure the dive didn't take place. Thank you for the information about Lawrence. It will be very useful. To be honest, it had crossed our minds that he might be a wrong 'un. Unwittingly, you helped us there. It was at my instigation that Blaine suggested you report to him what you'd found out. We wanted to see how he reacted. As we had anticipated, he took no action.'

That explained why Blaine had appeared to lose interest so quickly, thought de Silva.

'There was also a murder at a bar near the harbour,' he said. 'The victim was a fisherman called Mohen who had hired out his boat to a man I'm now sure was Max Larsson. Coming so soon after Jane and I had questioned Mohen about the man who'd hired his boat, I felt that the timing of his death might not be coincidental. Lawrence seemed keen to pigeonhole it as the result of a feud between neighbours. Once again, I thought he was overly quick to do so.'

'I see your husband likes to be very thorough,' said Reeve, smiling at Jane.

Jane smiled in return. 'Yes, he does.'

Reeve leant back in his chair. 'Now, my turn to fill you in a little more. For some time, British intelligence has been aware that there are agents working for the Nazis in this part of the world. We believe their primary objective is to disrupt British interests by supporting the violent faction of the nationalist movement. To the best of our knowledge, the movement isn't anywhere near as active in Ceylon as it is in India. Although there may be some pro-German feeling on the island, there's little evidence of strong opposition to the British. That, however, probably makes it an attractive location to target. If in the past it hasn't been watched too closely, it might make it easier for an agent to pass unnoticed.

'The other attraction is Ceylon's wealth of precious stones. In particular, the island's renowned sapphires. The mines at Ratnapura are, as I expect you're aware, an important source. At first, when small numbers of inferior stones started to disappear from there, petty pilfering was suspected. But when the thefts became more significant and in some cases, sapphires with no legitimate provenance were reported to be coming onto the overseas markets, we began to suspect there was more to it than that. Surveillance was organised and eventually the list of suspects was narrowed down, one of them being Larsson. We discovered he was taking a holiday in Galle, and it wasn't the first time. In view of the fact it's a coastal city that he might be using to get sapphires off the island, Blaine and I were given the job of following him to find out whether there was more to the visit than an innocent holiday.'

'Forgive me for interrupting,' said Jane. 'But isn't Larsson Swedish? Since Sweden's a neutral country, why would he want to help the Nazis?'

'You make a good point, Mrs de Silva. His father was Swedish, but his mother was German. Unfortunately, his loyalties appear to have erred in his mother's direction.'

'I see. Thank you.'

'We watched Larsson's movements and saw that over the course of several days, he set out each morning by boat and didn't return until late in the afternoon. Thanks to you, we now know that the boat was hired from the unfortunate Mohen. Overnight, Larsson moored it in a quiet area away from the main harbour. As far as I was able to tell, in the daytime he always went out to the reef. One possibility was that he was meeting a boat in that area and handing over precious stones. Alternatively, he was bringing something back with him, although that seemed less likely.'

Reeve drained his whisky. 'Another one, gentlemen? What about you, Mrs de Silva?'

De Silva and Blaine accepted but Jane shook her head.

'Perhaps some tea?' asked Reeve. 'I'm sure Hendry can rustle some up.'

'Thank you, that would be lovely.'

'It was no accident that Blaine's room is close to Larsson's,' Reeve continued. 'Blaine stayed back at the hotel most days and as soon as he was able to obtain a duplicate key, took the opportunity to search it.'

De Silva wondered how Blaine had managed to get hold of the duplicate. He doubted Reeve would enlighten them.

'Days went past, and we began to fear we were barking up the wrong tree. If Larsson was collecting something, he certainly wasn't storing it in his room. Equally, if he was delivering goods, he kept them elsewhere until he was due to meet his accomplices. Then an idea occurred to us. Might Larsson be using the reef as a place to hide his spoils? I contacted base and asked for naval divers to be made available. The day that Larsson was involved in the search for Miss Morris gave them the opportunity to investigate the area without being disturbed. When they dived at the reef, they found the wreck of a small boat. On board were two men who appeared to be only recently dead. There was no sign of fishing gear, or indeed anything to identify them.'

There was a pause while Pamela Hendry brought Jane's tea. As she served it, de Silva watched the gauzy white curtains hanging at the open windows billow gently in the breeze. He was grateful for it. He felt cooler and calmer than he had done earlier in the evening, but he was apprehensive about how the night would end. With everything he and Jane knew, he hoped Reeve really was happy to trust in their discretion.

'Blaine carried out another search of Larsson's room – more of a challenge as by now Larsson wasn't leaving the hotel – however he still found nothing. Nevertheless, we were convinced that Larsson had a connection with the men on the wrecked boat. Possibly, he'd wanted to find something they were carrying. In case he came back, I gave the order that their bodies were to be left where they were. In any case, if they were involved with him, they'd forfeited any claim to respect.'

The expression on Reeve's face was grim. De Silva's qualms about how the night would end went up a notch.

'We didn't want to arrest Larsson at that stage,' Reeve went on. 'Catching him red-handed was our priority. We agreed that the best way forward was to wait for him to make the first move. Naturally, it would have looked extremely suspicious if I'd tried to strike up an acquaintance with him, so I gave Blaine the job of keeping an eye on him. Last night his efforts went unrewarded, but of course tonight has been a different matter.'

Reeve looked at his watch. 'I expect you and your husband would like to get some sleep, Mrs de Silva,' he said briskly. He gave de Silva a searching look. 'Once again, I stress that everything that's occurred tonight must be kept under wraps.'

'You have our word on that, sir.'

There was a moment of silence; icy fingers crept up de Silva's spine.

'Good,' resumed Reeve in a brisk tone. 'When the time's right to bring in Helen Morris, your help may be needed, but otherwise, you're to leave everything to us.'

He turned to George Blaine. 'Escort our guests back to the hotel, will you? Make sure they get safely to their rooms then come back here.'

* * *

'Gracious, what a night it's been,' said Jane when they were safely back in their room. 'Poor George Blaine, he must be very tired after having to watch Max Larsson day and night. I hope Jocelyn Reeve lets him get some sleep now.' She smiled. 'But on the other hand, did you notice how happy he looked when he heard that Helen is alive?'

'Hmm. I can't say I did, but I wasn't really watching. I was too busy wondering what Reeve was going to do.'

'How do you mean?'

'I was worried he might think we knew too much. The way he looked at me, I felt as if a duck walked over my grave.'

Jane laughed. 'It's a goose, and you're letting your imagination run away with you. He was charming.'

'Oh, I agree with you there, but he has a job to do, and I expect that includes taking a strong line with anyone who gets in the way.'

'Well, we're safely back, aren't we? Not locked up in some dark dungeon.'

He grinned. 'I suspect that has quite a lot to do with my having a charming English wife who knocks out Nazi spies then drinks tea at four in the morning, behaving as if it's the most natural thing in the world.'

Jane shook her head. 'What nonsense you talk.'

But later, as de Silva drifted off to sleep, he reflected that he hadn't entirely been joking.

CHAPTER 23

For the next two days, de Silva and Jane spent their time relaxing at the hotel or taking drives into the countryside round about. True to their word, they said nothing about the real reason why Jocelyn Reeve and George Blaine had come to Galle.

'Try to relax, dear,' said Jane as she got ready for dinner on the second evening. She finished tidying her hair and put down the brush. 'I'm sure the two of them have everything under control.'

'I'm sorry, old habits die hard.'

'I'm as curious as you are to know exactly what's happening, but we have to accept that it's out of our hands.'

He sighed. She was right, but it was hard to throw off the restless feeling that dogged him. The only bit of information he'd managed to glean from a passing conversation with George Blaine was that a British officer from the Colombo force had been brought in to take Lawrence's place.

On the morning of the third day, however, his mood improved when Blaine approached him again, suggesting a stroll in the garden during which he told him he could collect Helen Morris from the village in the jungle.

'The official story is to be that she was frightened by a wild animal and took refuge there then lost her way in the dark,' said Blaine. 'And she's only just managed to send a message to the hotel. The new man from Colombo's spoken

179

to her aunt to ensure that this time she doesn't rock the boat. He's not told her about Reeve's and my involvement. She does, however, know that Larsson and Lawrence have been arrested, although she thinks it's on a charge of corruption rather than treason. You may tell Helen that too, but make sure she understands it's not for general publication.'

De Silva wondered how readily the story that Helen had been frightened by an animal and got lost would be believed by the other hotel guests. With luck, most of them wouldn't possess too enquiring a turn of mind. On the other hand, Harold Jenkinson and his wife might not swallow it so easily.

They had reached the summerhouse where de Silva had first spoken to Helen. Blaine sat down on the steps up to the small verandah and squinted into the sun. 'Reeve has agreed to my telling you more about what's been happening,' he said. 'After all, as I pointed out to him, we might never have tracked Helen down without your intervention. Larsson was convinced she'd come to grief and for a while, so were we.'

'It's good of you to say so.'

Blaine grinned. 'My pleasure. Larsson has confessed he's been working for the Nazis. As we suspected, he was planted at the mines in Ratnapura with orders to steal sapphires and bring them down to Galle to hand over to their couriers. The money raised was to be used to help fund the Indian nationalists' campaign against the British. As it turns out, it was even more fortuitous that we caught him this time because he'd brought something far more important with him. That metal cylinder Helen described to you contained plans of the mines at Ratnapura and details of the key people in charge there. I hardly need tell you how valuable they would be to the Nazis if they tried to occupy Ceylon.'

Jane came to join them, and Blaine repeated the story for her benefit.

'The men on the wrecked boat had come to collect the jewels and plans from Larsson several nights previously,' he continued. 'They'd set off from a larger boat waiting out at sea. They were probably unfamiliar with the reef, and they ran aground on the return journey after their rendezvous with Larsson. It won't have helped that the weather was stormy around that time. Maybe neither of them could swim, or they panicked in the darkness. Whatever the case, they didn't make it back to the main boat. Its captain radioed Larsson to tell him. After that, he went out repeatedly to dive at the reef in the hope of recovering the sapphires and documents that had gone down with the boat. He'd found them, and was burying them at the beach ready to hand over to another boat that he'd been informed was on its way, when Helen saw him.'

'So he was lying when he told her he was nervous of water,' said Jane.

'Most certainly. He claims Lawrence masterminded the plan to poison Elodie Renaud and her party to make sure they gave up their dive at the reef so there was no chance of them finding the boat before it had been stripped of the incriminating evidence. Unsurprisingly, Lawrence claims the plan was down to Larsson. Oh, and we still need to find the nightwatchman you saw. From your evidence, it seems a fair assumption he was working for one or both of them and responsible for actually killing Jai. Larsson and Lawrence both swear that if he did, he exceeded their orders but that doesn't wash. They'd hardly want Jai left alive to be questioned about what happened to him that night.'

'What about the murdered boatman, Mohen?'

Blaine shrugged. 'Lawrence is sticking to the story of a feud with a neighbour, but we'll get to the truth in the end. We suspect he wanted to make sure that Mohen was silenced. The man who killed Jai might have done the job, or maybe Lawrence had more than one villain in his pay. That's something we still have to find out.'

'And has the boatman who took Helen to the beach been freed?'

Blaine nodded. 'Lawrence confessed to buying the necklace in the bazaar and planting it in his boat along with the money.' He paused. 'Tell me, I'm interested to know when you reached the conclusion that Larsson was the man who attacked Helen. From what you told Reeve and me, she didn't see his face clearly and so wasn't able to give you a description, apart from the fact that the man was tall and dark.'

'He behaved strangely at times,' de Silva said. 'Harold Jenkinson mentioned he'd tried to talk to him on subjects which should have been of interest, but he hadn't been able to draw him out.'

The explanation sounded rather lame, thought de Silva. He felt uncomfortable admitting that it had only been on the night at the beach that they'd been sure Larsson was the man.

'I imagine that means you considered other suspects.' Blaine gave a wry smile. 'Me, for example? I could have fitted Helen's description.'

'We didn't consider you for long,' said Jane.

Blaine laughed. 'I suppose I should take that as a compliment. What about Reeve? Don't worry, this won't go any further.'

'I must admit, for a while we were convinced that he was our man,' de Silva said. 'For one thing, I saw him swimming early one morning. He was obviously very proficient, and the man Helen encountered had come in from the sea and looked as if he'd been diving out there, or at least swimming a fair distance.'

'Hmm. Interestingly enough, from the information we've been able to find about Larsson's history, he was a champion swimmer in his youth. Anything else?'

'I'm afraid Edith Pargeter doesn't have a very good

opinion of Lieutenant Commander Reeve,' said Jane. 'Because he seems to be wealthy and apparently hasn't joined up, she suspects he's involved with the black market. There was an occasion when Shanti and I saw him arguing with a member of staff outside the hotel, and we wondered if there was something in that. Perhaps the man was trying to get money out of him in return for keeping quiet about something.'

'Certainly, it was Helen's opinion that the man she saw on the beach was Reeve,' de Silva went on. 'She thought she'd surprised him in some kind of illicit activity, and he was prepared to kill her to silence her.'

Blaine grinned. 'I think I won't pass all that on, but I believe I can throw light on the business with the staff member. Reeve's car had a puncture the previous day. One of the staff took it to the local garage for repair and was late bringing it back. Reeve was waiting to get off to rendezvous with the naval divers and hear if they'd found anything at the reef and it held him up. He told me the fellow still had the nerve to ask for a tip. He was annoyed and only gave him one to get rid of him.'

He reached out to the nearby verandah post where there was some damaged wood and started to pick at a loose piece. 'By the way, I'm leaving Galle in a couple of hours. Larsson and Lawrence are being moved to Colombo and Reeve's sending me along to keep an eye on them. I'd be grateful if you'd say goodbye to Helen for me.'

'Are you sure you wouldn't prefer to do it yourself?' asked Jane.

A melancholy expression came over Blaine's face. He gave the piece of wood a sharp tug and it broke off. 'Best not. Troubled times, you know, and too much baggage. This isn't the first time my services have been required and I doubt it will be the last. Tell her… tell her I'm sorry.'

He stood up. 'I must be on my way. Packing to be done.

It's been a pleasure to make your acquaintance, Mrs de Silva. And yours, Inspector.'

'Oh dear,' murmured Jane as he walked off. 'How sad he looked. I think Helen Morris will be sorry too. But I fear they won't be the only couple divided by this dreadful war.'

CHAPTER 24

Soon after saying goodbye to George Blaine, de Silva set out to collect Helen. The journey seemed shorter than it had the first time. Often the way, he reflected, when you knew where you were going, or at least he hoped he did. He found the place where he had parked the Morris the first time and set off on foot. As he went deeper into the jungle, he had moments of uncertainty. It was a relief when he heard the sound of voices ahead.

His approach must already have been noticed, for soon a gaggle of children ran towards him. He handed out the sweets he'd stopped to buy from a roadside stall. The children crammed them into their mouths as they led him the rest of the way into the village. In the daylight, the huts looked less ramshackle than they had by night. He realised that the village was more prosperous than he'd thought. Tethered goats bleated, some of them with kids that suckled from the teats of their swollen udders. On a patch of ground that hadn't been built on, a wattle fence corralled four fat pigs that were rootling through a pile of fruit and vegetable peelings. Beyond that, women were working in a vegetable patch where tomatoes, peppers, and long green beans were growing.

The headman came out to greet him and they went to find Helen. They stopped at a hut that was larger than most of the others. Outside it, a woman was milling rice in a mortar with a long pestle whilst her companion was busy pounding something else with a smaller one. The spicy aromas of cardamom, coriander, pepper, and turmeric wafted to de Silva's nose. Another woman sat on a low wooden stool chopping jackfruit into small pieces and removing the seeds. Her neighbour was scraping coconut from a shell with a curved knife, releasing the sweet milky scent.

The headman led him into the hut. Its walls were blackened with smoke, and the air hummed with the chatter of women and the clattering of pots and pans. In one corner, an iron stove glowed red. A woman was cooking roti on the flat metal plate that lay on top of it. Helen was standing by the woman's side, watching. De Silva was relieved to see that she was smiling. The woman pointed in his direction, and Helen looked around and saw him.

'Inspector de Silva!'

'I'm sorry I couldn't come sooner.'

'There's no need to apologise. I'm sure you had your reasons, and everyone here has been so kind. I've been well looked after.'

'Shall we go outside?'

He turned to the headman. 'I need to talk to the lady in private.'

The headman nodded and led them to another hut that, from its size and quality, de Silva assumed was his own. They sat in the shade of the palm-thatched roof that overhung the front wall, creating a small loggia. De Silva watched Helen's expression as he explained the official storyline she was being asked to follow. By the time he'd finished, she was frowning.

'So, I'm not to tell anyone about the man who tried to attack me?'

'That's right. The police know it was Max Larsson.' At least he didn't have to lie to her about that, he thought. 'But they want to keep Chief Inspector Lawrence's part in the affair quiet.'

'How much does Aunt Edith know?'

'She's been told everything that you have.'

'Good, it would be hard if she and I couldn't speak freely.'

A woman came out from the hut carrying shells filled with coconut water. De Silva sipped the refreshing drink appreciatively.

'I wondered if George Blaine would come with you to fetch me,' said Helen.

De Silva felt a twinge of awkwardness. 'I'm afraid he had to leave Galle unexpectedly.'

'Does he know I've been found?'

'He does,' said de Silva, feeling even more awkward. 'He asked me to say goodbye to you and to tell you he was sorry not to do so himself.'

Helen was silent for a moment then she smiled with what was, de Silva was sure, forced brightness. 'Then I'll have to find myself a new tennis partner, won't I?'

She put her barely touched drink on the ground. 'I'd like to thank the villagers now,' she said. 'Then I'd like to go home.'

CHAPTER 25

Two days later

Tea tables shaded by parasols had been set up in the garden and Helen and her aunt were already ensconced at one of them. Helen smiled and beckoned Jane and de Silva over.

'I'm so glad you could join us,' said Edith as they sat down. 'We've taken the liberty of ordering.'

Her expression was benevolent. It softened her face and made her look almost pretty. De Silva decided that she must have been attractive as a young woman.

The invitation to tea had come earlier that afternoon. It would have been churlish to refuse, but although spending time with Helen Morris would be a pleasure, he had been less sure about her aunt's company. Still, perhaps the occasion would be more enjoyable than he'd expected.

Edith put a hand on his arm. 'I haven't had the chance to thank you properly for helping Helen. I dread to think what would have happened if you hadn't found her.' She lowered her voice. 'I was appalled to hear that we'd been so misled by Max Larsson. A thoroughly bad character. And Chief Inspector Lawrence! One doesn't expect a British officer to behave in such a disgraceful manner.'

Helen gave her aunt a quelling look. 'Hush, auntie. Someone might hear. Don't forget you promised the new inspector that you'd be discreet.'

Edith harrumphed but she simmered down, and they chatted amicably for a few minutes until tea arrived. When everything had been laid out and the waiter had departed, she split a scone then spread thick cream on one half and topped it with jam. 'Have you ever heard of the controversy over how scones should be eaten, Inspector?' she asked. 'People from the English county of Devon think that the jam should be put on first and then the cream, but the Cornish are adamant that the cream should be put on first and then the jam.'

To de Silva, it sounded like another example of the strange ways of the British, but clearly she was trying to be friendly, so he replied with a polite, 'How interesting.'

He enjoyed his tea and was glad to find that the conversation continued in a very pleasant vein. It seemed that in her married days in the colonial service, Edith had been acquainted with Archie and Florence Clutterbuck in one of their postings before they came to Nuala.

As he set about his second scone, however, in what he now knew to be the Cornish way, Edith's amiability vanished. Wondering what had caused the sudden drop in temperature and hoping it was nothing he'd said, de Silva looked up and saw Jocelyn Reeve and Pamela Hendry coming in their direction. She wore a stylish sundress patterned in black and white, and he was dressed in an open-necked shirt, and cream flannel trousers. The outfit gave him the relaxed air of a man who hadn't a care in the world. As he congratulated Helen on her safe return, Reeve was genial and friendly, but de Silva would have been surprised if he hadn't noticed Edith's hostility. He wondered if Reeve had any idea what it was due to. It was a pity she still disliked him, but it couldn't be helped.

Shadows were lengthening across the grass by the time they got up from the tea table and headed indoors.

'That was really very pleasant, wasn't it?' said Jane. 'I think you enjoyed it far more than you expected to.'

'I did. Like Florence, Edith Pargeter can be charming when she wants to be.'

'I wonder if they got on in the old days.'

'I imagine they were like two bull elephants circling each other.'

'Shanti! What a thing to say.'

De Silva chuckled. 'Only joking.'

He paused and turned to look at the garden, now bathed in the golden light that heralded the sunset. They watched as the sky flamed and then its vivid hues vanished with the onset of dusk.

'I think I'll do some packing before dinner,' said Jane as they stepped inside the hotel. 'It would be nice to leave in good time tomorrow so that we're not too late getting home. I'm looking forward to seeing everyone.'

'I hope Billy and Bella will forgive us for being away,' he said with a smile.

They went upstairs and de Silva let them into their room. On the table by the window there was a vase containing a bunch of red roses and beside it, a bottle of champagne.

'Gracious!' said Jane. 'Whoever can have sent them? Look there's a card.' She went over to the table and picked it up. As she read it, a smile came over her face. 'Shanti, you shouldn't have.'

He grinned. 'Oh yes, I should. If it hadn't been for you, Max Larsson would most certainly have drowned me. And I'm sorry that our holidays so far haven't turned out to be restful. First the cruise to Egypt and now this. Perhaps it will be third time lucky on the next one.'

'Somehow, I doubt it,' said Jane with a smile. 'But at least no one can say that they're dull.'

* * *

191

Many thanks for reading this book, I hope you enjoyed it. If you'd like to find out about my other books, please visit my website where you can leave any comments and sign up to receive my monthly email with news of promotions, events, and new releases.

https://harrietsteel.com
Facebook Harriet Steel Author
Twitter @harrietsteel1

HISTORICAL NOTE

This book is a work of fiction, but the idea for story was inspired by real events.

During World War II, most Ceylonese feared and mistrusted the Japanese, but some of those living in Japanese-occupied Malaya formed the "Lanka Regiment" of the Indian National Army, which had been established with the help of Nazi Germany to fight against British rule in India. There was a plan to transport the regiment by submarine to Ceylon to begin the independence struggle against the British on the island, but the plan came to nothing.

The island was not directly involved in the war until April 1942 when the Japanese air force bombed Colombo, followed a few days later by an attack on the naval base at Trincomalee. Previously, however, an airfield had been built near Galle and several RAF squadrons were sent to Ceylon. Several Commonwealth units were also stationed on the island for the duration of the war. Notably, Lord Mountbatten had his headquarters at Peradeniya, not far from the hill country. There was no conscription in Ceylon, but volunteering was encouraged, and many islanders did.

AN INSPECTOR DE SILVA MYSTERY

CHRISTMAS IN NUALA

HARRIET STEEL

CHAPTER 1

'The holly and the ivy,
When they are both full grown,
Of all the trees that are in the wood,
The holly bears the crown.'

Almost in tune, Inspector de Silva sang the carol under his breath as he returned from the police station that afternoon. It was the week before Christmas, a time of year he enjoyed. Even though he was a Buddhist, in common with many of his co-religionists, he thought of Jesus Christ as a Bodhisattva – a teacher whose life had been a blessing to the world.

Accordingly, he had no objection to celebrating the season. In fact, he relished it. He liked the festive spirit that livened up the British community, the colourful decorations, and the Christmas carols. Although he found most British food bland, much of the traditional Christmas fare appealed to his sweet tooth. He looked forward to the mince pies, the fruit cake with marzipan and icing, the crystallised figs and apricots, and of course, the plum pudding.

Inside the bungalow, he was met by the pleasing aroma of baking. His wife, Jane, rarely entered the kitchen – it was their cook's domain – but she broke the rule at Christmas. There were mince pies to be made, and the Christmas cake, baked weeks ago to her family recipe, to be fed with brandy at regular intervals.

When he put his head around the kitchen door, she smiled, brushing back a lock of hair from her damp forehead. 'Hello, dear.'

He gestured to the tray of mince pies, golden brown and warm from the oven. 'They look good. Am I allowed one?'

'Just one. The rest are for the sewing circle's Christmas meeting.'

She turned to their cook. 'Roll out the rest of the pastry trimmings and decorate the next batch as I showed you, please. When that's done, we should have enough.'

Later, they sat in the drawing room for a pre-dinner drink. 'Florence is giving her annual party at the Residence tomorrow evening,' Jane remarked.

The Christmas party at the Residence, the official home of the British assistant government agent Archie Clutterbuck and his wife Florence, was another thing that de Silva enjoyed. It was far jollier and more relaxed than Florence's usual entertainments. The only black spots were the beverages she served, one of them being mulled wine. He appreciated that the warm, syrupy mixture was probably very welcome on a frosty English night, but in the balmy climate of Ceylon, it was distinctly unrefreshing. The second offering was eggnog: a strange, British concoction of milk, eggs, sugar, spices, and whisky. He preferred his whisky unadulterated.

'I wonder what Florence has in store for us this year,' he remarked. There was normally an entertainer who put on a show to amuse the children of the British and the handful of local families invited. He had to admit, the performances usually amused him too.

'Apparently, she has a magician coming,' said Jane. 'He's Clarence Rushwell's nephew.'

A picture of Clarence Rushwell came into de Silva's mind. He was a curmudgeonly old man who rarely ventured away from home, but when he did, his wild grey hair, spindly figure, and old-fashioned clothes gave him the air of a Dickensian villain – Ebenezer Scrooge, perhaps. He lived on the edge of town about fifteen minutes' drive from Sunnybank in a house that de Silva had never visited, but it was reputed to resemble an ancient fortified manor. Although its appearance was medieval, however, the house had only been built in the late nineteenth century by the eccentric owner of the tea plantation that surrounded it. Sadly, the extravagance of the project, coupled with poor management of the plantation, had ruined the man, and he died a few years after building his dream home. Subsequently the house fell into disrepair and might have disappeared entirely, swallowed up by the jungle, if Clarence Rushwell hadn't bought it – gossips said at a knock-down price. Since then, he'd lived alone in a tower that formed part of the house.

De Silva recalled that Clarence's nephew Robert occupied a bungalow somewhere on the plantation. He had come across Robert Rushwell on numerous occasions and always thought him a decent, honourable man. He was a keen cricketer and in his younger days had apparently been a good all-round athlete too.

'I didn't know Robert Rushwell had talents as a magician.'

'Oh, not Robert. This nephew is a man called Count Cosmo Arcanti.'

'Where's he sprung from?'

'Italy. His late mother was Clarence's younger sister. She married an Italian count, and they lived in Naples. Cosmo, who inherited the title when his father died, was their only son. I hear that Clarence grumbled about him and his wife coming to Nuala, but now they're here, he's thawed a little. Countess Arcanti is very attractive and charming, which may have helped.'

'Have you met her?'

'Yes, Florence brought her in for a visit when I was helping at the junior school the other afternoon. The children were enchanted by her. She played with them for a long time and wanted to know all about the teachers too. Florence introduced us, and when the countess heard you and I would be coming to the Residence party, she said she very much looked forward to meeting you. She asked where we lived, and when I explained, said we must be near neighbours. She even apologised for not inviting us to visit her. She said that in Italy, it's customary to entertain neighbours all the time. Of course, I assured her no apology was needed, and I hoped she would visit us one day. The living arrangements at Clarence Rushwell's house sound unconventional to say the least. He refuses to have electricity installed, and everything from meals to hot water for washing must be carried up from Robert's bungalow. There's a generator for electricity and a kitchen there.'

'Why don't the count and countess live down at the bungalow?'

'Apparently, the count shares some of his uncle's eccentricity, and he's enjoying the medieval style of life. The countess confided that she hopes the novelty will soon wear off, and she'll be able to persuade him to take rooms at the Crown Hotel.'

'It sounds as if she'll have deserved some luxury by then. I look forward to meeting this couple. A count who is a magician. Unusual.'

'I agree. The countess told me it's a hobby of his. The Arcantis seem to lead a bohemian life. In Naples, they give parties where the count entertains their friends with conjuring tricks and illusions.'

'I'm rather surprised Florence Clutterbuck approves.'

'It's Christmas. She likes to let her hair down.'

Florence was also likely to be swayed by the fact that the Arcantis possessed a title, thought de Silva. She was rather a snob.

'Did you learn all this from your conversation at the school?' he asked.

'Some of it, but the rest of my information comes from the sewing circle. There's always someone there who knows what's going on in Nuala.' Jane lowered her voice. 'For example, everybody's known for a long time that the Phelps's daughter Anna and Robert Rushwell are sweet on each other. Do you remember her? She's a teacher and I introduced you to her at the school rummage sale last July. Well, Anna's mother's been hoping he'll propose, and she's convinced herself it will happen this Christmas. Mind you, she said that last Christmas. She'll be so relieved if he does. Anna isn't in the first flush of youth. She'll be forty soon, and Agatha Phelps does so want to see her happily married.'

De Silva chuckled. 'Her maternal duty will then be done, eh? Well, perhaps he'll propose at Florence's Christmas party, but we could try to help him along. Should I follow them around with a bunch of mistletoe?'

'You wouldn't dare! Seriously, I hope things work out well for them. Robert's a nice man, but his uncle is a different matter. Poor Anna Phelps might be taking on responsibility for a very difficult elderly relation.'

De Silva was puzzled. 'In that case, it surprises me that Mrs Phelps is so keen for her daughter to marry Rushwell.'

'I suppose she thinks Clarence won't be around much longer. He's elderly and not in good health. You have to remember that as she gets older, Anna's choices are becoming rather limited, and she is very fond of Robert.'

'I suppose they wouldn't have to stay in Nuala.'

'It's not that simple, dear. I understand that Robert feels responsible for his uncle, despite his faults. Apart from the Arcantis, who've only just come on the scene and may not plan to stay in Nuala, Clarence and Robert are each other's only living relatives. And then there's the plantation. Over the years, Robert's tried hard to improve it. Unfortunately, he's not had much success, but I think that's because his uncle is so against change. If Robert was in sole charge, he could probably make it profitable again. It might be hard for him to give up the prospect.'

'Is Robert Clarence's heir then?'

'I've heard so, and it seems only fair. Robert's been working for his uncle for many years, and people say the count is already wealthy.'

'Are these people the ladies of the sewing circle?'

Jane smiled. 'How did you guess?'

'But suppose Clarence leaves no money that Robert can use to rescue the plantation? Good intentions alone are rarely enough.'

'I've heard rumours there's no shortage of money. It's just that Clarence never agrees to spend a farthing more than he has to.'

CHAPTER 2

The following day, de Silva and Jane drove to the Residence for the party. As the grounds lacked spruce or fir trees, Florence had instructed the outdoor servants to festoon the palms along the driveway with lights. More twinkled on the columned portico of the Residence's elegant façade. The effect was magical.

In front of an enormous Christmas tree, shipped in for the festivities and glittering with baubles and lights, Florence and Archie waited in the entrance hall to greet their guests. Archie's concession to Christmas was a red bow tie to liven up his dark suit, but Florence had surpassed herself with a festive scarlet chiffon dress and numerous strings of pearls. In keeping with the informality of the occasion, Darcy, Archie's black Labrador, and Angel, Florence's shih tzu, were in attendance, Darcy with one eye on his master's whereabouts and the other on the canapés, and Angel condescending to wag his stumpy little apostrophe of a tail when anyone patted him.

'I'm *so* glad you could come,' said Florence, beaming. Her cheeks looked a little flushed. Charitably, de Silva put it down to the warmth of the evening, rather than overenthusiastic testing of the mulled wine and eggnog he assumed would be served.

'What a day it's been,' she went on. 'I was afraid nothing would be ready in time.'

Jane smiled. 'It all looks lovely. I'm sure it will be a wonderful evening.'

'How kind you are, my dear. Now, you *must* go into the drawing room and have some mulled wine.'

They passed into the drawing room, accepting glasses of mulled wine from one of the servants who stood by the door with a silver tray. *Eggnog must be off the menu this year*, thought de Silva.

'How pretty the room looks,' said Jane. They admired the swags of colourful paperchains that decorated the walls. The mantelpiece was festooned with holly.

'It must be from the tree Florence told me she planted when she and Archie first came to Nuala,' Jane said.

They settled down to enjoy the party, chatting with local acquaintances. Servants circulated with trays of sausage rolls and mince pies, and glasses of mulled wine were refilled. On a little stage set up at one end of the room, a group of children from the British school, dressed as angels, treated the guests to high-pitched renderings of Christmas songs and carols.

'That's Anna Phelps conducting them,' said Jane.

De Silva studied her. She was dressed in a berry-red frock piped with white at the collar and cuffs. Her hair was a mousey shade of brown, but it was thick and wavy, framing a youthful face. 'I don't remember her, but she looks a very pleasant lady,' he said.

'She is, and she's marvellous with the children.'

There was a stir over at the entrance to the drawing room and her attention was diverted. 'Oh look, that's Robert Rushwell coming in now. The couple with him must be the Arcantis.'

The count and his wife spent the first part of the evening strolling around with Florence to be introduced to the company. When it was Jane and de Silva's turn, de Silva found them very charming and unstuffy, despite their aristocratic status. They both spoke English well, the count with very little trace of an accent. He told them he had been educated at an English school.

'The count and his cousin Robert don't look much alike,' remarked Jane afterwards, in an undertone. 'Perhaps the count gets his good looks from his father.'

With his olive complexion and strong features, Count Arcanti certainly was a handsome man. His wife was equally striking, and both were tall. Robert Rushwell was of a similar height and build to his cousin, and had the same dark, curly hair, but even his kindest friend wouldn't have described him as more than pleasant looking. The count clearly took more care of himself too. His hands were smooth and well-manicured, whereas Robert's were sunburnt and roughened from his work at the plantation. The cousins also seemed very different in character, thought de Silva. Robert was a good fellow, but much more reserved than his cousin.

Eventually, the magic show was announced, and Cosmo Arcanti stepped onto the little stage where the children's choir had performed. De Silva hadn't known what to expect and had hoped the countess wouldn't have to submit to the indignity of being sawn in half, but he needn't have worried. Although the count donned a black cloak, top hat, and white gloves that gave him a dramatic air, and accompanied his act with frequent flourishes of a sparkling wand, he confined himself to doing a variety of tricks with cards, cups, and balls.

'What did you think of the show?' asked Jane as they drove home. 'I hope Florence wasn't disappointed.'

'I confess it was less of a spectacle than I anticipated, but as the count is an amateur, perhaps one shouldn't have expected too much.'

'I suppose not.'

At Sunnybank, they sat on the verandah for a while, admiring the stars. The air was still warm, although a light breeze stirred the trees. Jane was quiet; de Silva wondered whether she was thinking about Christmases past in England.

'I admit I do miss some things,' she said when he asked her. 'Snow on Christmas morning, carol singers coming to the door on a frosty evening. But the most important thing is to be with the people you love, and I'm here with you.'

He squeezed her hand. 'Thank you, my darling.'

They sat up for a little longer before deciding it was time for bed. De Silva wasn't sure how many hours he'd been asleep when the noise woke him.

Jane stirred. 'Whatever's going on? Who can be knocking at this time of night?'

'I don't know, but I'd better go and find out. It doesn't sound as if it's something the servants will be able to deal with.'

He hauled himself out of bed, pulled on his dressing gown and hurried to the front door. He heard a woman's voice outside, and she sounded very agitated. Quickly, he unlocked the door and opened it.

At first, he couldn't see her clearly against the bright moonlight, then his eyes adjusted, and a jolt of surprise went through him. It was Countess Arcanti. The hair that had been so elegantly arranged at Florence's party straggled to her shoulders, and she had exchanged her party frock for a coat thrown over a nightgown. All she had on her feet were thin slippers.

'Countess! What on earth has happened?'

She seized his hands in both of hers; she was trembling violently.

'Thank goodness I've found you! I went to the police station, but it was locked up. It was only because I was lucky enough to find someone who told me where you live that I'm here. I need help. Please come quickly!'

De Silva glanced past her to the drive. There was no car parked there. Had she run all the way?

She saw him looking, and her grip tightened. 'The car... I've never driven it before, but I had to find you. Cosmo will be furious with me.' She began to cry. 'My poor Cosmo! He may already be dead.'

'Who is it, Shanti?' De Silva heard Jane's voice. A moment later she was by his side, a look of dismay on her face.

Countess Arcanti gripped de Silva's hands even more tightly than before and turned to her.

'Mrs de Silva, I beg you, tell your husband he must help us. My husband and his cousin are fighting. I'm terrified one of them will be badly hurt.'

'Of course I'll help you, Countess,' said de Silva. 'But how did you get here?'

'I left without them noticing and drove here dressed as you see. I had no choice – the house has no telephone. If only I hadn't lost control of the car as I turned into your gate.' She paused as more tears flowed. 'It will be impossible to drive it now,' she said wretchedly.

'You mustn't worry about that,' said Jane. 'My husband will have our car out in a jiffy. You can tell him everything as you go along.'

De Silva hurried to the bedroom and pulled on his uniform. At the turnout from Sunnybank's drive, he saw a car with its bonnet buried firmly in the roadside ditch that was there to take rainwater from the road in the monsoon season. He would have to call in someone from the local garage, Gopallawa Motors, to tow it out in the morning.

Countess Arcanti hunched in the passenger seat beside him, her eyes fixed on the road. 'Go faster, Inspector, I beg you,' she said tensely. 'I am terrified of what will happen if they're left alone for too long.'

'What are they fighting about?'

'I don't know, but Robert is very drunk. At the party, I thought he was safe to drive home, but he must have had much more to drink when he got back to his bungalow. Cosmo and I talked about the party for a while, then I got ready for bed and Cosmo was about to do so when we heard Robert shouting beneath our window – we sleep on the first floor of the main house overlooking a courtyard, you see. He sounded very angry, and I begged Cosmo not to go down to him, but he said he wouldn't be accused of being a coward. When I looked out of the window, I saw them arguing. Then Robert struck my husband, and they started to fight. I was shocked to see that Robert could behave so violently and terrified of where it would end. I just pulled on this coat and ran to the car. They didn't see me drive away.'

A note of terror entered her voice. 'Inspector! I must ask you again to go faster! I think Robert will kill my husband if we don't get there very soon and stop him.'

'Try to calm yourself, Countess. The argument is probably over already.'

They reached the entrance to the Rushwells' property, and the Morris turned in. They bumped up a rough drive, passing a bungalow that de Silva assumed was Robert Rushwell's home.

At the top of the drive, a brick gatehouse with crenelated walls and narrow windows came into view. The central part was three storeys high, with another storey topping off the massive rectangular towers on either side. An archway that was easily wide enough for two cars to pass through pierced the wall of the central section. Beyond it, de Silva saw a courtyard with a range of buildings around it, some of them in a ruined state. He shivered at the air of gloom the place exuded.

'I suggest you stay in the car, Countess, while I find your husband and his cousin.'

Countess Arcanti's eyes flashed. 'No! I must come with you. I can't rest until I know my husband is safe.'

She threw open the Morris's door, jumped out and ran into the moonlit courtyard. There was no one there.

'We're too late!' she cried. 'How will we find them now?'

She glanced wildly around the range of buildings. There was a light in one of the upstairs windows in the building to their right. 'That's one of our rooms,' she said. 'They must be up there.'

De Silva followed her through a doorway and found himself in a dark hall, illuminated only by the moonlight filtering through high windows. There was a dank smell and he saw that the walls glistened with damp. He presumed that no fire had been lit in the cavernous fireplace for many years.

The countess headed for a staircase in one corner. 'Take care you don't fall,' she called over her shoulder. 'Robert's bungalow has a generator for electricity, but my husband's uncle refuses to have one. This house is dangerous at night.'

At the top of the staircase, there was another large room, but the antique four-poster bed, piled with bedclothes, was empty. The oil lamp, whose light they had seen from the courtyard, flickered on a windowsill.

The countess snatched up the lamp. 'They may have gone to Uncle Clarence's tower. We must try there.'

As he descended the stairs behind her, de Silva put a hand on the side wall to steady himself. The surface was cold and slimy to the touch. Back in the courtyard, he followed her back to the gatehouse's archway where a door into one of the towers brought them to an entrance lobby. There was no window, but in the light provided by the oil lamp, de Silva saw a spiral staircase to his right and beyond it, a door to a room. He glanced into the room as he went to follow the countess up the stairs and saw that it was empty.

The stairs were narrow and at the top of each flight there

was a small landing. On each one, there was a doorway to a room as there had been on the ground floor. His heart thumping with the effort of keeping up with the countess, de Silva only glanced into the rooms as he passed, but there was no sign of any furniture. Presumably the rooms were never used.

The countess shouted at him to hurry, and it was as they started up the stairs leading to the next floor that he heard raised voices. There was obviously a violent argument taking place, but he couldn't make out if there were two or three men involved, still less their identity. This sounded more serious than he had anticipated. What a fool he'd been not to stop at the station to get his gun. He supposed that was because the idea of having to shoot an Englishman was beyond his imagining. However, it might have helped him to take control of the situation.

The countess was still ahead of him as he hurried up the last few steps.

'We must be quick!' she cried. 'They're up here in Uncle Clarence's study.'

De Silva heard the count's voice. 'Julia, stay back! Robert has a gun.'

Her hand clasping her throat, the countess shrank against the wall. 'Robert!' she cried out. 'I beg you not to hurt my Cosmo!'

As de Silva reached the place where she had put the oil lamp down to one side of the top step, he saw an open door. Just inside the room, the bulky figure of a man standing with his back to them almost blocked the view, but then he moved a little to one side and for a moment, de Silva caught a glimpse of Count Arcanti beyond him. The yellowish light that illuminated his face revealed an expression of profound horror, before once again the man in the doorway moved, blocking the view.

'Robert,' pleaded the countess. 'Give up the gun. Talk to us.'

But Rushwell ignored her entreaties. With a black-gloved hand, he reached behind him for the door and pushed it shut, trapping himself and Arcanti inside the study. De Silva heard a bolt shoot across.

The countess threw herself against the closed door, hammering at it with her fists. A crash came from inside the study followed by another.

'We must get in,' she gasped.

De Silva studied the door. It looked very solid, but he had to try. He motioned the countess to stand aside. At the first blow, his shoulder throbbed, but the door didn't budge. As he prepared himself for another attempt, from inside the room he heard muffled cries and what sounded like furniture being overturned and smashed.

'The fireplace in our hall!' the countess cried. 'There are fire irons there. Perhaps we can use one of them to break the door.' She raced off down the stairs.

De Silva tried more blows with his shoulder, but soon he was exhausted. The sound of breakages had stopped, and there was an ominous silence. 'Open the door!' he called out.

There was no reply.

He heard the countess's footsteps and she soon appeared, catching her breath, and brandishing a poker.

'Here, try this.'

He gripped the poker and raised it to strike, then froze. From inside the study, a shot rang out, swiftly followed by another.

'Cosmo!' screamed the countess.

The shots spurred de Silva into action. As he hammered at the door with the poker, the countess watched with terror in her eyes. 'We're too late,' she said wretchedly.

'We may not be. Don't give up hope.'

The wood started to splinter as he redoubled his efforts but still the door held. Suddenly, she seized his arm. 'Someone is moving inside.'

De Silva stopped and listened; she was right. There were distinct sounds of movement, as if someone was trying to crawl towards the door. He pressed his ear to it and heard a faint voice calling for help. The door opened a fraction.

'Take care!' whispered the countess urgently.

'Julia!'

The countess's face lit up. 'My Cosmo! He lives. Push, Inspector! Push at the door.'

When the door finally opened, the study looked as if a whirlwind had swept through it. Furniture was upended, and papers were scattered over the floor. A puddle of ink from a broken inkpot lay on the desktop. One of the two candelabras in the room had been knocked over and the wax from its extinguished candles was dripping onto the floorboards. The candles in the one that was still standing swayed in the draught from an open window.

Count Arcanti crouched on the floor; one sleeve of his dress shirt was stained with blood. His face was chalk white and contorted with pain. Behind him, a trail of blood stretched back into the room.

The countess put down her oil lamp, sank to her knees beside him and cradled his head in her lap. 'My darling, you're wounded.'

'It's nothing – a scratch.'

In the dim light, de Silva saw that a motionless figure lay close by. A few steps into the room, he realised it was not Robert, but Clarence Rushwell, and the trail of blood came from where his body lay. De Silva went to him and felt for a pulse but found none.

'Where's your cousin?' he asked Arcanti.

'Gone,' muttered the count bitterly. 'He climbed out of the window, and I couldn't stop him. He shot my uncle. I'm sure that if he hadn't thought you were close to getting in and panicked, he would have killed me too.'

'Why were you arguing?'

'It was a stupid quarrel.' He stopped, as if he struggled to control his pain before he spoke again. 'I thought we were friends. I had no idea all the friendship was on my side.'

The countess looked up from binding his wounded arm with a strip of fabric she had torn from the hem of her nightgown. 'Inspector, is this really the time to be questioning my husband? He needs a doctor quickly. He is in shock and the wound is worse than he claims. His uncle refused to have a telephone, so a doctor will need to be fetched. Please go. I will stay here with him.'

De Silva glanced at the count. His eyes were half closed now. De Silva had little medical knowledge, but he knew shock could be dangerous if the count slipped into unconsciousness. The countess was right.

'Are you sure you can manage?'

'Yes. Please hurry.'

She touched the count's cheek. 'He's very cold,' she said, half to herself. 'Yes, that will be the shock. I must find a blanket to cover him.' She looked up at de Silva and urgency sharpened her voice. 'Please, Inspector, go!'

CHAPTER 3

'You've been lucky, Count Arcanti,' said Doctor Hebden when he and de Silva returned less than an hour later, and he had examined the count. De Silva had decided to go directly to Hebden's house rather than to Sunnybank to telephone. It wasn't much further and had the advantage that he could guide Hebden to the plantation if the doctor didn't know it.

'It's only a flesh wound but a nasty one,' Hebden went on. 'You have the countess to thank for her first-aid skills. She acted as competently as any nurse. You've lost some blood, but we'll get you down to the hospital and in a few days, you'll be right as rain.'

'Thank you,' the count said weakly. He looked desolate. 'But my poor uncle. It's too late for him, isn't it?' He glanced at his uncle's body which had been covered with a sheet.

'I'm afraid it is.'

Hebden turned to the countess. 'Shall I make the arrangements for the undertakers to fetch Mr Rushwell's body, ma'am?'

'We'd be very grateful. I want to be with my husband at the hospital.'

'Of course.'

Outside, the sky was turning the colour of pearl. Soon, the sun would be up. After Hebden had driven away with the Arcantis, de Silva went to Robert Rushwell's bungalow.

There was no car outside, and no sign of servants. He walked around to the back of the building where he found their quarters, lifted the latch on the door and went in.

The first room was stuffy and dimly lit. He heard a groan and saw that it came from a pallet bed in one corner where a man dressed in a loincloth was sprawled on top of a crumpled sheet. There was a strong smell of arrack. The man raised his head a few inches from the bed, grunted and turned onto his side. De Silva went over and poked him, none too gently, with his foot. He saw de Silva's uniform and sat up abruptly.

'Sahib!'

De Silva crossed to the room's only window and pulled aside the makeshift curtain, letting in the dawn light.

'Get up, man. Who are you?'

'I am the cook, sahib.'

Now that de Silva saw him more clearly, he noticed there were blisters on the man's forearms that might have been caused by kitchen burns. His hair was greasy, and he didn't look too clean. Thank goodness he wasn't the cook at Sunnybank.

'Is anyone else here?'

'Two more servants, sahib. They are asleep in there.' He jerked his head in the direction of an inner room.

'Well, you'd better all get up. Look sharp about it. I'll see you outside in five minutes.'

Five minutes later, the three men stood on the bungalow's drive and faced him. Their eyes were bloodshot.

'Where were you when your master came back last night?' asked de Silva after they had told him their names.

'Asleep, sahib,' said the cook. 'He said we could have the evening off.'

'Did he also tell you that you could get drunk?'

The men looked sheepish.

'Never mind. What I want to know is when you last saw your master.'

'Before he left to go to the Residence, sahib.'

'Are you sure that was the last time? You didn't see him go up to the main house here later?'

'No, sahib. Forgive us, but why do you ask this?'

'Because your master's uncle was attacked and killed last night.'

The three men's eyes widened. 'We know nothing about it, sahib,' said the cook unhappily.

'No one is accusing you. But if you see your master, you must come to the police station immediately. Do you know where it is?'

'Yes, sahib.'

CHAPTER 4

'I'm flummoxed by how he got down from that window without injuring himself,' said de Silva.

The sun was up, and it was already hot. He and Jane sat in the dining room at Sunnybank having a late breakfast. He scooped up the last of his egg with a piece of roti and ate it.

'Shall I ask cook to send something else in for you?' asked Jane.

De Silva wiped his lips and took a drink of tea.

'No, I'd better be on my way to the station. Prasanna and Nadar should be in by now. They'd better go and clean up Clarence Rushwell's study, then I want them to start looking for Robert. They can take their bicycles and search the area immediately around the property. I'll take the Morris and go further afield. But I fear it will be like looking for a needle in a hayfield, especially as Robert has a few hours' start on us.'

'A needle in a haystack, dear. I do hope it won't be that hard.'

At the station, he gave Prasanna and Nadar their instructions and they fetched their bicycles and rode away. Left alone in his office, he mulled over the case. The next thing he needed to do was report to his boss, Archie Clutterbuck, before he heard the news from anyone else. When he put in a call to the Residence, however, Clutterbuck wasn't there, so he left a message asking to see him at the earliest opportunity then telephoned the manager at Gopallawa Motors and asked him to recover the Arcantis' car. Finally, he made calls to the police stations at Hatton and Kandy, and as an afterthought, to his old colleague Inspector Chockalingham in Colombo. On his usual principle of no stone unturned, it would do no harm to try to find out more about the Arcantis.

He yawned. His night had been very short on sleep. Perhaps he'd close his eyes for a while. Settling back in his chair, he put his feet on the desk and folded his hands on his stomach.

The shrill of the telephone in the public room woke him. Irritably, he wondered why Prasanna or Nadar didn't answer it, then he remembered he'd sent them out to search for Rushwell. One of Archie Clutterbuck's staff was on the line. 'Mr Clutterbuck can see you in half an hour, Inspector,' she said.

De Silva thanked her and put down the receiver. He felt a flicker of regret for his nap and Prasanna's and Nadar's nonappearance. It would have been good to have some progress to report.

* * *

'I hope this isn't going to put a dampener on the festivities,' grumbled Archie when de Silva had explained the reason for his call. 'You know what store my dear wife sets by everything being tickety-boo at this time of the year.'

'Unfortunately, murder has a habit of happening at inconvenient moments, sir.'

Archie's brow furrowed then he gave a grudging nod.

'Very true, de Silva. Poor old Clarence Rushwell. I can't say I knew him well, but I'm sure there'll be those who mourn his passing.' Archie took a puff of his cigarette. 'Do I take it you and your men have had no luck with finding his nephew Robert yet?'

'Not yet, sir, but we've only been looking since this morning.'

'You say there was no car at the bungalow. He could be a long way from here by now.'

'I've alerted Inspector Singh down at Hatton and notified the Kandy and Colombo police. They're keeping a look out for him.'

'Good.' Clutterbuck stubbed out his cigarette. 'Well, keep me informed.' He scraped back his chair and stood up. As if attached to his master by an invisible thread, Darcy scrambled to his feet, tail wagging.

CHAPTER 5

Back at the station, the public room was empty. Prasanna and Nadar must still be out searching. Deciding it would be best to wait for them and see what, if anything, they had unearthed, he went into his office and left the door open. An hour later, he heard Nadar's familiar voice and went out to greet him.

'Anything to report?'

'We think we may have found his car, sir. It's in a lake about a mile from the house.'

De Silva frowned. 'Was Rushwell inside?'

'No, sir, but we think he can't be far away. We thought you'd want to know, so I came back straight away to fetch you.'

'Very well, I'll come. We'll take the Morris.'

And this time, he thought, he would bring his gun.

* * *

It was mid-afternoon by the time they reached the Rush-wells' plantation. About a mile beyond it on the road leading to Hatton, Nadar indicated they should turn left down a track.

'What made you come along here?' asked de Silva.

'Sergeant Prasanna and I thought it more likely that Mr Rushwell would drive away from town than towards it, so as not to be recognised. A fugitive who's been in a big fight could be injured and need somewhere to hide, at least until he's decided what to do next. There might be a remote hut he knew about, but we only had our bicycles and couldn't travel very far, so we decided to check each track off the road leading from the plantation that a car could drive down. This was the second one we searched.'

'Good thinking, Constable, I'm impressed.'

Nadar beamed.

'Now, we'd better crack on.'

Soon, the track became too rough for de Silva to be prepared to risk puncturing the Morris's tyres. He pulled her over to one side and they began to walk. The heat bore down on him, and flies blundered into his face. The surface of the track, though passable, worsened considerably before widening out into a grassy area with a very obvious drop at the far end. There, at the bottom of a steep slope, the lake sparkled in the sunshine. At the area closest to them there was a muddy strip of beach, and over to the left, a large expanse of reed beds. Otherwise, as far as the eye could see, the jungle grew right up to the shore.

'This way, sir,' said Nadar. 'The car's over here.'

The car had gone some way into the reeds, but its rear end was still visible through the gap its passage had created. As they reached Prasanna, de Silva saw that he wasn't wearing his policeman's boots or his socks, and his uniform trousers were rolled up above his knees. Mud coated his feet and there were splashes of it up his legs.

'I went out as far as I dared, sir. I don't think there's anyone in the car, but if you want me to go further—'

He looked warily at the gently waving reeds, clearly unnerved as to what might be lurking amongst them. A vision of snakes danced before de Silva's eyes.

The car wasn't all that far from the shore, probably halted by a submerged tree trunk or an outcrop of rock, but very likely, it wouldn't be long before its weight would take it below the surface and the reeds would close around it. Even as they watched, it shifted and settled deeper into the mud. It had been fortunate that Prasanna and Nadar arrived when they did, or they might never have found it. A stroke of luck for Rushwell too that he had got out in time. De Silva assumed the car was his. It seemed too much of a coincidence that someone else would have such a recent accident at this godforsaken spot.

'No need to go back in, Sergeant,' he said briskly. 'I'm happy to rely on your eyesight.' He didn't want to be faced with having to rescue Prasanna if the lad came to grief.

'Thank you, sir.' Prasanna looked very relieved, but his expression turned to one of comical dismay when he saw de Silva glance once more at his bare, muddy feet and legs.

'I'm sorry, sir. I know I'm improperly dressed.'

De Silva chuckled. 'I'll excuse you this time, Sergeant, but don't let it happen again. In any case, well done, the two of you.'

He looked around. The upturned hull of a boat, painted a peeling blue, lay a little way off along the beach. Out in the water several sturdy poles, each with another piece of wood jutting out at an angle, stuck up from the glassy surface of the water. De Silva was aware that older fishermen often liked to use them, so they could fish in the deeper water without getting their feet wet. The remains of fish guts, stinking in the heat, indicated that a catch had been landed on the beach recently. In the distance, he saw the outline of a few huts.

'There seems to be a village over there. They might have seen something. We'd better get over there and find out. Prasanna, don't forget those boots and socks of yours. You'll have to carry them. I'm sure some village maiden will help you to wash and dry your feet.'

As they set off, de Silva saw Nadar grin and nudge

Prasanna in the ribs. In return, Prasanna gave him back a more forceful nudge.

'Stop it, the pair of you,' de Silva said sternly, hiding a smile.

'Sorry, sir.'

The heat haze through which de Silva had spotted the huts was deceptive, and the walk took longer than he had anticipated. When they finally reached the edge of the village, a pack of mongrel dogs ran out barking. Prasanna picked up a stick in case they needed to fend them off, but the dogs halted a short distance away.

The village was small, comprising only nine or ten huts made of bamboo poles roped together in sections and thatched with palm fronds. The air smelt of woodsmoke and fish. Between the huts, the beaten earth was dun-coloured and dry. Old metal drums stood around, presumably to store water. A little way off, a large structure made of poles and palm matting displayed headless fish, their scaly bodies crusted with salt and laid out to dry in the sun.

A child saw them coming and ran off into one of the huts shouting something in a language de Silva didn't understand. The elderly villager who emerged after a few moments was dignified in bearing but so thin he was almost emaciated. His grey hair was cropped close to his head, and his skin was wrinkled and leathery. He leant on a peeled stick.

When de Silva greeted him in Sinhalese, he was silent at first, but then, to de Silva's relief, he answered in the same language. At least they would be able to communicate. Many of the fisher folk in Ceylon spoke only their local dialects.

By now, their arrival had gathered a small crowd of villagers. Men, women, and children stared at them, the younger ones giggling behind their hands. Many of the children were naked, but their skinny little bodies looked healthy enough, and their black hair gleamed. *The benefits of a diet of fish*, thought de Silva.

'Are you the headman?' he asked the elderly villager.

The man nodded.

'Have you seen a white man around here recently?'

Again, the man was silent.

'You won't be in any trouble if you tell me,' said de Silva.

'We found him at the lake. So much mud on him, we didn't know it was a man until we came near.'

'Was he alive?'

'Yes.'

'So where is he now?'

The headman leant on his stick and regarded de Silva shrewdly. De Silva was sure he understood but was probably waiting for a reward for his information. He felt in his pocket and brought out a handful of coins. A spark of interest appeared in the headman's eyes.

'These are for you if you take me to him.'

The headman took the money and led the way to one of the huts.

Once inside, it took a few moments for de Silva's eyes to adjust to the dim light. When they had done, he saw that there was a man lying on a mattress on the ground.

'I need more light,' he said.

The headman went to the door of the hut and called out. A younger man came with a burning stick and lit an oil lamp that was hanging from a beam.

Robert Rushwell's eyes were closed, and he lay still, but the gentle rise and fall of his chest showed he was alive. De Silva was surprised their arrival hadn't woken him.

'How long has he been like this?'

'Since we found him when we went to fish this morning at dawn.'

'Did you hear any noises in the night?'

'Noises every night,' said the headman with a shrug.

'Elephants come to drink. We do not go and ask them what they do.' He grinned at his own joke.

'What about the sound of cars, or people talking?'

The headman shook his head.

So, it was a mystery why Rushwell had driven into the lake. De Silva went over to the mattress to take a better look at him. He was naked under the rough blanket. Presumably, his clothes had been so filthy that the villagers had removed them. De Silva peeled back the blanket and inspected his pale torso and partially sunburnt limbs. Apart from scratches and bruises, they appeared to be unharmed.

His head was a different matter. On one side, the hair was matted with blood. De Silva felt the area and found a lump. He put his ear to Rushwell's chest; his heartbeat was reassuringly steady. He groaned and muttered something then turned on his side. He didn't seem to be in immediate danger, thought de Silva, but it was probably unwise to move him.

He stood up. 'I'm going back to Nuala. Prasanna, you and Nadar stay here and keep guard. If Rushwell wakes, send one of the villagers to me with a message. Whatever you do, don't let him leave. I'll be back as soon as possible but given the time of day you may well have to stay here for the night.'

CHAPTER 6

'Have you had any luck?' asked Jane when he returned to Sunnybank.

'We found him, but he's in no condition to answer questions.'

'Where was he?'

'At a fishing village by a lake a mile or so past his uncle's property in the Hatton direction. His car was in the water, stuck in some reeds, but he'd somehow managed to get out. Some villagers found him unconscious on the beach and took him back to their village. They don't know when the car crashed. They told me that they found it when they came down to the lake to fish around dawn. They say Rushwell's not been in any condition to talk since they found him.'

'Should we call Doctor Hebden?'

'I don't think there's any urgency. He's had a knock on the head, but I don't believe he's in immediate danger. His heartbeat and pulse were steady, so it's most likely he's just exhausted. I've left Prasanna and Nadar there with instructions to send a message if he comes to.'

'What do you plan to do next?'

'I won't make my report to Archie yet. He'd probably insist on my bringing Rushwell in, but he won't be going anywhere with Prasanna and Nadar on guard. Would you send one of the servants to tell their families not to expect them home tonight? I'd like another look at the uncle's house. There's something odd about this. Rushwell knows his way around the area. If he wanted to make himself scarce, why would he head for that lake? It's possible he wanted somewhere to hole up for a while, but the way down to the lake is treacherous. Surely, he could have found better places, and further away too. I had to leave the Morris a good way off from the shore and walk to save her tyres.'

'Might he have lost his sense of direction? After the scene the countess described with all the drinking and the fight with his cousin, he must have been in a terrible state.'

'It's possible, I suppose.'

Jane stood up. 'I'll go and organise the messages to Prasanna and Nadar's families, but then if you're going to the Rushwells' place, I'm coming with you.'

De Silva frowned. 'I'm not sure that's a good idea.'

'Two heads are better than one, dear. Anyway, I can't see there'll be any danger now. If Robert Rushwell is the murderer, he's safely under guard.'

Despite his reluctance, de Silva knew there was little point arguing. 'Very well,' he said.

'Do you think he is? The murderer, I mean.'

'I'm not sure who else it can be, but something about this business smells fishy, and it's not just the lake village.'

'I'll go and get ready.'

'And I'll fetch a torch to take with us. As Clarence refused to have electricity installed in his house, it'll be hard to find our way around without one.'

* * *

As they drove up to the plantation, de Silva noticed there were no lights on in Robert Rushwell's bungalow. The servants were probably idling in their quarters again. The main house was also in darkness, but the moon was rising over the line of trees that bordered the overgrown garden. When it was fully up, its light should make it easier to see, but for the moment their torch would have to do.

He parked the Morris and they walked towards the archway. Jane flinched as a colony of bats rose from the roof of one of the towers. 'Ugh, I've never liked bats,' she said. 'There's something so eerie about them.'

Inside the tower, they climbed the stairs to the study. The furniture was no longer in disarray and the bloodstains had been cleaned up. Prasanna and Nadar hadn't done a bad job.

Now that he and Jane had the study to themselves, de Silva let his torch beam range across the walls, illuminating shelves filled with dusty, leather-bound books. He noticed that the furniture in the room was shabby but included some interesting items. There was an almost life-sized standing figure of the Buddha, made of close-grained wood polished to a glossy golden brown, an antique celestial globe, and propped against one wall, a very large mirror with a gilded frame. On the wall above it, the brown wallpaper was torn in several places, revealing holes in the plaster behind. Clearly, the fastenings hadn't been strong enough to support the mirror's weight. Its frame was chipped along the base, perhaps from when it had fallen. De Silva also noticed a tear in the rug that poked out from under it.

Moonlight shone through the window that Rushwell had apparently used for his escape after he shot his uncle. Jane opened it and looked out.

'It's beautiful here when one sees it like this, but I don't think I could live in such an isolated spot.'

De Silva came to join her. 'I agree.'

He studied the size of the window. 'It's certainly large enough for a man to climb through, but it's a long way to the ground. I wonder how Rushwell managed to get down.'

'He might have used this creeper.' Jane reach for a

handful of the creeper that grew up the wall and gave it a tug. 'But it doesn't seem very steady.'

'Shall we have a look upstairs? Clarence's bedroom should be up there.'

With only the torch to show the way, it was very dark on the stairs. De Silva climbed the first few steps then froze as something damp and soft brushed his hand. With a shout, he recoiled, almost knocking over Jane who was behind him holding the torch.

'Shanti! Whatever's the matter?' She flashed the torch beam up the stairs then laughed. 'It's only cobwebs.'

A large spider scuttled away into a crevice in the wall. Grimly, de Silva watched it go. 'Anyone can make a mistake.'

The bedroom on the top floor contained no furniture except for a bed and an old wardrobe. The clothes inside were shabby and smelled of mothballs. If Clarence Rushwell was as wealthy as he was reputed to be, what a shame he seemed not to have enjoyed his money a little more.

They left the bedroom and went downstairs and out to the garden. Under the window that Rushwell had presumably jumped from, the torch beam illuminated a patch of weedy plants that straggled along the base of the wall.

De Silva frowned. 'There's no sign they've been damaged. If he did escape this way, he must have managed to jump clear. But I can't help feeling that the facts don't add up. Let's say Rushwell landed relatively unhurt, as it seems he must have done if he was able to drive his car away; what caused the lump on his head? It's in an unlikely position for it to have happened when he crashed his car. And why did he leave his cousin alive but kill his uncle?'

'Head wounds can bleed and swell badly, even if they're relatively minor. As for why he left the count alive, perhaps since he knew you and countess were outside the study, he was too afraid he'd be caught to think straight. All the same, I agree it does seem odd.'

'From what I've heard about him, he's a phlegmatic sort of chap. I know the circumstances were extreme, but I wouldn't have thought he was the type to panic. And why would he want his uncle or his cousin dead? It's a pity the countess couldn't tell us what they were arguing about. The count's story wasn't helpful either. It wasn't a good time to press him for more information, but I need to question him about what he meant when he said that he found out all the friendship was on his side.'

Jane touched his arm and put her finger to her lips. 'Did you hear that?' she whispered. 'Over there in the bushes – something moved.'

De Silva listened. She was right, and the something was too large to be a bird or a small animal. A shiver went through him. Dangerous creatures might be on the prowl in this lonely place. He put Jane behind him and eased his gun from its holster.

'Do you think we should go back inside?' asked Jane in a low voice.

'Yes; but move slowly.'

His heart began to beat faster as they edged back towards the gatehouse. Suddenly, a bush swayed. A shadowy figure darted out and started to run fast in the direction of the drive.

'I'm going after them,' he said quickly. 'You go back inside where you'll be safe.'

Jane waited until he had gone a little way then followed.

De Silva's lungs ached as he ran. In his younger days, he thought ruefully, he would easily have caught up with the intruder by now. As Robert Rushwell's bungalow came into sight, he forced himself to put on a spurt and close the gap.

The figure disappeared behind the bungalow. He raced around the corner of the building in pursuit and saw that it was a woman. She headed for a car that was parked on the back driveway, pulled open the driver's door and scrambled in. He heard the engine start then stall as she tried to drive off. It gave him time to reach the car. She struggled to hold on to the door as he tried to open it, but he was stronger than she was. Then he saw her face. It was Anna Phelps.

CHAPTER 7

De Silva and Jane watched Anna Phelps as she sipped the hot tea one of their servants had brought in. One glance at the state of the kitchen in Robert Rushwell's bungalow, and Jane had insisted they take her back to Sunnybank. Jane had accompanied her in Anna's car, declining to answer her questions as to what was going on. She seemed a little calmer than when they'd found her, but it was clear to de Silva that tears were still not far away. Even though she had tried to run away from the scene of a crime, he didn't want to be too hard on her. He would be very surprised if she was involved in Clarence's murder. All the same, he needed to know why she had been at the plantation.

'I came to see Robert,' she said shakily. 'We were supposed to meet at the club this afternoon, and he didn't come. It's not like him to let me down.'

'Did he talk to you about his cousin?'

'Sometimes.'

'What did he say about him?'

'Robert didn't know the count and his wife until they came here. We were surprised at first that they'd travelled all this way to visit relations they'd never met, but the count said that it was one of his mother's last wishes that he should visit her brother Clarence.'

'Did Count Arcanti give a particular reason for his mother encouraging the visit?'

'Well, Clarence can be very difficult, particularly as his health has worsened over the last few months. He was often mean and ungrateful with Robert, and I imagine he could have been the same with his sister. According to the count, his mother was nevertheless very sorry she and her brother had grown apart. She wanted the family to be reconciled, and she'd grown too old to make the journey herself.'

'How did Robert feel about the visit? Did he say anything to you?'

'Nothing specific, although I had the impression that he wasn't quite sure what to make of the Arcantis. But then Robert doesn't find new people easy at the best of times.'

She frowned. 'Inspector, why were you and Mrs de Silva at the house? Is something the matter? Robert's not come to any harm, has he?'

'I'm afraid I have bad news for you,' said de Silva. He spoke with careful deliberation. 'Clarence Rushwell has been murdered. Count Arcanti was wounded in the same incident, and Robert is missing.'

Anna Phelps turned pale. 'You can't possibly believe this has anything to do with Robert! Why, he wouldn't hurt a fly. He never even talked back to his uncle, whatever the provocation, and despite everything, he put his heart into keeping the plantation going. I'm sure he didn't have a grudge against his cousin. It's just he didn't know him well.'

'Miss Phelps, I'm afraid we have testimony to the contrary. Countess Arcanti claims that her husband and Robert had a violent argument in the early hours of this morning after the party at the Residence. There was a fight, and the countess came to me for help. When I returned to the house with her, I saw Robert in the doorway to the study threatening his cousin with a gun. Before I could intervene, he shut the door in my face and bolted it. Two shots followed. When I finally gained entry to the room, Clarence Rushwell was dead, and the count wounded. There was no sign of Robert.'

Tears brimmed in Anna Phelps's eyes and spilled down her cheeks. 'I don't believe it. It must be a terrible mistake. The countess probably imagined what she saw. I expect she's prone to being excitable.'

'I'm sorry, but I was there.'

A stubborn look came over Anna Phelps's face. 'You're mistaken. Robert wouldn't hurt anyone. Let me help you find him. He'll talk to me, and I know he'll be able to explain everything.'

She stopped and looked closely at de Silva. 'Are you sure you don't know where he is?'

She was no fool, thought de Silva, but he kept an impassive expression on his face. He didn't want her becoming too involved.

'I can't tell you anything more at this stage.'

'So, you do know where he is! I insist you tell me.'

'We understand your feelings, my dear,' Jane said gently. 'But if Robert is innocent, he has nothing to fear. Now, I think you should go home. My husband will drive you.'

There was a long pause then Anna Phelps shook her head. 'I can drive myself. Just promise me that when you find him, Robert will have a fair hearing. I know he's innocent.'

* * *

'I'm glad you were here,' said de Silva when he returned from taking Anna Phelps back to her car. 'I don't think I would have managed as well without you.'

'Poor girl, the news must have been such a shock. I think you were wise not to tell her where he is. The sight of him would only have distressed her more.'

De Silva glanced at the clock on the mantelpiece. 'There's been no message from Prasanna and Nadar, and it's very late to go back to the lake now. It can wait until morning. Let's hope Robert Rushwell is fit to be questioned by then. I want to hear his side of the story.'

'I'm afraid after this, there's not likely to be a Christmas engagement for Anna, or one at all,' said Jane sadly.

'Unfortunately, I have to agree with you. Even though she believes he's innocent, things don't look good for Rushwell.'

CHAPTER 8

He set off the next morning for the lake. Once again, the last part of the journey was arduous, and he had to drive very slowly, watching for hazards. Mosquitos buzzed into his face and the dry air parched his throat. He was within sight of the water when he saw Constable Nadar coming from the other direction, wheeling his bicycle over the rough ground. He was fanning his face with his cap, but when he spotted de Silva he quickly slapped it back on his head. In the circumstances, de Silva refrained from telling him off for removing the cap on duty.

'Good morning, Constable. Were you coming to find me?'

'Yes, sir. Mr Rushwell is awake now. He's still very weak, but Sergeant Prasanna and I thought you would want to talk to him.'

'Well done, Constable, lead on.'

In the stuffy little hut, de Silva informed Robert Rushwell of the charge against him then listened carefully to his story. Should he believe the man? He decided to make Rushwell go over it again.

'You say you don't remember anything from the time you went to fetch your car keys for your cousin until you found yourself in the reeds. Mr Rushwell, forgive me, but I think any reasonable person would find it hard to credit that you succeeded in freeing yourself from such a dangerous predicament.'

'I remember a violent impact of some kind that revived me. It was dark, but I realised I was trapped in my car. I could feel water around my feet. I managed to force the door open and get out, but I immediately sank into mud. It was only the thought of what would happen to me if I stopped trying to free myself that kept me going. I may only have been struggling through that reed bed for minutes, but it felt like hours before there was solid ground under my feet. After that, I must have passed out again.'

'Let's go back to the events immediately after you left the party at the Residence.'

Rushwell tried to raise his head from the mattress but fell back, a grimace of pain on his face. 'I've told you all about that, Inspector,' he said hoarsely.

'I'd like you to tell me again.'

'I drove home with my cousin and his wife, dropped them at the house and went home, intending to listen to some music on the gramophone before going to bed. There was no argument and no fight. I'd given the servants the night off, so I was alone at my bungalow. I had a lot on my mind.'

De Silva wondered if he was referring to his relationship with Anna Phelps. He waited for him to go on.

'To be frank with you, Inspector, I'm in love with a lady and I'd like to ask her to marry me, but what with the state of the place and the difficulties with my uncle, how could I ask her to throw in her lot with me? The only answer was to leave and ask her to come with me, but that would be fraught with uncertainty. It's all out of the question now anyway,' he added bitterly. 'I certainly can't ask her to marry a man who's been accused of murder. I didn't do it, but I'm sure no one will believe that.'

If he was innocent, de Silva pitied him.

'I had a couple of glasses of whisky,' Rushwell went on. 'That probably made me start to feel drowsy. I was about to get undressed when I heard someone knocking on the door. I didn't look to see what time it was. I can only tell you that it was still dark. With poor Uncle Clarence's worsening state of health, I'd been expecting a crisis for some time. I was anxious to answer the door and find out what had happened.'

The furrow between his eyebrows deepened. 'I'd like some water, please.'

De Silva nodded to Prasanna. 'Try and find some that's safe to drink.'

'Yes, sir.'

'My cousin Cosmo was at the door,' Rushwell went on. 'He was very agitated. I had to ask him to speak more slowly, so I could understand what he was saying. When he'd calmed down, he told me I was needed urgently at the main house. Uncle Clarence was in a very bad way and asking for me. I'd already had to drive us to the party because Cosmo had been having some trouble with his car and didn't want to risk taking it out until the garage had a chance to look at it. He asked if he could take mine to go for Doctor Hebden. Of course, I said yes, and turned away to go and find the keys for him. After that, the next thing I remember is regaining consciousness at the lake, as I've already told you.'

Prasanna reappeared with a glass of water. Gratefully, Rushwell gulped it down.

'Do you recall the villagers finding you on the beach?'

'Dimly. I knew I was being carried somewhere.'

'Who do you think knocked you out?'

'My cousin, Cosmo. Who else could it be?'

CHAPTER 9

Jane shuddered. 'What a horrible thought. Poor Robert Rushwell might easily have drowned.'

'It's lucky he keeps fit and could extricate himself from his car. A lot of people wouldn't have been able to.'

'What about this business of not being able to remember how he got to the lake? Do you think it's true?'

'It's possible.'

'And do you think it was Cosmo who hit him?'

'It's a reasonable supposition, and Rushwell certainly believes it was his cousin.'

Jane frowned. 'Then if Robert was already unconscious, who was the man you saw in Clarence Rushwell's study?'

'Either Robert's lying, or we're missing something,' said de Silva. 'Something that's staring us straight in the face. I'll go to the hospital tomorrow and see how the count's getting on. Perhaps that will provide some inspiration. In the meantime, it's in the best interests of the investigation that Robert stays where he is, out of sight and looked after by Prasanna and Nadar. I'd better get another message to their families.'

* * *

'Inspector, have you found my cousin yet?'

Cosmo Arcanti's head rested against a soft heap of

pillows. The sunshine streaming through the window of the hospital room showed there was more colour in his cheeks than there'd been when de Silva last saw him.

De Silva had decided not to reveal yet that he knew where Robert Rushwell was. 'We're still working on the case, sir, but I'm very glad to see you looking better.'

The countess, who sat in the chair beside the bed, fixed de Silva with her dark eyes. 'I can't rest until I know that monster has been caught.'

Arcanti reached for his wife's hand. 'Julia, my love, I'm perfectly safe here. You mustn't upset yourself.'

'How can I help it? He might have killed you, as he killed your poor uncle.'

'As the countess rightly pointed out,' intervened de Silva, 'our last meeting wasn't the time for questions. But I'd be grateful if you'd answer some for me now, sir.'

'Of course.'

'Do you have any idea why your cousin shot your uncle?'

'He was angry. He and my uncle had argued about the plantation that day. I'm afraid the old man was very stubborn. Robert was obviously becoming increasingly frustrated by the difficulties our uncle put in his way, but he seemed to be enjoying himself at the party that evening, so I thought that, for the moment, the argument had blown over. After we came back from the Residence I hoped he would go quietly to bed, but instead he started drinking again. He got it into his mind that I was working against him too.' He shook his head sadly. 'I think my cousin is a lonely man, and lonely people can do strange things.'

'Did he say in what way he thought you were working against him?'

'He accused me of trying to persuade our uncle to change his will in my favour. It was nonsense, of course, and anyway, I'm sure Uncle Clarence wouldn't have gone through with it, even if I had tried to influence him. Under all the bluster, I believe he knew he would never manage the plantation without Robert.'

'Had you heard your uncle threaten to change his will?'

The count shrugged. 'Yes, but I did not take it seriously. He seemed to relish playing my cousin and me off against each other. On more than one occasion, I told Robert not to take any notice.'

'Were you to benefit if the will was changed?'

'A blunt question, Inspector. My uncle hinted at it, but I have no need of the money and know nothing about growing tea. I made it clear to Robert that I wouldn't accept.'

'The countess saw you and your cousin fighting in the courtyard before she left to call for my help. What happened in the end?'

'Robert got the upper hand and knocked me to the ground. After that, he stormed off. My first thought was for Julia. I wanted to reassure her I was safe, but when I went inside, to my dismay, she wasn't there. Then I noticed that the car had gone too. I was doubly anxious, for although at home in Italy she's occasionally driven some of our cars to amuse herself, it's only been away from public roads and with me beside her in case she gets into difficulty.'

He smiled at his wife and took her hand. 'I know you wanted to help, my love, and it was very brave of you, but you must learn to drive properly before you do such a thing again. I'd only gone a little way down the drive,' he continued, 'before I realised that it might take me a long time to find Julia. I ought to make certain my uncle was safe first. He wasn't in the habit of locking his doors, and the alarming thought occurred to me that if Robert was prepared to fight me, he might also attack my uncle. I saw a light in the bungalow and assumed Robert was back inside, but I couldn't be sure he would stay there.'

Arcanti paused to drink some water from the cup his wife held to his lips. 'Strangely, the oil lamps were still lit on the landings. When I got up to his study, I found my uncle hadn't gone to bed but had fallen asleep in his chair. As I was trying to wake him to persuade him to lock himself in until I came back from searching for Julia, I heard footsteps on the stairs. I went to the door and saw Robert with a gun in his hand. The rest you know.'

He rubbed his forehead wearily, and his wife stroked his arm. 'You're tired, my darling. You must rest as Doctor Hebden advised. The inspector understands you can't answer any more questions, don't you, Inspector?'

De Silva stood up. 'Of course. Thank you for your help so far. If I may, I'll come back soon and let you know how matters are progressing.'

'Thank you.'

* * *

With Prasanna and Nadar still at the lake village guarding Rushwell, the station was quiet. De Silva decided to telephone Gopallawa Motors to find out if they had recovered the Arcantis' car from outside Sunnybank.

'The driver of our breakdown truck brought it in yesterday, sahib,' said the manager. 'The damage is not too bad. The front fender is bent, and the paintwork will need to be attended to, but when that is done, the car should be as good as new.'

De Silva's ears pricked up. He was surprised there was so little physical damage. 'Can you estimate how fast the car was going when it crashed?'

'Not fast. Two or three miles an hour at a guess. Forgive me for asking, sahib, but when the work is finished, where should I send the bill?'

'I'll deal with that later. Leave the work for the moment and keep the car at your garage.'

Gopallawa sounded dissatisfied, but he agreed. After assuring him that he would be paid eventually, de Silva put down the telephone. The conversation had been most interesting.

CHAPTER 10

'I'm sorry Prasanna and Nadar had to stay at the lake village for another night,' said Jane.

'Oh, it will do them no harm to put up with a bit of discomfort. I had to in my early days in the force. The important thing is to keep Robert out of sight until we find out more.'

The afternoon sun beat down on the lawn at Sunnybank. A small brown lizard was basking at the top of the steps to the verandah where de Silva and Jane had just finished having their lunch in the shade.

'I suppose I'd better telephone the Residence,' he said. 'Archie Clutterbuck will want to know how things are going.'

'Will you stay for some tea afterwards?'

'Yes, if he doesn't want to see me at the Residence.'

His mind was troubled as he went to make the call. He wished he had something more definite to tell Archie. This matter of the identity of the third man, the one he had seen in the study, still perturbed him. If Rushwell was telling the truth, who had it been?

'The only sensible conclusion is that Rushwell's lying,' growled Archie when they had talked for a while. 'Bring him back to town and charge him. After that, make the arrangements to transfer him as soon as possible to the gaol at Kandy. They have more resources down there than we do to hold him until a hearing can be set up and that may not be for some time. The courts won't be sitting until the New Year now.'

Reluctantly, de Silva admitted to himself that Archie was probably right. First, there was the evidence of his own eyes, and then what he'd heard from Count Arcanti. Clarence had taunted Robert that he would change his will, and Robert didn't trust his cousin. It could easily have been the case that Robert simply snapped and could take no more. So why did he still have doubts?

'De Silva?'

'Yes, sir.'

'Did you hear me? I said let me know when you've charged him. I'd like to put the Arcantis' minds at rest, and Mrs Clutterbuck is nagging me to wrap things up quickly now Christmas is so close.'

'I hear you, sir.'

Loud and clear, he thought wryly as he returned to the verandah.

* * *

'You don't look happy, dear,' said Jane. 'What does Archie want you to do?'

'I have to bring Rushwell back to Nuala and charge him, then arrange for him to go down to the gaol at Kandy to await trial.'

'Poor Anna Phelps. This will be such a shock for her.'

She paused, studying his expression. 'Shanti? What's on your mind?'

'It may be nothing, but I spoke to the manager at Gopallawa Motors this morning. His people have looked at the Arcantis' car. Considering that the countess told me she ended up in the ditch at our gate because she lost control of the steering, I was surprised how little damage the car sustained.

'What did the manager say exactly?'

'That the car wouldn't have been going faster than two or three miles an hour at the most. Yet the countess said she couldn't stop in time.'

'Why would she lie?' Jane paused to consider for a moment. 'Unless she wanted to make sure you were the one to leave the scene and go for Doctor Hebden. That would leave her alone with the uncle and her husband. But what was she planning to do?'

'I'm not sure, but it's occurred to me that it could be the Arcantis who wanted Clarence dead, and the man I saw in the doorway might have been an accomplice who was waiting at the house when they got back from the party. If that was the case, however, how did he get there and then vanish into thin air afterwards? There was no sign of a car at the house.'

They lapsed into silence. The lizard suddenly darted from one side of the verandah's top step to the other; its tongue flicked out to catch an insect before it resumed its motionless disguise.

'They're clever little creatures,' remarked Jane, noticing it. 'You wouldn't know he was there now. Nature is very adept at deceiving the eye.'

'Well, I'll be off to the lake village,' said de Silva, standing up. 'If I must bring Rushwell in, I'd better get on with it. I won't wait for that tea.'

'Will you be home in time for dinner?'

'I fully intend to be. Once Rushwell's tucked up in one of the cells, Prasanna or Nadar can take over again.'

CHAPTER 11

He came home that evening leaving Robert Rushwell guarded by a slightly more content Nadar. The constable hadn't been relishing the prospect of yet another night at the lake village.

Jane was in the drawing room.

'Mission accomplished,' he said. 'Although I must admit, I'm not entirely happy about it. Rushwell's still denying everything, and I find it hard to believe he's a murderer.' He sighed. 'But I suppose Archie's right. The obvious conclusion is that he did it.'

'It may be the obvious conclusion,' said Jane. 'But I think it might be the wrong one.'

'What?'

'I've been thinking about it all afternoon. It was the lizard that started it. The creature gave me the idea of the eye fooling the mind.'

'Go on.'

'Just suppose that Robert couldn't have committed the crime because he wasn't really there.'

'What are you talking about, my love? I saw him.'

'You may only have thought you saw him.'

'Are you going back to the idea that Robert had an accomplice?'

'No, I think there might just have been two people in the study: Clarence and Count Arcanti.'

De Silva frowned. 'So, who killed Clarence Rushwell?'

'The count, then he wounded himself in order to mislead you. Do you remember the mirror that was propped up in the study? The one that had obviously come off the wall.'

De Silva cast his mind back to the scene and Jane's idea started to become clear. 'Do you mean that when I saw Robert threaten Cosmo Arcanti, what I really saw was Arcanti's reflection?'

Jane nodded. 'He was only acting as if he was being threatened.'

'Wait a minute, let me think a bit more about this.' He paused for a few moments.

'Shanti?'

'Now I look back on it, it was suspiciously convenient that the countess chanced to meet someone that night who knew where we lived. It's more plausible that she and the count had everything planned in advance. It would be easy to find our address in a telephone book.'

'Yes, it would. Let's say the Arcantis moved that mirror to a position near the door where it would have filled up most of the space that anyone coming in would see. You told me you only caught a glimpse of the count's face when the man you thought was Robert briefly stood aside.'

De Silva considered the idea. 'But surely the gilt frame would have been visible? I would have realised there was a mirror there.'

'Not if the frame was covered with a dark cloth of some kind, and the Arcantis kept the lights low.'

De Silva recalled that as Clarence Rushwell had refused to install electricity and the only lighting in the house came from oil lamps and candles, the lighting had been very dim. Now that he thought about it, the candelabra that had remained upright could have been placed in a position that would throw light onto the face of whoever was standing in the doorway: an image that would be reflected in a mirror angled for that very purpose.

Both Cosmo and Robert had worn evening dress at the party. They were of similar height and build, with the same colour hair. The man that he had believed to be Robert Rushwell had been wearing black gloves. Was he really Cosmo and had he worn them to hide his smooth, manicured hands, so different from Robert's roughened ones, and avoid it being too obvious from the reflection in the mirror that it was Cosmo, not Robert, who had closed the door in de Silva's face? When the countess had called out Robert's name from the landing outside the study, that might have been the signal for Cosmo to execute the illusion.

'So, you're suggesting that the count shot his uncle and then wounded himself. The idea does have possibilities.'

'I'm glad you think so. I also suspect Cosmo may already have killed his uncle by the time the countess came here to get help. Clarence would have been far too likely to make trouble if he had still been alive when you and the countess reached the study. The first shot you heard was probably fired out of the window. The count then wounded himself, trying to do as little damage as possible, and as Doctor Hebden confirmed his wound was a minor one, he succeeded. Before he shot himself, the count moved the mirror back to its original place. The noises you heard when you were outside the study trying to get in were the sound of him doing that as well as knocking over furniture. His only problem was that he couldn't hang the mirror back up on the wall on his own. While you went to get Hebden, the countess had time to dispose of the gun, but she wasn't strong enough to rehang the mirror by herself either.'

'My goodness! Where did you get all this from? Surely not just the lizard.'

Jane smiled. 'I admit there was more to it than that. I read a mystery novel – last spring I think it was – where the villain used a similar illusion to hide his crime.'

'It's an ingenious idea, but I'm not sure how Archie will take it. He may dismiss it out of hand.'

'You might remind him that the count practises magic and illusionism. Maybe he's a much better magician than his performance at the party suggested. I'm not saying he knew of the book, but he and the author might have had a similar idea.'

There was a silence.

'Very well,' he said at last. 'You may have hit on the answer, and I'll run the risk. But first, I'd like to go back to the house and have another look around.'

* * *

There was no sign of activity at Robert's bungalow. It looked as if the servants de Silva had met had left, perhaps permanently. He wondered if it was because they didn't want to answer any more questions.

At the main house, the door to Clarence Rushwell's tower was unlocked. Up in the study, he ran a hand over the mirror and tried to lift it. 'It's heavy,' he gasped after trying for a few moments. 'Do you really think Arcanti could move it on his own?'

'Let me show you,' said Jane.

Pivoting the frame from one bottom corner to the other, she succeeded in moving the mirror several feet then stopped to catch her breath. 'There. If I can do it, I'm sure he would be able to.'

Between them, they moved the mirror to the wall opposite the door. It was already quite dark in the room, but Jane closed the curtains. As de Silva moved one of the candelabras to a corner of the room and lit the candles, it occurred to him that it was odd that only one of them had fallen over when most of the furniture had been overturned.

'We must cover the frame,' said Jane. She looked around. 'There's nothing suitable here. I'll go and get some of those clothes from the bedroom.'

In the bedroom, she opened the wardrobe and took out two of the jackets, a voluminous old-fashioned cloak, and some long scarves.

'I think that will do,' she said, standing back to survey her work when she had brought them downstairs and used them to hide the mirror's gilded frame.

De Silva studied the arrangement. 'I saw the count's face very briefly, but there was enough light to make him clearly recognisable. If I was seeing his reflection, why didn't I see candles reflected in the mirror too?'

'He must have been very careful how he positioned them. The mirror wasn't necessarily against a wall. It could have been propped up by furniture, closer to the door and at an angle.'

They spent a few minutes moving the candelabra, the black-draped mirror and – using it to prop the mirror up – Clarence's desk, from one place to another, until they achieved the result they wanted.

'I think this is as close to the scene as we'll get,' said de Silva at last.

'Good.' Jane faced the mirror. 'Now, we must imagine that I'm Count Arcanti, and see if my idea works.'

CHAPTER 12

'It's an ingenious idea,' said Archie Clutterbuck when de Silva telephoned him the next morning, 'I'm intrigued to know where you got it from.'

Even though it was the season of goodwill, de Silva suddenly feared that if he told Archie the whole truth, lizard and all, he might consider such an approach to the case a little too eccentric. 'It was after a discussion with my wife,' he said carefully.

Archie chuckled. 'I see.' De Silva wondered how many of his boss's ideas came from his wife, Florence.

'However, I wouldn't like to stand up in a court of law with nothing else to support the case for the prosecution.'

'I appreciate that, sir, but we also have the information from Gopallawa Motors about the Arcantis' car. I think the countess was lying about not being able to control it. I believe she crashed into the ditch outside my house deliberately, so that we would need to use my car to go for Doctor Hebden, giving her time to dispose of the gun that killed Clarence Rushwell. With your permission, I'd like more time to pursue the idea before I send Robert Rushwell down to Kandy.'

He heard a harrumph at the other end of the line, then, after a pause, 'Yes, the lack of damage is surprising. Well, I suppose there's no harm in giving the theory some consideration. You have twenty-four hours, de Silva, but I'm not promising anything. Now, I have other matters to attend to, so I'd better be going. We'll speak again in due course.'

Only moderately encouraged, de Silva decided to go down to the station to check on his prisoner.

Robert Rushwell was despondent. It was only to be expected, thought de Silva. He wouldn't mention Jane's idea and raise any hopes that were quite likely to be dashed.

'Inspector Chockalingham telephoned yesterday from Colombo, sir,' said Prasanna. 'I told him we didn't know when to expect you, but I would ask you to call him back when you came in.'

'Get him for me now, please. I'll take the call in my office.'

A few minutes later, Prasanna put his head round the door. 'I'm sorry, sir. Inspector Chockalingham is out now and not expected back at the station until later.'

That was a nuisance, but there was nothing he could do about it. 'Say I'll be in all this afternoon and ask him to call me as soon as possible when he returns.'

Later that afternoon, the telephone rang. He picked up the receiver and heard his former colleague's voice.

'Good afternoon, de Silva, I have news that I hope you'll be pleased to hear. It's about this couple, Count and Countess Arcanti, who you asked me to enquire about. The Customs and Immigration Office confirm that they arrived in Colombo a little over a month ago. I've been to the Colombo hotel they gave as their first address. The manager says they stayed for three nights. The count wasn't well and remained in his room for the first two days, but the countess went out a few times.'

'What kind of hotel is this?'

'A small one and very cheap. Didn't you tell me that they claim to be wealthy?'

'They do.'

'Odd, eh? And they were in tourist class, not cabin class, on the ship from Naples.'

'Did you find out anything about how they travelled up from Colombo?'

'The hotel manager said they left by car. He wasn't sure, but he thinks they planned to drive all the way.'

'Did you manage to find out where they got the car from?'

'I'm not sure yet. I have a few more garages to contact. All I know so far is that on one of her forays from the hotel, the countess came back with it: a black Delage. Perhaps they saved their money to splash out on that.'

It was the same make of car that the countess had crashed outside Sunnybank.

'The manager remembers it,' Rudi Chockalingham continued. 'I doubt his usual clientele drive that class of car if they drive one at all.'

'You said the count was unwell and confined to his room, so who drove the countess?'

'She drove herself.'

'I see. That's interesting news. Her husband told me she was very inexperienced and had never driven on a proper road.'

'Do you want me to keep on asking around the garages?'

'If it's not too much trouble, but I think you may already have given me the information I need.'

* * *

Archie Clutterbuck's study had escaped Florence's Christmas fever, but as he was shown in by one of the servants, de Silva thought that his superior looked hunted. Perhaps he was afraid that if he stayed in one place for too long, his wife would drape him in tinsel. He listened while de Silva recounted the conversation with Rudi Chockalingham.

'Good work,' he said when de Silva came to an end,

surprising him. When he'd first mentioned Jane's idea to Archie, he hadn't been particularly encouraging.

'I've been doing a bit of ferreting about of my own,' Archie went on. 'Strictly unprofessional, and to be kept between ourselves. The manager of the Bank of Kandy tells me that despite old Clarence Rushwell's meanness, he was a very wealthy man. It occurs to me that might have some bearing on the case.'

'It certainly might, sir, and I'd say it's beginning to look as if the Arcantis aren't as well off as they make out.'

Archie took a cigarette from the packet of Passing Clouds on his desk, lit it and shook out the match. 'All we have to do now is think of a way of testing out your theory. What do you suggest?'

De Silva had considered that on the way to the Residence, although not seriously expecting it was a question he would need to answer.

'If we confront the countess, she's bound to deny everything. I think we need to set up the same situation as on the night of the murder.'

'And hope to startle her into giving herself away, do you mean?'

'Exactly, sir.'

'My wife has already given her a bedroom at the Residence for when she isn't at the hospital with the count. She mentioned to my wife that she wants to go up to the house to retrieve some things she left there. I'll offer one of the official cars and a driver to take her over later this afternoon. She's due back from the hospital by teatime, so I'll arrange it for around five o'clock. I'll follow at a discreet distance, leave my car at the bungalow, and walk the rest of the way. By the time we arrive, it should be dark.'

Over the course of the next few minutes, they thrashed out the remaining details of their plan, then Archie nodded. 'Good. I think we have it all covered. Just make sure you have everything ready, de Silva.'

'I will, sir.'

'Oh, and by the way,' he said with a broad grin as de Silva reached the door. 'Mrs Clutterbuck is convinced that Mrs de Silva's hit on the answer.'

That was support from an unexpected quarter, thought de Silva. He smiled to himself as he drove home. If Florence got into the habit of teaming up with Jane, they would make a formidable pair and he might as well retire.

CHAPTER 13

He and Jane stood on the roof of Clarence Rushwell's tower, gazing out over a billowing sea of green.

'I wonder if he often came up here,' she mused. 'If he did, I can understand why he wouldn't leave the place, but not why he let it become so dilapidated.' She looked at the setting sun. 'Not much longer until it's dark. Do you think we should go down?'

'Probably.' De Silva's brow furrowed. 'I hope our plan will work.'

'Of course it will. Florence was going to tell the countess she was unable to accompany her, and I've offered to help collect up her possessions and pack them. She won't be expecting you, but we'll say you joined me at the last minute because you'd like her assistance with some papers that have just come to light. All you have to do then is ask her to come up to the study with you to see them.'

'What do I say if she wants to know what these papers are about?'

'Tell her they concern Clarence's investments. If she's as greedy as we suspect she is, she won't be able to resist.'

'But what if she refuses?'

Jane smiled. 'You'll have to use your charm.'

They checked the study one last time as they passed it. The mirror was in position, carefully draped as it had probably been on the night of Clarence Rushwell's murder.

What was left of the daylight had been excluded and the only artificial light came from the candelabra.

Down in the courtyard, they listened for the sound of the official car coming up the drive. De Silva looked at his watch. 'Six o'clock,' he said. 'What if she doesn't come? All this planning will be wasted.'

'Oh, I'm sure she will.'

A few moments later, they saw a car's headlights coming slowly up the drive. The official car stopped in front of the gatehouse. A chauffeur got out and went round to hold the door open for the countess.

'Mrs de Silva,' she said as she emerged. 'How kind of you to offer to help. There are only a few things to collect. It won't take long.'

'It's no trouble,' said Jane with a smile.

De Silva stepped into the light and the countess noticed him for the first time. If she was alarmed by his presence, she didn't let her expression reveal it.

'What a pleasant surprise,' she said sweetly.

'When I heard that my wife was coming, I suggested I accompany her,' he said. 'I found a few papers in the late Mr Rushwell's study that I would be grateful for your opinion on.'

The countess frowned. 'I can't imagine how I can help but naturally if you wish it, I will do my best. How could I refuse the man who saved my poor husband and caught his uncle's murderer?'

'Thank you, ma'am, you're very kind. If it's not inconvenient, I suggest we go to the study first. I have business to attend to in town, so perhaps my wife can come back with you in the official car when you've had time to pack up your possessions.'

'Certainly.'

On the way up the stairs to the study, the countess gave no indication that she suspected anything was afoot. De

Silva wondered if she was really as calm as she seemed to be. Perhaps she had such confidence in the trick she and her husband had played that she wasn't afraid of being unmasked.

The door to the study came into sight. Still talking, the countess waited for him to open it for her. When he did so, he quickly took a step to one side, just as the man in the doorway had done on the night of the murder.

Mid-speech, the countess froze as she stared at her reflection in the glass, then she exploded in fury. 'What is this outrage?'

Before he had time to stop her, she turned and ran down the stairs, straight into the arms of Archie Clutterbuck.

CHAPTER 14

'Both of them still insist that the idea of murdering Clarence Rushwell and trying to put the blame on Robert came from the other one,' said de Silva as he and Jane got ready for the carol service on Christmas Eve.

'The important thing is that Robert is in the clear. Anna Phelps was skipping about like a five-year-old at the rehearsal this afternoon. Robert has proposed and she's accepted him.'

'Apparently, the Arcantis learnt from the count's late mother that Clarence was likely to be very wealthy. The count had already run through all his own money, and he wanted them to come to Ceylon in the hope of getting Clarence's fortune for themselves. When they arrived, they were disappointed to find the plantation so rundown, but a few discreet enquiries suggested that there was still plenty of money. The countess claims the count knocked Robert out when they arrived home after the party and forced her to help put him into the car. The count drove him to the lake and made her follow in their car.'

De Silva remembered how her eyes had shone with tears as she claimed to have begged Cosmo not to do such a wicked thing. 'It would have been enough if his uncle left us a little money,' she had said.

'She claimed that after Robert's car went into the water, she made her husband come away because she hoped

Robert might somehow escape, but that seems unlikely. Her husband's story is that it was her idea, and he was just a pawn. As I guessed, Clarence was already dead when the count went to Robert's bungalow to borrow his car. He and the countess accuse each other of firing the shot that killed Clarence. I doubt we'll ever know the truth, so they'll be charged with conspiracy.'

'What a charming pair,' said Jane.

'If they hadn't miscalculated the speed at which the car would sink, they might have got away with their crime.'

'I suppose that as it was dark, it was hard to tell how much mud there was. I expect they were in a hurry to get back to the house and carry out their trick. The car must have been only partially submerged when they left the scene, but they probably believed that its weight and the camouflage the reed bed would provide would do the rest.'

'A choice that proved to be their undoing.'

'Have you discovered whether Clarence changed his will in favour of the count?'

De Silva nodded. 'Fortunately, he didn't. But of course the law would disqualify Cosmo from inheriting the plantation and the money in any case. Everything goes to Robert.'

* * *

At church on Christmas morning, a large congregation had assembled. On either side of the steps to the choir, greenery and orchids cascaded from tall pedestals. To the left stood the Nativity scene. Something of a Nuala heirloom, it had been made many years previously by one of the Residence's outdoor staff who had a genius for carving wood. De Silva had always liked the patient donkey with its amiable expression. This year, the three kings had been given a pick-me-up in the form of new robes made by the ladies of the sewing circle. The jewel-coloured brocades gleamed against the pale stone of the church wall.

To the right of the pulpit, the choir was marshalling in the vestry. De Silva caught a glimpse of Anna Phelps organising her small charges who traditionally joined the adults for the occasion. The organist started to play, and they processed to their places, followed by Reverend Peters, resplendent in his Christmas robes.

Her duties over, Anna Phelps joined her parents and Robert Rushwell in one of the front pews. As the congregation rose to their feet, he turned with a smile to hand her a hymn book. Soon, the church was filled with song:

'The holly and the ivy,
When they are both full grown
Of all the trees that are in the wood
The holly bears the crown.'

Printed in Great Britain
by Amazon

77928249R00164